He stood altogether too close and she thought he might kiss her again.

As if reading her thoughts, he said, "Do not worry. I will not outrage your grandmother by kissing you here in front of her house, as much as I'd like to. I have enjoyed our ride, Isabel."

"So have I. Thank you, Richard."

"It was my extreme pleasure. Enjoy your visit."

Isabel watched him mount the seat again, take the reins, and drive away. Richard was such an enigma, she simply did not know what to make of him. A thief and a flirt and a manipulator of people, he could also show compassion for a wounded soldier and feel compelled to offer help. And make her head spin with a kiss.

It was not until she turned to reach for the door knocker that she realized her reticule was far too light. She opened the drawstring and uttered a frustrated cry.

The brooch was gone. The wretched man had stolen it again.

Other AVON ROMANCES

CANDICE HERN

Her Scandalous Affair

AVON BOOKS
An Imprint of HarperCollinsPublishers

This is a work of fiction. Names, characters, places, and incidents are products of the author's imagination or are used fictitiously and are not to be construed as real. Any resemblance to actual events, locales, organizations, or persons, living or dead, is entirely coincidental.

AVON BOOKS
An Imprint of HarperCollins*Publishers*
10 East 53rd Street
New York, New York 10022-5299

Copyright © 2004 by Candice Hern
ISBN: 0-06-056516-0
www.avonromance.com

First Avon Books paperback printing: December 2004

Avon Trademark Reg. U.S. Pat. Off. and in Other Countries, Marca Registrada, Hecho en U.S.A.
HarperCollins® is a registered trademark of HarperCollins Publishers Inc.

Printed in the U.S.A.

10 9 8 7 6 5 4 3 2 1

*Dedicated with thanks
to the Braintrust:*

*Carol Culver, Diana Dempsey,
Barbara Freethy, Lynn Hanna,
Barbara McMahon, and Kate Moore.*

*With their help,
and a little chocolate,
this story was born.*

Chapter 1

June 1814

"And so you must find the Mallory Heart and bring it home at once. No matter what it takes."

Richard Mallory stared at his grandmother in astonishment. The Countess of Dunstable was a stately, reserved woman who had never, as far as he could recall, made a flippant remark or jest in her life. He had to assume she was quite serious.

He stood straight and tall as he faced her, with hands clasped behind his back in a position of formal ease he had employed so often when addressing a superior officer. And there was none more superior than his grandmother. She sat ramrod stiff on the edge of a gilt French chair that had seen better days.

"Let me be certain I understand," he said. "You called me home not because Grandfather is dying, but because you want me to locate a family jewel that has been missing these past fifty years?"

"It is because the earl is dying that the jewel must be restored to us. He has been most agitated about it."

"Has he?"

Richard had been raised by his grandparents from the time both his mother and father perished in an overturned carriage when he was still in leading strings. In all those years, he could remember only a single occasion when his grandfather had mentioned the Mallory Heart. Richard had been about eight years old when he first heard the story of the large heart-shaped ruby from his older brother, and had asked his grandfather about it. The earl had confirmed its existence and how it had come into the family, but had otherwise been quite reticent on the subject. Even at so young an age,

Richard had understood it to be a topic best avoided. He always assumed his grandfather felt guilty that the jewel had been lost on his watch.

"Yes, he seems most upset about it," the countess said, her own distress evident in the tight lines around her mouth and the slight tremor in her voice. "About not wanting to . . . to die before it has been restored to the family."

"And you summoned me from France to find it? Was there no one else you could have called upon?"

It was the wrong thing to say. She narrowed her eyes in a look of displeasure he had known well as a boy. She had always favored his brother, Arthur, the heir to the earldom and the most charming, considerate of men. Richard had been the troublesome brother, always into mischief. But Arthur had died last year and now Richard was Viscount Mallory and his grandfather's heir.

"I understood the fighting was over," she said. "You are needed here now. You ought to have returned last year."

When Arthur died. Richard had not even learned of his brother's death until four months after the fact. He would have come home if he could, but he'd been otherwise occupied. "You know it was impossible for me to return, Grandmother. My regiment—"

"Was engaged in some battle or other." She dismissed the event with a wave of her hand.

"Vittoria." He spoke through clenched teeth and made an effort to curb his irritation at her cavalier disregard for what the army had done to keep her, and the rest of England, safe from Bonaparte. He'd lost several good men during the charges that day. Vittoria had been an important victory, not one to be so easily dismissed. But the countess had never approved of his soldiering. It had been his grandfather who'd understood his restlessness and bought him a commission in the Dragoon Guards.

"I am sorry I could not come home sooner, Grandmother. I was heartsick to hear about Arthur's death, believe me, but the war did not allow time off for grieving. However, with Bonaparte routed at Toulouse and sent packing to Elba, I was able to leave my regiment as soon as I received your urgent message. I was worried about Grandfather."

"As you should be."

"I will go up to see him now. It has been too long and I have . . . missed him." It was true.

4

Richard had spent little time at home these last dozen years while the wars raged on the continent. Even so, he was still devoted to the man who'd raised him, who'd taught him about duty, about honor, about what it meant to be a man.

"He will be pleased to know you have returned safely," his grandmother said. She cleared her throat. "As am I."

He smiled. It was the closest thing to approval he was ever likely to hear from her. "And I should like to ask him about the Mallory Heart."

"No!" Her eyes widened with anxiety. "You must not mention it to him, Richard. It upsets him too much and his heart is too weak. I *beg* you not to distress him."

"His condition is that serious?"

"He is dying."

She kept her emotions in check, as always, but sorrow was evident in the slight hitch in her voice, and a sharp pang of sympathy shot through his gut. The anticipated loss of his beloved grandfather weighed heavily on his own heart. Though Richard had never had as close a relationship with his stern grandmother, she surely loved the earl as much as he did. His death would rip a hole in both their lives.

He took a deep breath, then asked, "How long?"

"The doctor says a month or two at most, though additional strain on his heart could take him at any moment. That is why you must not mention the jewel. It is one of the topics that seems to upset him the most."

"I wonder why?"

She lifted her shoulder a fraction. "It is a private matter between the earl and me. All the previous countesses of Dunstable have worn the Mallory Heart. It has always been a special . . ." Her voice cracked and she took a moment before going on. "It was a special love token presented by each earl to his countess as a symbol of the bond of marriage. Your grandfather feels guilty that he was never able to recover it and present it to me. I have told him that he mustn't worry about it, that I have never needed a special jewel to know . . . to know how he feels. But he will not let go of the notion of restoring it to the family."

"I had no idea it was that important to him."

"It has belonged to the Mallorys since the time of Queen Elizabeth. I thought it would bring him peace to know it had been recovered. But if you tell him you are going to search for it, and then are unable to find it, that would surely kill him. It is better he does not know you are searching. But then, if you *do* find the jewel, it would be a blessing."

"Nothing would please me more than to give him a bit of peace before . . ." He paused, unable to say the words. "But how the devil—forgive me—am I to find the blasted jewel? It's been missing over fifty years. I thought it had been stolen."

"It was. But I have heard of a woman who has recently been seen wearing a jewel that could only be the Mallory Heart."

His brows lifted. "What woman?"

"I don't know. That is what I am hoping you will discover. Lady Aylesbury told me of seeing a jewel that she thought resembled the one she'd seen in our family portraits. She does not, of course, know of its loss or of its importance to the family. She merely remarked upon the resemblance. But it must be the Mallory Heart. There could not be two such unique jewels. Lady Aylesbury did not, unfortunately, know the woman who wore it, and lost sight of her shortly afterward."

"When was this?"

"Back in April, at one of the victory balls held

in town before Louis the Eighteenth returned to France."

"She is someone of rank, then, to have attended such an event."

"Apparently."

"And you want me to find this unknown woman of the *ton* among the crowds currently celebrating in London? A daunting task, ma'am."

"Whoever she is, surely she will wear the jewel again, especially with all the balls and fêtes still taking place and so many important people in Town. But I don't care who she is, the jewel does not belong to her. She has no legitimate claim to it."

"And so I am simply to march up to her—assuming I find her—and ask her to hand it over?"

She shrugged. "How you obtain it is up to you."

"Perhaps the best thing would be to offer to buy it from her."

"You cannot do that. It is an extremely valuable piece. Our circumstances are not what they once were."

An understatement, to be sure. Richard had not failed to notice the shabby appearance of the house and grounds. He wondered if that had something to do with this sudden need to retrieve the long lost Mallory Heart? Did his grandfather want it returned so the family could sell it to finance repairs to the estate?

"Do you, then," he said, "expect this unknown woman simply to agree, willingly and without protest, to part with the jewel?"

"I don't care what you have to do to get it back. The earl has bragged enough of your efforts on the battlefield and in certain other apparently clandestine operations. I must assume you have the wits to locate and retrieve one small jewel. You were always full of cunning. Steal it, if you must."

His eyes widened. "You would have me turn thief?"

"It was stolen from us, after all, so it will not really be stealing, but only returning it to its rightful owner."

Before he dies.

"What a grand time to be in London. So many important people. So many parties. It really is quite wonderful."

Lady Isabel Weymouth smiled at her tittering cousin, an elderly spinster who seldom left the house in Chelsea, much less partook of elegant society. Her pale, thin hand rested on her breast as she sighed with pleasure. It seemed Cousin Min was content to live vicariously through reports she read in the newspapers and fashion magazines, and through Isabel's own firsthand accounts of this glittering summer of celebration.

It was indeed a grand time, and Isabel was determined not to miss a single moment of the excitement. "Yes, it has all been rather dazzling," she said. "And tomorrow's ball should be no exception. The Regent is expected to make an appearance. And the Duke of Wellington."

"Oh, my." Cousin Min gave a little squeal of pleasure.

Isabel's grandmother smiled indulgently at her cousin. Gram had never been as interested in Society as Cousin Min, though they had lived together for years. Isabel's grandfather had left only a modest jointure for Gram, and she had invited her cousin to share expenses for the small house in Chelsea. Neither woman, though, had any income to speak of, and they maintained the sort of circumspect existence typical of so many women left alone and without resources. It was a lesson Isabel took to heart.

"You know that we have high hopes for you," Cousin Min said.

"It *is* a splendid opportunity." Gram sent Isabel a speaking glance.

She did not pretend to misunderstand. The metropolis was teeming with nobility and aristocrats come to celebrate the Peace. Wealthy aristocrats. Unmarried wealthy aristocrats. Isabel, more so even than her elderly champions, was determined to bring one of them up to scratch.

She needed a husband.

"I shall do my best," she said.

"And all those handsome soldiers," Cousin Min said with another wistful sigh. "I wish we could have seen the troop review in Hyde Park."

"It would have been much too crowded, Min," Isabel's grandmother said. "We would not have been able to see much, I suspect."

"Ah, but there's nothing more dashing than a scarlet coat, is there?" Cousin Min said. "In my day, it was the greatest wish of every girl to be seen on the arm of a handsome officer. And I daresay London is overflowing with them just now. You could do worse, my dear, than to find yourself a red-coated soldier."

But she could also do much better, and Isabel intended to do so. A soldier was generally a younger son with little or no fortune. Isabel needed—and wanted, to be perfectly honest—a fortune.

When Sir Rupert Weymouth had died almost two years ago, leaving Isabel a widow, he'd also left behind a mountain of debts. The truth of her circumstances had shaken her to the core. She and Rupert had lived high and fast, thriving in the whirlwind of the *ton*. Isabel had no idea they had been living on credit. And she had no intention of letting anyone else know either. It would be beyond mortifying to have her situation bandied about as the latest *on dit*. She had retrenched as best she could, but there was really only one option that insured she would not end up alone and poor like Gram and Cousin Min.

She would marry a rich man.

Both Cousin Min and Gram were determined she should marry again. They did not know the extent of her circumstances, and in fact believed Rupert had left her a comfortable fortune. They only wanted marriage for her because she was still young, not quite thirty, and had not been

HER SCANDALOUS AFFAIR

lucky enough to have children. So they knew she was looking for a husband. They just did not know she was looking for a rich husband.

"Though I have a special fondness for soldiers," Cousin Min said, "I imagine you could look higher. You might even attract the attentions of one of the visiting dignitaries. A foreign prince, perhaps." Her eyes widened with excitement. "Or any of our own nobility who will be at the ball tomorrow."

Isabel laughed. "I promise to set my sights on no less than a Royal Duke." When her cousin sucked in a sharp breath, Isabel added, "But seriously, you must know that I am not elevated enough to be invited to the most elite gatherings. Certainly not the Burlington House ball tomorrow night."

"Not that one, perhaps, but there are so many other balls," Cousin Min said, "and some of the dignitaries must surely make an appearance at one or two of them. You did say the Regent was expected at the Inchbald ball."

"Lady Inchbald is certainly making it known that she expects him," Isabel said. "Perhaps it is wishful thinking on her part, but I shall keep my fingers crossed."

"Then you must wear your very finest dress," Cousin Min said. "And your best jewels."

Isabel must have visibly blanched, for her grandmother quickly said, "You must wear my diamonds, my dear."

Gram had a lovely diamond parure from her years spent in India. Her circumstances had never been desperate enough to sell them, and Isabel had made it clear she would never allow it. She would sell off everything she owned before she would let Gram part with any of the beautiful keepsakes she still had from her days with Grandfather.

"Oh, yes, the very thing!" Cousin Min said. "You have lovely jewels of your own, of course, but Emmeline's diamonds would be perfect for such a grand occasion."

Isabel smiled at her grandmother, and wondered if she had guessed at the truth. "That is very kind of you, Gram. I was much complimented the last time you loaned them to me."

"Then you must take them," Gram said. "Run along upstairs. You know where to find my jewel case."

She did indeed. And Isabel knew what else was in that case. Something much more tempting than diamonds.

* * *

Richard stood in the Long Gallery and stared out the window. The visit with his grandfather had shaken him. He had not been prepared for how old and frail the earl looked. He had always been a large man, tall and broad shouldered, just as Richard was, but he seemed almost small and withered and as pale as the bed linens. The hand Richard had grasped was thin and knobby and spotted with age, the skin papery and thin.

It had been an effort to hold back tears. "Grandda," was all he could say for several minutes. But the pleasure in the old man's blue eyes had warmed his heart. They had spoken briefly about Toulouse and then about Greyshott.

"It is a sorry legacy," the earl had said in a raspy whisper. "I wish I could have done better by you than to leave you this expensive old pile of stone."

"I love this old pile, Grandda. I shall do my best to put it to rights again."

At that point, his grandfather had become a trifle agitated, and the nurse fluttered about, trying to shoo Richard from the room. But he had managed one more brief exchange.

"I must leave right away for London," he said.

"Of course," his grandfather whispered. "You must have your share of the celebrations."

"I have some business there, but will return as soon as I can. Wait for me, Grandda."

The old man knew what he meant. He shook his head and managed a smile. "I will be here when you return," he said. "I am not ready to cock up my toes just yet." But he fell back against the pillows, exhausted, with the nurse hovering over him.

Richard hoped it was true. He was not ready to say good-bye, though clearly he would have to prepare himself to do so in the near future. And then all of this—the unkempt grounds he surveyed from the window, and the decaying house with its chipped plaster, peeling paint, and worn furnishings—would be his. Even if the wars were not over, he would have had to come home to take over the reins of Greyshott.

It was not something he looked forward to. He'd never wanted to be the earl. Arthur had been groomed for the role and Richard never once envied him for it. He was not the type of person to settle quietly in the country. The thought of such a life made him shudder. He would rather ride into battle again. With the blood rushing hot through his veins and heart pounding, he never felt more alive. He loved army life—the camaraderie of the camps, the excitement of planning strategy and tactics, the thrill of a successful campaign, well-planned and well-executed.

The life of adventure, though, was lost to him now. He would soon be responsible for all of Greyshott and its people. In fact, as heir he was responsible now. He would have a brief word with the steward before leaving for London.

Richard might be inheriting an impoverished estate, but he was not without resources of his own. He and Arthur had each received a small inheritance from their mother, and now he had Arthur's share as well. He was also in possession of long arrears of pay, a substantial sum he held in cash. And there was the prize money he'd collected over the years. He'd been too busy to spend it, but had invested it instead. Very wisely, as it happened. Richard had, in fact, a very tidy nest egg to fall back on. Greyshott would need it.

Images of renovations and repair, of draining fields and rotating crops brought a frown to his brow. He would do his duty and leave soldiering behind, but by God he would miss the adventure.

He turned back toward the room and gazed at the line of portraits along the opposite wall. He walked to stand in front of a portrait of the first Countess of Dunstable painted in 1598. She wore the Mallory Heart on her bodice, just below her left breast. Richard moved to study it closer. He had better memorize what it looked like if he was to recognize it pinned to a modern breast.

It was a large ruby in the shape of a heart, surmounted by a gold crown studded with smaller rubies, and pierced by two gold arrows with diamond points. The crowned heart was surrounded by what looked like a white ribbon with writing on it in gold. The whole was suspended from a large lover's knot of gold and diamonds. A more cloyingly sentimental piece of jewelry he could not imagine. But it was certainly unique and should be easily recognizable.

He moved down the line of paintings to find that each countess was shown wearing the same jewel. Even as fashions changed, the jewel remained prominent. Until he reached the painting of the seventh countess. The portrait of his grandmother did not include the ruby heart. It had been painted during the first year of her marriage. The jewel must have gone missing about that time.

Richard heaved a sigh. More than fifty years later, how the devil was he supposed to find the damned thing? Was he to mingle with the beau monde, searching every woman's bodice for the distinctive ruby heart?

He smiled. There *was* a sort of titillating appeal to the quest. He laughed aloud at the horrid pun, but could not deny that a survey of every woman in London was not exactly a disagreeable assignment. Perhaps this would be one final campaign, before taking on the responsibilities of the earldom.

One last adventure.

Isabel reached under the jewel case and pressed the secret lever. The tiny hidden drawer popped out from the side, and she looked over her shoulder to ensure she was not observed. Confident that she was quite alone, she removed the flannel bag from the drawer and opened it. The large heart-shaped ruby spilled out onto her hand.

She had first seen the remarkable brooch as a girl, when she had watched her mother rummage through Gram's jewels shortly after she had returned from India when Grandfather had died. There had been more jewelry in the case in those days.

Isabel's mother, ever a slave to fashion, had easily picked out the pieces she would like to borrow, and discarded others as hopelessly outdated. Including the ruby heart.

"You still have this heavy old thing?" she had said to Gram. "You really ought to have it taken apart and the gems reset into something more fashionable."

Gram had taken the heart back and said she would never dream of doing such a thing. Isabel's mother had muttered something about a waste of good stones and turned her attention to the diamonds, which she thought had much more potential. Isabel, however, had not been able to tear her eyes from the jewel. She had fallen in love with the ruby heart at first sight, thinking it the most magnificent and romantic thing she'd ever seen. While her mother was distracted, she had seen Gram reach beneath the case to spring the hidden drawer. She deposited the brooch in the drawer and quickly closed it. Isabel had pretended not to notice.

Over the years she would sometimes sneak into the jewel case and release the secret drawer just so she could gaze upon the glorious brooch. It was obviously quite old, and Isabel had spun all sorts of fantasies about its history, especially after she had found a translation for the Latin inscription on the white enamel surrounding the heart: "Perfectus Amor Non Est Nisi Ad Unum." It meant "True Love Knows But One." It was almost enough to make a young girl swoon.

But in all that time she had never once asked Gram about it, for she would have had to admit knowing about the hidden drawer. It had been much more romantic to hold that secret to herself.

When she had been married to Rupert, Isabel had enough jewels of her own to forget about the ruby heart. He loved to buy her expensive, elegant jewelry, and Isabel had loved him for it. She had not, of course, known he was mortgaging away her future to buy the jewels.

Almost all of it was gone now, sold to pay off debts and to keep the household running. But Isabel was not willing to let her friends, and Rupert's, know that she was forced to sell her jewels to survive. Instead, she had a good paste copy made of each piece before it was sold. When she wore the paste stones, everyone assumed they were the same genuine pieces Rupert had lavished upon her, and Isabel would never disabuse them of that notion. To do otherwise would tarnish not only her own reputation but Rupert's as well, and she could never do that.

But a few months back, when Gram had offered to loan her the diamond parure because it so perfectly suited a particular evening dress, Isabel had remembered the ruby heart. Without Gram's knowledge, she had taken it and worn it to a victory ball. It was the night she had met Lord Kettering for the first time. The very rich Lord Kettering. The antique brooch had been a good luck charm that night.

Isabel thought the big heart with all its bold sentimental devices would look just right on the gown she was to wear tomorrow night, which was trimmed with patriotic bits of red and blue as well as gold fleur de lis. As an emblem of love, perhaps the jewel would give her at least a symbolic edge as she set out to attract the attention of Lord Kettering.

She replaced the brooch in its cloth bag and tucked it into her reticule along with the diamond parure. When she made her way down-stairs, she sent up a silent prayer that Gram would forgive her for taking the jewel again. She felt like a thief, but there was something about the ruby heart that drew her to it, an al-most irresistible force that had called out to her from the first time she'd laid eyes on it.

Its power certainly came from its message. Not only the words about true love but the many symbols that reinforced it. When she wore the brooch, perhaps its power would in-spire someone to fall in love with her.

And if it was truly powerful, that someone would be a rich man.

Chapter 2

"**O**h, Ned. Not again."

Isabel's younger half-brother had pulled her behind a large urn in the ballroom at Inchbald House. Damn him. She had other things on her mind this evening and would rather not deal with another of Ned's crises.

"It's just this one more time, Iz, I promise. And I'll pay you back as soon as I come round again."

"It's always just one more time with you," she said, wishing he had left this bit of news for another day. She shook her head and gave a little groan, for she was no match against those puppy-dog eyes. "I really cannot keep bailing you out of these scrapes, Ned. My circumstances are . . . not as secure as they might be."

Her brother grinned, knowing he'd won. "Come on, Iz, it ain't that much. And you're my only hope, what with Mother in Italy and all."

Their mother was now the Contessa Giachetti. She had married the count, her third husband, a few years ago and had not returned to England since. Isabel wondered if she would return now that the wars were over. Not that she had ever provided much in the way of maternal support. She was the flightiest of women, but she *was* their mother.

"You won't miss a measly hundred pounds," Ned said, completely oblivious to the fact that she would very much miss it.

She would have to find something else to sell to raise the cash. But Ned, with his loose tongue, was the last person in whom she would confide. In many ways he was as capricious as their mother. Without considering the consequences, without thinking at all, he would spread her secrets all over town before she could blink an eye.

"The way old Rupert flung his blunt around town," Ned said, "he's sure to have left you a bundle. Besides, I've seen Kettering sniffing about. You'll land yourself in another honey pot before long, I daresay."

"Hush, Ned." She looked round to be certain no one had heard. "Try not to spoil my chances by scaring the poor man away."

"Sorry, Iz. Only joking. Didn't know you was in serious pursuit."

"It's not serious. Yet. But I wish to keep my options open, if you please, so I would appreciate a bit of discretion. In fact, I shall demand it if you want me to help pay off your vowels. You will not have another sou if I hear you have been spreading tales about me. I will not have my name in the betting books, Ned."

"Of course. Lips sealed and all that." He nudged her in the ribs. "Would be a pretty feather in your cap, though, old girl, to snare Kettering. Rich as Croesus, they say."

She was well aware of Lord Kettering's prospects. Isabel had done her research. She could not afford to align herself again with a charming spendthrift. She knew who was plump in the pocket and who was mortgaged to his eyeballs. She knew who was overly fond of the gaming tables and whose estates reaped the best profits. Most important of all, she knew who were the ten richest unmarried men in England under the age of forty.

Lord Kettering was one of them. There were nine others, of course, but the young earl was the only one of the ten who was not painful to look upon. He also spent most of his time in Town and seemed to enjoy Society, which was important to Isabel.

She supposed that going after a rich, handsome, social husband made her shallow and selfish. But she loved moving in the highest circles of Society. She loved the glitter and glamour, the balls and parties, the theater and the Opera, music and dancing, the beautiful fashions and the dazzling jewels. She loved it all and always had.

Was it so wrong to enjoy the pleasures of Society and not wish to give them up?

"I will make myself scarce," Ned said, "and allow you to concentrate on drawing Kettering's attention. Shouldn't be too difficult. Stunning dress, Iz. You look quite beautiful, in fact."

She looked down and straightened her skirts, biting back a grin. This "stunning" dress had been remade from two older ones, altered beyond recognition with bits of lace and chenille from another dress used to create a deep flounce, the waist shortened, and the back made fuller in the latest mode. Thank goodness Isabel and her maid, Tessie, were both clever with a needle. In her straitened circumstances Isabel could no longer patronize the most fashionable modistes, but she could not bear to be anything less than stylish.

"Doing it too brown, my boy," she said to her brother. "I've already agreed to lend you the hundred pounds."

His hand gripped his chest in mock outrage. "No such thing, I assure you. Honestly, Iz, you do look very pretty."

"For a dried-up old widow?" She smiled and touched his hand before he could pretend to object. At eight-and-twenty she would seem ancient to a boy almost seven years younger. "Ah, there is Phoebe. Run along, Ned. But stay away from the card room, I beg you. Drop by tomorrow afternoon and I will have your money."

"Thanks, Iz. You're a real sport." He kissed her on the cheek, grinned, and disappeared into the crowd.

A real sport, indeed. Isabel often wondered if she ought to stop bailing Ned out of trouble so he would learn to take responsibility for his actions. He was very young and would curb his enthusiasms soon enough. In the meantime, she hated to put a damper on his high spirits. If only those spirits weren't so expensive.

Isabel stepped in front of the urn and caught the eye of her friend Phoebe, Lady Challinor, who waved and made her way through the crowd.

"La! What a glorious squeeze." Phoebe stood close to Isabel's side and swept the room with her gaze. "Have you ever seen such a night? I heard, by the by, that the Burlington House ball is an utter bore and most of those attendees are beginning to arrive here."

"Lady Inchbald will be pleased."

"She will have an apoplexy if the Regent does not show up. And the new Duke of Wellington. She is counting on them, you know."

"But the Burlington House ball was in the duke's honor. Surely he cannot leave it so early."

Phoebe giggled. "Perhaps he will sneak away before anyone notices."

"It is difficult *not* to notice the duke. Or his nose."

Phoebe covered her mouth with her fan and giggled again. She was a good friend but could be dreadfully silly at times.

Isabel glanced about the room to see if she could locate Lord Kettering. Her gaze landed on a group of new arrivals still gathered near the entrance to the ballroom. There were several officers in red coats, but no Lord Kettering. Her eyes were just about to move on to the next group when one of the soldiers turned around.

Her breath caught in her throat. *Oh, my.* He was tall and handsome, to be sure, with dark hair and features chiseled in the classical lines of Roman sculpture. But she had seen handsomer men. No, it was something else. The way he held himself, the way he moved—there was a sort of aura of command about him, and not just because he wore a scarlet coat and a chest full of gold braid. The room was full of red coats, but this man took in the room as though he owned it. His eyes raked the crowd in slow scrutiny as though ensuring that everyone in attendance was worthy of his company.

"Phoebe," she whispered, "who is that officer near the door?"

There was no mistaking which officer she meant. Phoebe had noticed him, too, as had every other woman in the room, no doubt. "I have no idea," she said. "Let me see what I can discover."

She whispered in the ear of the woman at her other side, who shook her head and whispered to the women next to her. And so it went until the room was fairly abuzz with curiosity.

It took no more than a moment for the answer to make its way back to Phoebe. "He is Viscount Mallory, heir to the Earl of Dunstable and a major in the Dragoon Guards. He is unmarried and just returned from France." She gave a little sigh as she stared openly at him. "My, what a magnificent specimen. If it were not for his lamentable lack of fortune, I would recommend him to you as fine husband material, my dear. Very fine, indeed."

The tidbit about the viscount's prospects, or lack of them, was no news to Isabel. Her research had uncovered widespread rumors that the old earl's fortunes were at low ebb. And in any case, she had dismissed the absent heir as unavailable since his regiment was still in France. Now that he had returned, she could only lament those empty pockets. Even from across the room he had set off a certain stirring in her body she had not experienced in a very long time.

After all, financial security was not the only benefit of marriage.

Though Isabel kept to herself the particular requirements of her matrimonial quest, Phoebe did not need to be told that she was looking. She simply assumed, correctly for the most part, that every unmarried female was on the hunt for a husband. And no man without a fortune was worth consideration. For marriage, anyway.

"I could, of course, recommend him for something less formal," Phoebe said, with a mischievous twinkle in her eye. "But then Lord Kettering might be put off. He is ever so proper, and you certainly do not want to put a spoke in that wheel. I, on the other hand, have no such impediment." She grinned wickedly.

"Except for Challinor."

Phoebe shrugged. "Yes, I suppose he might take it ill. I declare, sometimes it can be quite tiresome to have a husband so besotted. Poor Challinor, I—Isabel! The man is staring at you."

Isabel turned her head toward the door and her gaze collided with Lord Mallory's. Even halfway across the large room, the intensity of that look caused her skin to prickle and flush, and she almost forgot to breathe. He stared boldly at her for what seemed an eternity, then bent to speak to the woman at his side.

When Isabel was finally able to look away, she saw that it was Lady Althea Bradbury to whom he spoke, a woman she knew casually. She was the daughter of an earl but had outraged her family some years ago when she'd married a common soldier. He must be one of the other scarlet coats in their group. She looked toward Isabel and nodded.

"He is coming this way," Phoebe said in an excited whisper. "Good heavens, my dear, what a coup. Out of this entire company, that sublime creature has singled *you* out. How perfectly marvelous! Just look at the way he moves, how the crowd stirs in his wake. There is a certain air about him, don't you think? A hint of . . . what? Danger?"

"Arrogance."

"More than that, I think. Ooh, it fair gives me shivers just to watch him. I swear I cannot take my eyes off the man." She must have done so nevertheless, for an instant later she said, "Dear me, there is Lord Kettering as well, coming this way. And Sir Henry Levenger trailing behind. I am fairly certain neither of them is coming to pay his respects to me." She reached for Isabel's arm and gave it a quick squeeze. "My goodness, this *is* your lucky night."

33

Isabel smiled and fingered the ruby heart pinned to the high waist of her dress, just below her bosom.

It was almost too easy.

This was his first evening in Town, and only his second social event, and yet Richard was fairly certain his quest was over. Unless he was mistaken, he'd found the Mallory Heart, though he would not know for sure until he got a closer look.

Richard gave a quiet sigh as he considered how short-lived this last adventure was to be.

Thank God for Lady Althea and her social connections. The wife of Colonel Bradbury, Richard's commanding officer, seemed to have a nodding acquaintance with just about everyone in the beau monde. She had guided him through the rather intimidating gathering of the nobility at the Burlington House ball. Richard had never rubbed elbows with such an elevated crowd in his life. But it had been his military rank and not his courtesy title of viscount that had granted him admission to that august company. Officers of every sort had seen their consequence rise in the wake of

Toulouse, none more than cavalry officers such as Richard.

Althea, proudly wearing her war-hero husband on her arm, had introduced Richard to scores of ladies. Most of them were of a certain age, with stately bosoms and plumed turbans, but none of them sported a heart-shaped ruby. The crowd was so large, though, that there were surely scores of women he never even clapped eyes on. The task his grandmother had set him had seemed ridiculously daunting.

Until now. What a piece of luck that Althea had found the Burlington House crowd a bore and suggested that the Inchbald gathering might be more interesting. And so it was.

The large ruby brooch winked at him from beneath the elegant bosom of one of the loveliest ladies in the room. Lovely and proud and supremely confident. When he'd caught her eye—or, more precisely, when she'd caught him staring at her—she had returned his gaze with a frankly appraising look of her own. As he followed Lady Althea and Colonel Bradbury through the crowd, the woman watched his approach with a slight lift of her brows and the merest quirk at one corner of her mouth, as though his obvious interest both amused and intrigued her.

When they finally reached her, she had become part of a small group, including several other men whose interest was rather blatant. And no wonder. Upon closer inspection she was a real beauty. Not in the classical way, but beautiful nonetheless. Lord, how he had missed the fair-skinned women of England.

She was taller than most of the women around her, and slender, with a long neck accentuated by the upswept style of her hair. That hair was honey gold, lighter than it had appeared from across the room where he had thought it brown. But she had moved slightly so that she stood almost directly beneath a chandelier and the candlelight burnished the gold in her hair. Her eyes still held that hint of amusement, and he could not be entirely sure of their color. Not brown, but not quite green either. They seemed to be flecked with all sorts of colors. And her mouth. Egad, it was the most tempting feature of them all. It was a bit too wide for perfection, but the lips were full and sensual, and still quirked up into an intriguingly provocative smile, as though she was aware of every private thought in his head.

Or so she believed.

He casually dropped his gaze to the brooch at her breast, and was assured in an instant that it was indeed his family's missing jewel. It was an exact duplicate of the one he'd seen in all those portraits in the Long Gallery at Greyshott. The heart-shaped ruby was enormous and all those boldly sentimental bits—the piercing arrows, the crown, the lover's knot—gave it a very old-fashioned look. Richard was no expert on women's fashion, but he believed the heavy piece was not the sort of thing considered stylish. Yet somehow it looked just right on her.

He wondered how the devil this woman, who could not be much above five-and-twenty, came to have it in her possession. The dashed thing had been missing over fifty years.

"Good evening, Lady Weymouth," Althea said, addressing the ruby-wearer. "A lovely ball, is it not?"

"Indeed it is. A grand squeeze." She smiled more fully and it beamed across her face like a light held up to dazzle him.

"We have just come from Burlington House, and I will tell you in confidence that it was deadly dull. Already I can tell this ball will be much more entertaining. Oh, but you have not met my husband, have you?" She tugged Brad-bury by the elbow and brought him closer to her side. "Colonel Bradbury. Joseph, this is Lady Weymouth."

"Your servant, my lady." Bradbury took her hand and kissed the air above it.

"I am pleased to meet you, Colonel. I hope you will not find it tedious to hear one more of-fer of congratulations, and heartfelt thanks, for routing that horrid little Corsican at last. You are great heroes to us, you know." Her glance flickered to Richard. "All of you."

"Thank you, Lady Weymouth," he said. "We are certainly happy to be home again, and at peace. Will you allow me to introduce a fellow officer? Major Lord Mallory."

She looked full at him, her greenish-brown eyes a bit wary, but still flickering with interest. "My lord," she said and offered her hand.

Richard took it, but did not kiss the air above it. He brought the silk-covered fingers to his lips, while one of his own fingers managed to find the opening of the glove at the underside of her wrist and touch the bare skin very briefly. Her eyes widened slightly at the presumption, and she discreetly retrieved her hand.

"Lady Weymouth," he said. "Your servant."

"And this is my friend, Lady Challinor," she said, indicating the dark-haired beauty who he'd only barely noticed at her side.

"Lady Challinor." Richard bowed, and did not reach for the lady's hand. Nor did she offer it.

"What an unusual brooch," Althea said, and he could have kissed her. "It looks quite old. A family heirloom?"

"Yes, it is," Lady Weymouth said, and touched the ruby with one gloved finger.

"It is a beautiful piece," Richard said, studying it once more. When he lifted his eyes to hers again, they were twinkling with mockery. She thought he was ogling her bosom, and of course he was. All in the line of duty. He decided to test her.

"It looks to be several hundred years old," he said. "It must have been in your family for a long time."

"Yes, it has" she said, "for ages and ages."

He watched her closely and saw not a flicker of discomposure. She was a very skillful liar.

"I envy you such a grand old jewel," Althea said. "And you wear it with such flair. You will bring the Elizabethan style back into vogue."

At that moment, one of the other gentlemen hovering nearby, a golden-haired good-looking chap, inched forward. "The next set is beginning," he said. "I believe it is mine, Lady Weymouth?"

"Of course, my lord," she said, and took his arm.

"May I be so bold," Richard said before she could take one step away, "as to hope you will honor me with the next free set?"

She lifted her brows, but said, "Of course, my lord. The second set after this one, if you please."

He bowed to her and she walked away with the fair-haired gallant. Another gentleman claimed Lady Challinor, and the others drifted away, leaving Richard alone with the Bradburys.

"She is quite lovely, is she not?" Althea said, her eyes dancing with merriment. She had been surprised and delighted when he'd asked for an introduction. All women must be born with a need to play matchmaker.

"Lady Challinor?" he said. "Yes, she is very beautiful."

Althea laughed and slapped her fan on his arm. "Lady Weymouth, you wretch. It was she who caught your eye all the way across the room. Was it love at first sight?"

Richard smiled at her. "Nothing like it. I was

merely attracted by the enormous ruby at her breast." Which was quite true, of course, though the breast itself was attractive enough.

"Nonsense. I daresay it was her hazel eyes."

Ah, hazel. He'd wondered how to describe their color. Hazel certainly sounded prettier than greenish-brown.

"Leave the man alone, Althea," the colonel said, chuckling softly. "He can manage quite well on his own, I promise you. Though I suspect, Mallory, you had best steel yourself for the onslaught of female interest that a handsome unmarried officer is liable to generate just now. They think we're all heroes, you know."

"As you are," Althea said and gave her husband a warm smile, which he returned. She turned her attention to Richard and said, "Her husband was Sir Rupert Weymouth. The poor man died of a fever not quite two years ago. He was a dashing young fellow as I recall. They were seen everywhere. A very popular young couple."

Richard appreciated those details, though not for the reasons Althea would assume. He wondered if the jewel had come through the husband. Perhaps he would do a bit of probing into the affairs of the late Sir Rupert Weymouth.

"A widow, eh?" Bradbury gave him a wink over his wife's head.

During his years in the Peninsula, Richard had somehow always managed to find a beautiful Spanish or Portuguese woman to help wile away the long lonely days, and nights, between engagements. His commanding officer would therefore be astonished to learn that dalliance with the lovely widow Weymouth was not uppermost in Richard's mind. Not yet, at least. He needed to understand how she happened to be in possession of his family's jewel before he could seriously consider those intriguing eyes and that beguiling mouth.

"I confess I do not know her well," Althea continued, "but she is always pleasant and cheerful. And attractive enough to catch your eye across the length of a ballroom."

She was most definitely attractive enough, but it had not been her pretty face that had caught his eye.

"I thank you for the introduction," Richard said. "I look forward to our dance when I shall hope to get to know the lady better."

Much better indeed. He was determined to discover why she had lied about the Mallory

Heart belonging to *her* family, and then he must contrive a way to return it to *his* family.

This last adventure might not be over so quickly after all. And it just might prove to be considerably more entertaining than he'd expected.

Chapter 3

Isabel saw him moving through the crowd toward her. Phoebe was right about Lord Mallory's affect on those around him. He caused a bit of a stir, and she wondered if he was even aware of it. Women turned to watch as he passed, some craning their heads slightly to get a better look. Men glanced his way as well, though perhaps only to see what had caught the attention of their ladies.

She took a steadying breath as he approached to claim his dance. She was no less immune to his appeal than any other woman in the ball-room, but she was resolved to ignore that appeal. He was certainly one of the more attractive men in the room, and made even more so by the dashing red coat. But she would not lose her good sense to a pair of broad shoulders and a magnificent uniform. She was no green girl, after all. There were more important considerations than good looks, such as the waning fortunes of his family. She could not afford to be distracted from her purpose by scarlet-coated charm.

Especially after Lord Kettering had shown such obvious interest during their dance earlier. Even Sir Henry Levenger had been particular in his attentions, and though his fortune was no match for that of the exceedingly rich Lord Kettering, it was considerable enough.

Either of those gentleman, and several others as well, were more suitable for her needs than the impoverished viscount major.

When he reached her at last, he made an elegant bow. "I believe this is our dance, Lady Weymouth."

He held out his arm for her and smiled. It was a smile that lit his blue eyes and sent little creases echoing out from the corners of his mouth like parentheses. And suddenly the large, slightly intimidating soldier with the beautifully chiseled face was transformed into a very charming man. It was enough to make any rational woman weak in the knees.

Isabel took his arm and he led her to the dance floor where couples began to form lines for a country dance. They stood across from each other while they waited for the music to begin, and he took the time to study her. His blue gaze surveyed her from head to toe with disconcerting leisure and came to rest with casual impertinence on her bosom. When his eyes returned to her face, he winked at her.

The presumptuous scoundrel! How dare he ogle her like that in public?

She glared back at him and wondered, for only the tiniest instant, if she would prefer him to ogle her in private? Isabel pushed that wayward thought aside at once. Yes, it was flattering to be the object of a handsome soldier's flirtation. Very flattering indeed. But he was not the man for her.

The dance began. She took his outstretched hand as they moved into the first figure. The ebb and flow of the movements took them apart and brought them together again, and then again. The man was an unconscionable rogue. He did not attempt conversation so they could concentrate on the lead couple calling the steps. But each time they came together in a movement, his eyes met hers and flirted. Each time they passed across the line or stood side by side, he made sure their shoulders touched briefly, seemingly by accident. Each time they joined hands his fingers ever so gently stroked hers before he let go, reminding her of the way he'd touched her bare wrist when he'd kissed her hand.

Isabel could not help but wonder if she was the only one he flirted with so openly, or if that was simply his nature. She watched as the figures led them briefly to other partners, as he took the hand of the woman on her left and led her into a turn. He acted the complete gentleman, charming but not flirtatious. And the woman showed no signs that he'd done anything improper. Apparently he had singled out Isabel for his most shameless flirtations.

Her vanity was stirred, to be sure, and she was very tempted to flirt right back. If she were still married she would not have hesitated to do so, for she would have had Rupert for protection and both she and Lord Mallory would know it was merely a game. As a widow, however, such blatant flirtation spoke of a different game altogether. One she was not willing to play if she anticipated keeping Lord Kettering's attention.

It was to be hoped that the rich young earl was not watching them at the moment. When she scanned the room she found him in another line, dancing with her friend Lydia Pearsall. She prayed to heaven he had not witnessed anything untoward, like the major's frequent glances at her bosom or her own unguarded interest, and that Lydia was singing Isabel's praises in his lordship's ear.

When the first dance ended, Lord Mallory led her out of the line and said, "You have danced several sets already and it is overly warm in here. May I suggest we sit out the rest of this set? And perhaps enjoy a glass of champagne instead?"

Isabel was more than a bit wary of his intentions. No doubt he found flirtation difficult during a country dance, though he had certainly done a fine job of it. How much more determined would he be without the confines of steps and figures to impede his purpose?

Since he was already leading them away from the dance floor, though, it would be awkward if she requested they return to the line.

"All right," she said. "I would enjoy a glass of champagne."

She had rather hoped it would take him most of the remaining time in the set to find it, but he managed to signal a footman carrying a tray of champagne glasses who was at their side in less than a moment. Lord Mallory took two glasses, and dismissed the footman with a glance. She took the champagne he offered and said, "It must be your military training."

"What must be?"

"Your ability to get people to do your bidding with no more than a look."

He smiled. "I beg you will forgive my overbearing manner. I have been away from Society too long. I confess I am accustomed to command."

"And do you always get what you want? What you command?"

He gazed down at her with those piercing blue eyes and impossibly long eyelashes. "Frequently. But not always."

The husky timbre of his voice sent a shiver dancing down her spine. But Isabel was resolute against his charm. At least she tried to be.

He took her elbow and guided her toward a set of French doors leading to a terrace. "Let us get some fresh air, shall we?"

He led her outside where several other couples had preceded them. At least she would have the protection of their company. Isabel did not think it wise to be alone with Lord Mallory. She did not know if she could trust that resolve of hers to remain steadfast. He was a very attractive man, after all.

He walked toward the side of the terrace and leaned back against the balustrade. He raised his glass to hers. "To new friends," he said.

She touched her glass to his and then took a fortifying swallow. The best way to distract a man's attentions, her mother had always said, was to get him to talk about himself. "You were at Toulouse, I understand."

The tactic was only mildly successful. Like many soldiers he assumed ladies' sensibilities were too fragile to hear any but the most cautious generalities of war and battle. He seemed surprised at her questions about other battles—respectable, genteel women were not supposed to read newspapers, after all—though he did admit to having been involved in some of the major campaigns. Still, it was apparently not a subject he wished to discuss with a lady, and he very neatly turned the discussion back to her.

"I have only just arrived in town," he said.

Obviously. Isabel went everywhere and such a man would have been noticed.

"You must tell me what sort of victory celebrations I have missed."

He deftly led her through a discussion of all the major events since the spring, when the restored French king came to London, and later when the Tsar of Russia and his sister made such a stir, along with the King of Prussia and other allied leaders. She told him of the grand parties and balls, the special Opera performances, the formal proclamation of peace, the troop reviews in Hyde Park, and the Queen's official welcome reception for the new Duke of Wellington.

"It seems I have come too late and missed all the best entertainment." He shifted his weight slightly so that he stood closer to her.

"Not at all. There is still a great deal of entertainment ahead." She gave a silent groan when his grin made her realize how her words could be construed. She took a step back. "There are several more fêtes planned, and a Grand Jubilee next month."

"I shall look forward to them," he said, and his gaze dropped to linger on her bosom again.

Isabel was rather proud of her bosom, but

this was really too much. When his eyes lifted to hers she glared at him, hoping he would feel the sharp edge of daggers in her gaze.

Apparently not, for he smiled rather sheepishly. "Forgive me for staring, Lady Weymouth, but I have a particular interest in old jewelry."

Nonsense. He had a particular interest in her bosom. She continued to glare.

"Truly, I am fascinated by your brooch."

He was definitely fascinated by something, but she seriously doubted it was Gram's brooch. She did, though, have to give him credit for a novel approach.

"I am a collector of sorts," he said. "I hope you won't think me too forward, but I'd like to make you an offer."

Good God. She could not believe he was going to be so bold. Did he really imagine she would allow herself to be set up as his mistress? A pang of anxiety gripped her insides as she wondered if he somehow knew of her circumstances? "I beg your pardon?"

"I would like to buy the brooch," he said.

Isabel expelled a shuddery breath of relief. He had not thought her that low, thank heaven. But his offer was shocking nonetheless and a different sort of uneasiness prickled her skin. Her fingers reached instinctively for her grandmother's brooch. The one she had no business wearing.

"You wish to buy it?"

"Yes. It is of great interest to me."

"No. I'm sorry, but I cannot sell it."

"I would pay a good price."

"It is not for sale, my lord. It is an old family piece."

"Is it?"

Something in his tone chilled her, and his eyes studied hers too closely, as though searching for some sort of vulnerability. For a moment, she had an odd sensation that he knew the ruby was not hers and that she ought not to be wearing it. But that was foolishness. How could he possibly know?

She was letting her imagination run wild. He was simply an impertinent man using the brooch as an excuse to stare at her breasts, and she was feeling guilty for not asking permission to borrow the brooch.

"Yes, it is an old family jewel and I am very attached to it. For sentimental reasons, you understand."

"It has been handed down to you, then?"

A knot of anxiety twisted in her stomach, but she held onto her composure. "Yes."

"One of those old pieces with centuries of family history and legend attached to it, no doubt."

"Yes, of course. And nothing would tempt me to part with it."

"Nothing?" The flirtatious glint was back in his eyes.

"Nothing. And I do believe our set is finished, Lord Mallory."

He did not trust her.

Richard escorted Lady Weymouth back into the ballroom where she was quickly claimed by her next partner. She looked back at him over her shoulder as she walked away and flashed him an enigmatic smile. Was it only his imagination or was there a hint of triumph in her eyes?

He did not trust her.

Although his grandmother would have objected, Richard had decided to make an offer to buy the brooch as the easiest means to his end. He had rather expected she would take his offer, perhaps after a bit of quibbling over price.

After all, she could not have come by it in any manner that was legitimate, so getting rid of it and making a tidy profit in the bargain seemed an ideal situation.

Yet she refused to sell it.

There was definitely something smoky going on, though. He was certain of it. Tension shimmered and rose off her like a fever as soon as he'd mentioned the brooch. She was uneasy and anxious even as she claimed it had been handed down to her. Clearly she was lying.

Though the jewel was stolen fifty years earlier, Lady Weymouth apparently knew something about it. If only she had not lied about it being in her family for hundreds of years, he might have told her the truth. If she had said, for example, that her father had purchased it for her mother years ago, he would have felt comfortable telling her what had actually happened. He would assume her father had not known it was stolen property, but would have pleaded his case to return it to the Mallorys, and perhaps she would have accepted his offer to buy it.

Instead, she persisted with the fiction that it had been in her family for centuries. Lady Weymouth was not, however, an accomplished liar and her intriguing eyes easily communicated the lie.

So, retrieving the jewel was not going to be a straightforward, aboveboard operation.

In anticipation of such, he began to formulate a plan to get back the Mallory Heart as soon as he'd seen it, but it meant that he must make a public show of his interest in Lady Weymouth. He had used every weapon in his arsenal of charm, flirting with her openly at every opportunity.

In truth, it had not been a complete ruse. She was a beautiful woman and it would be no hardship to seduce her. Richard knew how to entice a woman with his eyes, his smile, a clandestine touch here and there, a hint of innuendo in his words. The glimmer of interest in Lady Weymouth's hazel eyes had been unmistakable, and he was certain his efforts had been successful.

Until he'd mentioned the brooch.

And so now he would have to put a more irregular plan into operation. It rankled that he was about to stoop into an area that might put his honor at question. For as an officer and a gentleman, there was nothing more important to Richard than honor. But he used his grandmother's words as license to do what had to be done.

It will not really be stealing, but only returning it to its rightful owner.

There was still a bit of reconnaissance required before putting his plan into action, and so he made his excuses to Bradbury and Lady Althea and quietly left the ball.

An important ball such as this one brought out a small army of street urchins looking to make a few coins by sweeping pavements, holding horses, carrying link torches, or any other small service they could offer. Richard found one and paid him to discover which carriage belonged to Lady Weymouth. Sometime later, the boy came back looking chagrined.

"T'aint no coach what belong to no Lady Weymouth, cap'n. Nor a hired 'un either."

Damn.

"But there be a fancy coach belongin' to a lord summink-or-uffer, an' she come in it wif 'im."

Well now, this could make things interesting indeed. Of course, it was likely only a friend or relative who'd driven her to the ball. She was an attractive, young widow, however, and she could very well have a lover who'd escorted her to the ball and would be taking her home. That could make Richard's plan a bit more tricky.

He put a few more coins in the wide-eyed urchin's hand and asked him to follow while Richard arranged for his own transportation. He had to walk several streets over to find a free hackney, and agreed to pay an exorbitant fee to have the driver wait there until Richard needed him. He then turned again to the boy.

"I want you to go back to the lord's carriage, the one Lady Weymouth came in. As soon as the carriage is called, I want you to run back here and tell me. There's an extra tuppence in it for you if you find out which direction the carriage will be headed."

"Right y'are, cap'n. Coachman's a gormless ol' prat what's been tipplin' a few. 'E'll sing like a birdie if I moon over 'is cattle enuf."

"If you can get him to tell you where Lady Weymouth lives—where he picked her up and where he'll drop her off—it'll be worth more than tuppence to you. Just be sure to get back here the instant the coachman is called to bring the carriage around."

"I'll be quick as a bunny, cap'n. I ain't called Jack Nimble fer nuffink."

An hour later, after several elegant carriages had passed by, Richard wondered if this had been a fool's errand. Either the boy had received a better offer and would not return, or the lady was determined to dance until dawn. He paced in front of the hackney while the driver dozed on the box.

The sound of running feet on the cobbles caused him to turn in time to see young Jack come bounding around the corner at breakneck speed. He almost collided smack into Richard before coming to a halt right in front of him.

"His nibs jus' called for 'is coach, cap'n," the boy said in a breathless voice. "Name's Lord Challiner or Chanceller or summink like. 'Im an' 'is lady brung Lady Weymouth wif 'em."

Ah. No lover then. She'd come with her friend, the dark-haired beauty she'd introduced to him.

"And I know where they's goin'," Jack said, puffing out his thin chest with pride. "She lives at Portman Square, coachman said. That's where 'e picked 'er up."

"Well done, my boy," Richard said. He plucked a few coins from his pocket and dropped them into the urchin's dirty palm. "There's a bit extra for your promise to keep my questions to yourself. Do you understand, Jack Nimble?" He used the same uncompromising tone of voice that put the fear of God in raw recruits.

"Yessir, cap'n." The boy's eyes had grown huge as he gazed at the tiny fortune in his hand. He looked up and grinned. "I never laid me peepers on yer. Ta!" And he disappeared around the corner, no doubt in a hurry to see how much else he could earn for the evening.

Richard jostled the sleeping jarvey awake and asked him to drive to Portman Square. He should arrive well ahead of Lord Challinor's carriage, which would be slowed by the heavy traffic around Inchbald House. It was only a short distance, and Richard thought it would have been just as easy to walk. The hackney dropped him at Seymour Street and drove away, the well-paid driver muttering about the queer notions of the swell set.

Richard surveyed the scene. It was a large square with an oval-shaped garden in the center, surrounded by a simple wrought-iron fence about four feet high. The locked gates kept the garden for the private use of the square's residents. Richard gripped the top rail, lifted himself up, and swung over to the other side.

Fortunately for his purposes, the garden was rather spare in its plantings. He could easily view all four sides of the square without the obstruction of too many trees. The disadvantage was that there was little cover for him, and his red coat would stand out like a beacon if anyone were watching. He moved toward the center and tried to make himself inconspicuous among the shrubbery.

He had barely taken cover when he heard the sound of an approaching carriage. Richard watched as it came to a halt on the eastern side of the square, and he silently moved from one cluster of bushes to another, hunching low, in order to see who exited the carriage and which house she entered.

It was not Lady Weymouth. An elderly couple descended from the coach and walked up the steps to a house where the lamps were lit and a butler or porter held the door open. While he watched, Richard heard the sound of another carriage across the square.

He hurried through the bushes to the southern side of the square, but the carriage turned right and finally came to a halt on the west side, in front of a small but elegant brick house three bays wide. The ground and upper floor windows were plain, but the first floor sported Italianate arched windows and iron railings. The front door echoed the windows of the floor above, with a brickwork archway and a simple fanlight. Two lantern poles flanked the door, but were not lit.

A single woman descended from the carriage. Richard recognized the dress at once. It was Lady Weymouth. She turned to wave to her friends in the carriage and walked up the steps to the front door. Richard crept closer and took cover behind a large bush.

He was surprised to see that no servant opened the door, and that Lady Weymouth let herself in with a key. There was only a faint light inside the entrance, perhaps only a single candle. When the door closed, light continued to flicker behind the fanlight for only a few minutes before all went dark. A moment later, a hint of light glinted from the lower part of the first floor window above the doorway, then filled the window, and disappeared again.

She was moving upstairs, then, carrying her candle. The second floor window was illumined briefly before darkness fell again. Richard waited to see if one of the second floor windows would show light, but the front of the house remained dark. Her bedchamber must be in the back of the house, which was quite perfect for his plan.

He counted houses in each direction and memorized the roof lines. Then he left the cover of the garden and walked around Berkley Street to the mews. It was easy enough to identify Lady Weymouth's house from the back, and there was light in one of the second story windows, escaping through the edges of closed draperies. A brick wall enclosed the back of the property, accessible by a small wooden door. Richard gently pushed, and it swung open.

The small garden he entered was formally laid out, but somewhat unkempt. A sort of shed structure was built against one wall of the garden, and it was covered in an ancient-looking vine of some kind with thick branches that spread onto the back wall of the house.

So, Richard had the information he needed. Lady Weymouth had a very inattentive, or very small, staff. Her bedchamber was in the rear of the house on the right, with an accommodating vine near its window. That last bit of intelligence would hopefully not be needed, but a good reconnaissance officer took in every detail of the terrain.

The charming Lady Weymouth might not want to sell the ruby brooch. But by tomorrow afternoon, Richard would have it in hand nevertheless.

Chapter 4

❦❧

"Major Lord Mallory, my lady."

Isabel looked up at the maid's announcement, and remained seated as he crossed the room. She ought to have known he would show up. "Good afternoon, my lord."

"Lady Weymouth."

He was not wearing his regimentals, and she was almost sorry to note that he looked every bit as large and commanding in ordinary dress. She had rather hoped it had been merely the red coat that had made him so appealing. He stood straight and tall, his military background apparent even without the uniform.

"I trust you have recovered from the exertions of last night's ball?" he said.

"As you see." She indicated the room full of friends, and a few interested gentlemen, who'd come to call. Phoebe caught her eye and lifted her brows slightly at the newcomer. Isabel had told her of the major's bold flirtations at last night's ball, and Phoebe had been agog with curiosity, certain the man had fallen in love at first sight. Isabel did not believe love had anything to do with it. But the huge bouquet of flowers she'd received that morning seemed to confirm his interest.

She could not return that interest, of course, but the rather intoxicating attentions of an intriguing gentleman were hard to ignore.

"I am seldom too tired to receive my friends," she said. "It is very kind of you to call."

Before he could respond, Isabel's attention was turned away by Lord Francis Gilliard, who asked her opinion of the latest pantomime at Drury Lane. As she had not yet seen it, she allowed him to expound at length while her gaze darted discreetly across the room to where Lord Kettering stood, chatting with Phoebe. There were so many callers today— everyone full of news and gossip from last night's entertainments—that Isabel had not been able to spend much time with him.

She sent him a smile and he nodded in acknowledgment.

Isabel reluctantly returned her attention to Lord Francis, but could not help noticing that Lord Mallory was moving back toward the door as though he intended to make his escape. Perhaps he was put off by the number of people in her drawing room. No doubt he had hoped to find her alone so he could flirt with her again.

That notion caused her to smile, and Lord Francis paused in his lecture and beamed. Isabel allowed him to believe the smile had been for him. She had to keep all her options open, after all, in case Lord Kettering could not be brought up to scratch.

Lord Francis had just launched into more description of the new pantomime when Lydia Pearsall approached.

"I must be off, my dear," she said. "I promised Dolly Richardson I would meet her at Hatchards."

Isabel rose and took her friend's arm as they walked to the door of the drawing room. "It was lovely of you to drop by, Lydia. Shall I see you and Oliver tonight at the Easton musicale?"

"Yes, and wait until you see the fetching new pink topaz necklace he bought me, the dear man." She leaned closer and lowered her voice. "Do you not miss having a husband to drape little tokens of affection about your neck and wrists? Lord Kettering might be just the thing, my dear. But you might have to nudge him a bit. He is rather shy, you know."

"Hush, Lydia! He might hear you. And if you must know, I am doing my best to nudge."

"Good girl. Then I shall leave you to it."

When Lydia left the room, Isabel realized Lord Mallory had quietly departed. It seemed a bit cowardly for an army officer to quit the field so soon, but she shrugged off her disappointment. It was just as well he'd gone, she supposed. He would be likely to interfere with her concentration as she attempted a bit of nudging.

She strolled to the corner of the drawing room where Lord Kettering still chatted with Phoebe. She put on her best smile and went to stand beside him.

"We were just speaking of last night's ball," Phoebe said, "and how Lady Inchbald must be crowing with triumph today."

"The Prince *and* the new duke," Isabel said. "It was indeed a coup."

They spoke about the illustrious guests for a few more moments, until Phoebe made an excuse to go have a word with Sir Henry Levenger.

Lord Kettering smiled, and his eyes clearly signaled his pleasure in finally having her to himself. At least, that is the way Isabel chose to interpret the look in those gray eyes.

"And what did you think of our new duke?" he asked.

Isabel shifted her position to stand a bit closer. "He appeared most . . ." She was momentarily distracted by the sight of Lord Mallory lounging against the doorframe. "Most impressive."

"He is, is he not?" Lord Kettering continued to speak, but Isabel found it hard to pay attention. Her eyes kept drifting to the door.

Had he changed his mind? Had he realized it had been faint-hearted to leave, and so had returned?

Or had he never left at all and been wandering about?

Oh, please not that. Please let him not have been exploring the house. If he had done so, he would know the truth of her circumstances and she would be mortified.

Isabel turned her back to the door and concentrated on Lord Kettering, who was such a pattern card of propriety, it would never even occur to him to snoop around someone's home without permission.

As she listened to Lord Kettering talk about his brief conversation with the Duke of Wellington, Isabel tried to convince herself that his disinclination to do anything improper did not make him dull.

He really ought to leave. He'd done what he'd come to do and all his training told him to get the hell out of there before the enemy discovered him. But an irresistible curiosity brought him back.

Richard looked about the elegant drawing room, which was furnished with what looked to be high quality, expensive furniture and a large, very beautiful Turkish carpet on the floor. It was the room of a prosperous and fashionable member of the upper class.

And it was the only room of its kind in the house.

He'd had no trouble sneaking upstairs to find her bedchamber. Not a single servant had challenged him. In fact, the only servant he'd seen was the housemaid who answered the door and escorted him to the drawing room.

When he'd reached her bedchamber, Richard had been astonished at its stark appearance. Besides the bed, which had no curtains, there was only a dressing table, a small chest of drawers, and a clothes press. No paintings or ornaments decorated the walls, but there was a large faded square above the fireplace. No carpet covered the floor, and there was only a small, worn rug next to the bed. The heavy draperies at the window were the only items in the room that matched the elegance of the drawing room below.

It was a room that had been stripped of everything valuable.

Even the dressing table was almost bare. No sterling in sight, there was only a simple ivory set of combs and brushes and one porcelain scent bottle with a chip on its stopper. A pen-work box sat on a table, and Richard guessed it was a jewel case. He lifted the lid and found he'd guessed correctly. The case was loaded with jewelry: diamonds and emeralds and sapphires, necklaces and bracelets, brooches and earrings.

Not all the valuables had been removed after all.

The one thing he sought was not there, but easily discovered in a drawstring flannel bag sitting on the table. She had not even tried to hide it, for this was obviously a room in which a visitor would not be welcome.

Which meant no lover was welcome either. Interesting.

Richard did not believe the stark, private bed-chamber was simply a reflection of its owner's character. Clearly the lady was suffering a financial setback.

He thought of the rest of the house and realized no door had been open, with the exception of the drawing room. On his way back downstairs, Richard opened a few doors and found every room almost stripped to the walls, confirming his suspicions.

He stood now in the only well-furnished room in the house and stared at the lady holding court. She had rejected his offer to buy the brooch, though it was obvious she could use the money. The excuse she had given was a complete sham, so why had she refused to sell?

Could it be that she already had a buyer? Was it possible she had become so desperate that she

72

had resorted to jewel theft, and then fenced the goods to make an income? Were all those other pieces crowded into her jewelry case stolen as well?

Perhaps she had another plan in mind to repair her fortune, and the thievery was only a temporary, desperate measure. Even now, she was paying particular attention to the fair-haired gallant he'd seen at last night's ball. Richard would wager a monkey the man was plump in the pocket.

Something—no doubt the imp of mischief that still came to perch on his shoulder now and then—urged him toward the corner where the blond chap and Lady Weymouth were in conversation. She had seen Richard but had looked displeased and turned her back to him.

"It is indeed gratifying," she said as he approached, "to have so many friends come to call. But I am afraid any such gathering pales after last night's ball and its celebrated guests."

"Nonsense," Richard said as he sidled up beside her. He was amused by the tiny start she gave at his sudden presence. "No gathering could be considered pale when graced with your luminous beauty."

She turned and glared at him, but he gave her

73

his most charming smile, and her annoyance visibly faltered. She gave him one of her provocative half-smiles, where one corner of her mouth quirked up to tease him. "A pretty compliment, my lord. Lord Kettering, may I introduce to you Major Lord Mallory?"

"My lord." Richard gave him an infinitesimal bow.

His blond lordship's brows lifted slightly as he acknowledged Richard. But Richard ignored him as he concentrated on the lovely widow.

"I trust you received my humble floral offering?" he said in his most seductive voice.

"Oh, yes. Thank you." Her tone was polite but her eyes said she wished he would go away.

He had no intention of doing so. "It was the least I could do," he said, keeping his voice low and intimate, "after the very pleasant time we spent together last evening."

Her eyes widened and she looked delightfully flustered. She turned to Kettering and said, "The major and I danced a set together at the Inchbald ball."

"And it was the most fascinating half hour I've spent in a very long time."

Richard reached for her hand, held it in both of his—a precaution, in case she attempted to pull away—and brought it to his lips. She wore no gloves today. Her skin was soft and smelled sweet. Roses. She must bathe in rose water. He inhaled the delicious fragrance. She inhaled a sharp breath.

"I have been away too long, you see," he said, still holding her hand. He made surreptitious little circles with a finger on her palm, and he felt the faint tremor that traveled up her arm. "It has been too long since I had the pleasure of dancing with a beautiful woman. I pray you will honor me with that pleasure again soon."

"Y-yes, of course," she said, and he allowed her to retrieve her hand.

"Excellent. I shall look forward to it. And to becoming better acquainted. Now, I believe you have other guests arriving and I have over-stayed my welcome. I bid you good day, Lady Weymouth." He pressed a hand to his breast and bowed. He turned to the golden-haired lord, who eyed him curiously, and nodded. "Kettering."

Richard strolled to the doorway, turned for one last look, and found Lady Weymouth staring at him. Her lips slightly parted, her intriguing eyes softened with curiosity, she looked good enough to eat. Richard forced his feet to take him away. He'd just taken her brooch; he had no business thinking of other things he would like to take.

No, he had to finish his assignment before he could consider anything more personal. He had to deliver the Mallory Heart back to his grandfather so he could properly present it to his wife before he died.

Richard could not, though, seem to shake the idea of coming back to Town and calling on Lady Weymouth again. Idiot. He was too easily seduced by a pair of intriguing eyes and a provocative mouth. He must remember that he could not trust a woman who had his family's property in her possession, and who was quite possibly a thief. Lady Weymouth was not the woman for him.

He had just passed through the front gate when he heard footsteps behind him.

"Mallory?"

Richard turned to find Lord Kettering coming down the steps. Damnation. He hoped he was not about to be warned off by a jealous suitor.

"I wonder if you could spare me a few moments," Kettering said.

"Of course."

"There is a small tavern a few streets away. I would be honored if you would allow me to buy you a pint. I should like to talk with you about something."

"All right," Richard said. It was an odd way to warn off a rival, but he could use a good pint.

"We could take my carriage, or yours if you prefer, but it might be more pleasant to walk. It is only a short distance."

"I took a hackney," Richard said, "and a walk would be fine."

"Splendid. Let me just have a word with my coachman to meet us at the Boar's Head in an hour or so."

An hour? What the devil did this fellow have to say that would take an hour? It would take Richard no more than a minute to tell the man he was leaving Town and was no threat to his courtship. It occurred to him that he ought to warn Kettering that the woman he was courting was quite possibly a thief. But that was really none of his business, and if the man fell into her trap he likely deserved it.

Kettering returned and led the way down Seymour Street. "You must wonder why I wanted to speak to you."

"I am curious, yes."

"Well, you see, I knew your brother."

Richard stopped walking. "Arthur?"

"Yes. He was one of my closest friends. I hadn't realized you had returned from France, or I would have looked you up. Arthur spoke of you so often. He was very proud of his brother the soldier."

Richard swallowed back a lump that had suddenly formed in his throat. He continued walking, keeping his eyes straight ahead so Kettering would not see his face. "I am very pleased to meet one of his friends. I saw him so little these last years." It was one of the things that pained him most about being away at war for so long. He had lost that time forever, and would never see his brother again. "You must tell me all about him."

"I will, happily. He was a great gun, you know. I could tell you such stories." He chuckled softly. "But there is something specific I wish to tell you about. I think you should know how he died."

"I would appreciate knowing more about that," Richard said. "I heard only that it was a hunting accident."

"It was no accident."

"What?" Richard came to a halt again and

grabbed Kettering by the arm. "What do you mean it was no accident? Tell me what happened."

"I will. But here is the tavern. Let us find a private table and order a couple of pints."

Richard could hardly breathe, much less speak, so he allowed Kettering to lead him to a dark corner and send the waiter off to procure two pints of ale. He was rigid with fury. If the gunshot that had killed his brother had not been accidental, there was only one other explanation.

"Tell me." He kept his voice low but the sharp edge of command came naturally.

"Wait for the ale. I think you will need it."

"Kettering, I swear I will leap across this table and throttle you with my bare hands if you do not tell me what happened."

"Ah, here it is." The burly waiter slammed two large pewter tankards on the table and walked away. "Now drink," Kettering said, "and I will tell you everything."

Richard took a long swallow, then glared at Kettering.

The man opened his mouth to speak, closed it, then took a drink of ale. Richard leaned across the table menacingly.

"Tell me."

Kettering took a deep breath. "He was shot in a duel."

Oh my God. "A duel?"

"I am afraid so. It was kept a great secret, so there was no scandal. Your family does not know."

"No, we do not know."

"That was Arthur's wish. He begged us all to keep the truth from your grandfather. Said he had a weak heart and it would kill him."

"Yes, it would have done." As it was killing Richard now. "Who was it?"

"Lord Ridealgh. You will not know of him, I daresay."

"No. Who is he?"

"A minor baron. A hotheaded fool."

"He called the duel?"

"Yes."

"Why?"

Kettering looked squarely at him, studying him intently as though judging how much to say. "Ridealgh accused Arthur of having an affair with his wife."

Richard swore.

"It was not true, of course. But Ridealgh was set on satisfaction. Arthur fired in the air. Ridealgh did not."

"Bloody hell."

"Arthur was mortally wounded, but did not die right away. He made us all swear to uphold the fiction of the hunting accident. He especially did not want you to know."

"Why?"

"He feared you would kill Ridealgh."

"And so I will. Where do I find the blackguard?" Richard made as if to rise from the bench.

Kettering held up a hand to stop him. "He is already dead, so there is no need for you to hunt him down. That is why I thought it safe to tell you, despite my promise to your brother. I thought you had a right to know the truth. If the story ever came out somehow, I wanted you to know Arthur was innocent. He was a man of honor and faced Ridealgh bravely."

Richard settled back on the bench and heaved a sigh. "Yes, he would do that. Thank you for telling me. It was painful enough not to have been here when it happened, but to have carried around a lie would only make it worse. I appreciate your honesty, Kettering. You were indeed a good friend to him."

"There are others who were his friends, who were there that day, and they would be honored to meet you. As it happens, we are all gathering at Tattersall's tomorrow morning to have a look at some cattle. A cavalry officer's eye would be much appreciated. Will you join us?"

Richard had planned to ride back to Greyshott in the morning, anxious to turn over the ruby brooch. But the chance to meet his brother's friends and learn more about all the years he'd lost with him was simply too tempting to pass up.

"Do the others know the truth of the duel?" he asked.

"Yes. We were all there."

"And they will not mind talking about it? I should wish to hear more about this Ridealgh fellow. And his wife."

"I have told them I was going to admit the truth to you, so I am certain they would be willing to talk about it. After we decide on the horses, we can share a bottle and a bird and tell tales about your brother."

"I would like that. Very much."

There might still be time to ride to Greyshott in the afternoon. That damned brooch was burning a hole in his pocket and he wanted to be rid of it.

"Excellent. We'll meet at Tatt's at noon. There's

a bay gelding I have my eye on, and I'd welcome your opinion."

"I am happy to oblige."

"And I confess I would welcome advice of another sort as well." He gave a sheepish grin. "You must tell me what you think of Lady Weymouth."

Richard groaned.

Chapter 5

The ruby brooch was missing.

Isabel searched everywhere, but the jewel was nowhere to be found.

She had dressed with care for the Easton musicale, donning a dress cunningly refashioned from an older one and updated with hand embroidery and seed pearls. The latter had once been part of a wide cuff-like bracelet, but Isabel had sold the large turquoise clasp and not replaced it, so the pearls were put to a new use. When she opened her jewelry case to retrieve a necklace of green paste stones that looked exactly like the emeralds Rupert had given her, she saw her grandmother's diamond parure and decided to wear it instead of the faux emeralds.

It was then she had realized the more important of Gram's jewels was not where she'd left it, in its protective bag on top of the dressing table.

Isabel stood in the middle of her bedchamber, frozen with panic. She could not lose the ruby heart. She could not. What would she tell Gram? She uttered a horrified moan at the thought of confessing to her grandmother that she had not only borrowed the brooch without permission, but had lost it. She knew in her heart that the brooch had special meaning to Gram, or she would not have kept it locked away in a secret drawer. How could Isabel possibly tell her it was missing?

She went into the corridor and called out for Tessie, who was in one of the other bedchambers that had been made over into a makeshift sewing room, where all of Isabel's "new" clothes were fashioned. Tessie came at once.

"Yes, m'lady?"

"Tessie, have you seen that big ruby brooch I wore last night?"

"The one in the little drawstring pouch?"

"Yes, that's it. Have you seen it?"

Tessie walked into the bedchamber and

pointed to the dressing table. "I seen the pouch right there."

"When?"

"This morning, when I tidied up."

"Well, it is not there now."

The color drained from Tessie's face and her eyes grew huge with alarm. "I din't take it, m'lady. I swear I din't."

Isabel touched the girl's shoulder in reassurance. She trusted the young maid, as she did each of the few remaining members of her household staff. Since she'd had to let so many of the servants go, those who remained behind were steadfast in their loyalty to her.

"I know you didn't take it, Tessie. But the fact is, the brooch is missing. Do you have any idea what might have happened to it?"

"No, m'lady. But it got to be here somewheres. Let me have a look 'round."

Isabel left the girl on her knees, searching under the bed, and went to question the other servants. She ran into Thomas, the lone footman on the staff, on her way downstairs. He hadn't seen the brooch except when she'd been wearing it, but promised to keep an eye out for it.

The housekeeper generally knew all that went on in the household, so Isabel sought her out. Mrs. Bunch doubled as the cook these days, but all the staff was under her management, and she made sure everything ran smoothly. Isabel found her down in the kitchen setting out bowls and knives and other items for tomorrow's meals on the big worktable in the center of the room, while the scullery maid, who doubled as a tweeny, scrubbed the dishes and pots from tonight's dinner.

"I'm that sorry, my lady," Mrs. Bunch said in response to Isabel's query, "but I haven't been up to the bedchambers all day. And I sure as heaven haven't seen a ruby heart laying around down here. Lordy, what could have become of it? Daisy? Girl, have you been upstairs to her ladyship's bedchamber today?"

The scullery turned from her work and said, "Only this mornin', t' empty the slops, ma'am."

"And did you see a cloth pouch with a jewel inside?"

"In the slops?"

"No, you stupid cow," Mrs. Bunch said, causing the girl to wince. "On the dressing table."

"T'ain't my place to look at no dressin' table," Daisy said. "That be Tessie's job. I ain't seen nothin'."

Mrs. Bunch looked at Isabel in frustration. "I

do not know what to say, my lady. Surely it will turn up."

"Where's Danny?" Isabel asked. "Perhaps he knows something about it."

"He's out back. Shall I call him?"

"Send him upstairs. I want to see if Tessie's had any luck."

Isabel returned to her bedchamber only to find Tessie in tears.

"I can't find it nowhere, m'lady. I've looked and looked."

"Thank you for trying," Isabel said. She thought she might break into tears herself. What the devil was she going to do?

"It were that one you borrowed from yer grandma, weren't it?"

Isabel nodded, unable to speak.

"Oh, my lady. What you gonna do?"

"I don't know, Tessie," Isabel replied in a tremulous whisper. "I really don't know."

"It don't make no sense. Nobody's been up here but me. You had all them callers, o' course, but none o' them woulda had a reason to come upstairs."

Isabel drew a sharp breath. One of them might have had a reason.

I have a particular interest in old jewelry.

Was it possible? She recalled Lord Mallory's brief and unexplained disappearance from the drawing room that afternoon. Surely he had not gone upstairs and stolen the jewel. Even if his family's fortunes had declined, she could not imagine a major of the Dragoon Guards and the heir to an earldom would resort to jewel theft.

No, he was an incorrigible flirt, but not a thief. She would not believe it.

"Yer wanted t' see me, m'lady?"

Danny Finch stood in the doorway. He had a shock of straight brown hair that never stayed neatly combed for more than a few minutes, and dark eyes that looked older than the freckled face into which they were set. He was small for his age, which Isabel guessed to be about thirteen. He had been a part of the staff for almost four years, since the day Rupert had caught him in the act of trying to pick his pocket. Instead of turning the boy over to Bow Street, Rupert had felt sorry for him and brought him home. Isabel's husband was as much a slave to fashion as she was, and it had become fashionable to have very small tigers perched up on the rear seat of a gentleman's curricle. So he had turned Danny over to the head groom to train as a tiger.

Since Rupert's death, there had been no need for tigers after all the carriages were sold. But Isabel had found it impossible to turn Danny out when she reduced the staff. She had grown very fond of the boy and feared he would fall back into a life of crime. So she kept him on as a sort of under-footman who did all sorts of tasks and ran any errand Isabel or Mrs. Bunch required.

"I seem to have misplaced a piece of jewelry," she said.

A furious look came over the boy's face. "It weren't me! You knows I don't do that no more. An' even if I did, I'd never take nuffink wot belonged ter you."

"Oh, Danny, I was not accusing you. I know you would never do such a thing. I trust you completely."

The boy blushed and smiled. "Thank you, m'lady."

"I was just wondering if you saw anyone come upstairs today when I had callers."

Danny shrugged and looked away. "Not really. Only that one bloke."

"What bloke?"

"That tall, dark-haired feller."

Damn and blast. Anger began to simmer in

the pit of her stomach. "You saw a tall, dark man going upstairs?"

"Comin' downstairs."

"That scoundrel!" He'd been in her bedchamber. He'd taken her grandmother's precious jewel.

Danny paled. " 'E weren't s'pposed to be up there?"

"No, he was not." Isabel almost spat the words.

Danny muttered a vulgar oath. "Sorry. Thought the feller was . . ."

"What? You thought he was what?"

"A friend."

"A friend?"

"You know. Special sorta friend. 'Andsome devil like that. Lookin' right at 'ome and all. I jus' figgered 'e was yer . . ."

Good God. Isabel felt her cheeks flame. She supposed if she ever did take a lover, she could count on Danny's discretion. "Well, he isn't. But I'm very much afraid the man is a thief."

"Yer don't mean it. That toff?" Danny shook his head in disbelief. "Well, waddaya know. So then, wotcher want me to do?"

"Do?"

"Yer want it back, dontcher?

Isabel eyed the boy quizzically. Suddenly he was no longer the young under-footman. He was the scrappy street urchin who picked pockets for a living. "Of course I do. It belongs to my grandmother and I must return it to her."

"Then there's only one thing ter do."

"What?"

"Steal it back."

Richard had risen early in preparation for the return to Greyshott. He'd leased the chambers on Tavistock Street for the rest of the summer, having assumed his quest would take longer to accomplish. Rather than trying to break the lease, he'd decided to keep the rooms. He just might return to Town after all.

Richard had traveled on horseback for so many years, over so many miles, that he could not bear to be confined inside a carriage for any length of time, so he had ridden into London and planned to ride back to Greyshott. He'd sent John Tully, his batman, to the stables to ensure their mounts were ready for the long ride into Hampshire later that afternoon. Tully had served Richard for so long he had asked to come to Greyshott with him. He knew Richard was going to have to sell out, even if his grandfather recovered, and Tully had offered his services.

The batman aspired to be a valet, which Richard thought to be a waste of an excellent soldier. But with the wars over, the man was simply looking to his future, and that was why Richard had brought him along to London. If he wanted to succeed as a valet, he needed to see how men who were not soldiers dressed, to learn who were the best tailors, where to buy the best neckcloths, and so on. But Richard was not accustomed to having a valet and did more for himself than Tully liked. And so while it was just the two of them, Tully continued to play the role of batman, or a gentleman's gentleman, doing every sort of service for Richard.

Richard's clothes were neatly folded and arranged on the bed ready for packing. Tully had refused to stuff them into the small saddlebag until he was absolutely certain they would be leaving that afternoon. He did not like to risk wrinkled shirts in case the trip was delayed, as it might well be, depending on how long Richard spent with Kettering and the others. Instead, Tully had prepared everything so that it could be packed and ready within a few moments. The little pouch holding the Mallory Heart lay next to Richard's shaving kit.

Richard picked up the pouch and removed the brooch. It was large and heavy, taking up half the length of his palm. The heart-shaped ruby was one of the largest he'd ever seen, and there were too many diamonds to count in the arrow tips and the lover's knot. The thing must be worth a small fortune. He wondered again if his grandfather actually wanted it back so he could sell it. If that was indeed his plan, Richard would talk him out of it. He had enough money of his own to make the needed repairs and improvements at Greyshott. And besides, his grandmother deserved to have the brooch, as had all the countesses before her.

He studied the inscription that encircled the heart, the words he had not been able to read in the paintings. It had been years since his school days at Winchester, but he was pretty sure the Latin translated to "true love knows only one" or something close to that. He supposed even his rather severe grandmother deserved such a tribute, however late in life.

A knock on the door interrupted his musings. He replaced the brooch in its pouch and returned it to the orderly arrangement of items ready to be packed for travel. He opened the door expecting to see the landlord, and was startled to find Lady Weymouth instead.

Damn and blast.

She must have discovered the brooch was gone and come to accuse him of taking it. He ought to have left for Hampshire at the break of dawn instead of agreeing to meet with Kettering. He was in for it now.

Yet it was not an angry woman who stood before him. Quite the contrary. She wore her most brilliant smile, the one that had dazzled him momentarily at the ball. She did not have the look of a woman bent on vengeance.

"Lady Weymouth. I am surprised to see you."

"Are you?" Her eyes held a look of quizzical amusement. "You should not be. May I come in?"

Richard had been away from Society for a long time, but even he knew it was not entirely proper for a woman to visit a gentleman's chambers alone. His hesitation compelled her to speak again.

"Please, my lord. I have taken pains to be discreet in coming here, but if you insist on keeping me standing outside your door I fear someone may eventually take note."

Richard stepped aside and gestured for her to enter. "Of course. Please come in."

She did, and it happened that she was not in fact alone. A liveried page followed her, holding her parasol. The bewigged boy, dressed in silver and green satin, kept his eyes deferentially lowered and remained a few paces behind his mistress. She strolled into the room with the confident air of one who was perfectly comfortable visiting a bachelor's rooms. She looked especially pretty in a white dress and a short green jacket, with a soft bonnet in the same green fabric.

Thoroughly puzzled by this invasion, Richard was somewhat at a loss. If she wasn't here to accuse and berate him, then why had she defied propriety and come to his rooms? She had not struck him as an eccentric.

Richard closed the door and walked to stand beside the fireplace. She remained posed elegantly in the middle of the sitting room. "Won't you sit down?" He indicated a pair of chairs in front of him.

"I would rather not," she said.

Her eyes moved slowly down his body and up again, and Richard's mouth went dry. She lifted one eyebrow as her eyes met his again, quirked up her lips in that seductive half-smile he'd seen before, and came to stand close to him. So close he could smell the scent of roses that clung to her skin. She lifted a gloved finger and touched one of the buttons on his waistcoat. "You did say you wished to become better acquainted, did you not?"

Good God. A sudden heat coursed through him, primitive and base, an instinctive male response to a signal of female interest. Was she suggesting what he thought she was suggesting? Did this visit truly have nothing to do with the ruby brooch?

Well, well, well. What an interesting development this was.

"I did," he said. He grasped the hand that played upon his chest and brought it to his lips.

She gave his hand a little squeeze, then kept hold of it while she softly stroked his fingers. Richard's groin tightened.

"I thought so." Her voice had taken on a soft velvety tone. "And I wish to know more about you as well. There were always so many people around us, I was not entirely certain that you understood your wish to become . . . better acquainted was reciprocated."

It was surely the most blatant invitation he'd

ever received. The woman was not only a thief but a seductress as well. He was completely and irresistibly fascinated. "And you came by especially to tell me?"

"I hope you do not mind?"

"I am delighted, my lady."

She smiled and leaned closer. "I am so glad. If we are to be friends, you must call me Isabel."

He had not known her name. It suited her. Its sibilant beginnings suggested whispers and intimacies. He tried it out. "Isabel."

"I like the way it sounds when you say it."

"It is a beautiful name. Isabel. And I am Richard."

"Richard."

She said it so softly it made him imagine hearing it in his ear as she lay beside him in bed. He felt like he was in the presence of a practiced courtesan. But he remembered that stark, simple bed chamber and could not imagine it as a den of seduction. He was thoroughly bemused and confused, but also very much aroused. He almost dipped his head to kiss her when he caught sight of the page boy, standing still as a statue in the corner.

She saw his glance and said, "Do not worry

about my page. He is paid to see nothing, hear nothing, and say nothing."

"He is not your protector, then?"

She laughed. "Heavens, no. He is simply a charming accessory I don now and then when my dress happens to match one of his liveries. Speaking of uniforms, I notice you do not wear yours during the day."

"No, only on formal occasions when I am on leave."

"It is a very handsome uniform."

"Ah. Then it was my scarlet coat that caught your eye."

"It was the man in the scarlet coat."

She still kept his hand in hers, resting against his chest, as she shifted positions slightly, turning away from the window so that her back was to it. Richard turned with her, and the way she looked at him, he had the impression the shift in position was to see him in a better light.

"Or the blue coat," she said. "It hardly matters."

Her eyes were very green today—perhaps a reflection of the green jacket—with gold flecks and brown depths, and even a hint of turquoise around the edges. The eyes that looked back at him from the shaving mirror each day were a pure blue, and most of the women he'd been intimate with during the last several years had eyes of the darkest brown. It was fascinating, therefore, to see so many different colors in her eyes.

When those captivating eyes moved to his lips, he was lost.

He snaked an arm around her waist, drew her to him, and kissed her.

And something ignited between them. Something quick and hot, as though an electrical charge jolted through them both, creating a steady roaring in his ears. It was not simple lust or sexual fire, though there was that, to be sure. It was more a fierce curiosity to know the full measure of each other, to test each other's mettle in mutual fascination.

Their hands were still clasped and crushed between them. He released her fingers and wrapped his arm tightly around her shoulders, pulling her closer. Her freed hand twined itself in his hair. The other had circled his waist and moved up his back.

Her lips parted against his and he thrust his tongue deep in her mouth. Isabel gave a little moan and pulled back. Richard lifted his mouth a fraction. He opened his eyes to find hers wide and uncertain, as if she was stunned by her own charged response and didn't know what to do.

This was the practiced courtesan?

Richard did not give her a chance to consider the situation, for *he* knew exactly what to do. He brought his mouth to hers again and coaxed her lips apart.

This time, when he touched his tongue to hers, she answered in kind, and her response sent shafts of heat darting through his body. His hands slid over the soft fabric of her dress, tracing the curve of her shoulder, her spine, her hips, and finally her nicely rounded bottom.

She jerked away again, roughly and completely, stepping back out of his embrace. Her eyes were still wide, as though the whole business had shocked and surprised her.

Which surprised Richard, for after all, *she* had come to him.

He lifted his eyebrows in question.

"I . . . I think I made a mistake. I shouldn't be here." She motioned to her page and said to him, "Please check outside. I don't wish anyone to see me leave here."

The boy nodded and left.

"I am sorry you feel you must leave," he said and touched her shoulder.

She shrugged off his hand. "It was a foolish idea. You will think me some sort of . . . wanton. I assure you, I do not usually do this sort of thing. I do not know what got into me."

Richard placed his hands behind his back and studied her. She really did look flustered and embarrassed. And utterly enchanting. "I am sorry you think it was foolish. I thought it was quite pleasurable. And I believe you did, too."

She flushed deeply and would not meet his eyes.

"If you prefer, we can pretend this encounter never happened. I am leaving Town today in any case."

"Oh. Then I am mortified to have imposed myself upon you. Ah, here is my page. Is the way clear, Danny?"

"Yes, m'lady."

"Then, I shall take my leave. I am sorry to have interrupted your travel preparations, Lord Mallory."

She made a hasty retreat through the door. As

she hurried down the corridor, he called out, "Good-bye, *Isabel*." She did not respond.

Richard closed the door, leaned back against it, and let out a long, slow breath.

What the devil had just happened?

Danny sat beside her in the hackney coach and scratched his head. He'd removed the dreaded wig and muttered something about trained monkeys.

"Least we got it back. 'Cept fer these rum kicks," he said, tugging at his satin breeches, " 'twas the easiest sham I ever run."

Easy for Danny.

Isabel sat in silence as they bounced along Oxford Street on the way back to Portman Square. Danny was a streetwise boy who'd no doubt seen a great deal worse, but she was embarrassed that he had seen that kiss, that he had seen Lord Mallory's hands roaming all over her body. The fact that he'd known of the plan all along, had even helped to devise it, did not make it any easier to know that he'd been watching.

It had seemed the perfect plan. Lord Mallory had distracted her with his bold flirtations and seductive manner, knowing just exactly how to keep her flattered and intrigued and off guard. All so that she would not suspect his true purpose.

But two could play that game, and she'd decided to give him back a little of his own. She would employ all the feminine wiles at her disposal to distract him while Danny searched for the jewel. And she need never worry that he would reveal she had broken every rule of propriety to come to his chambers. He wouldn't dare, for she would then reveal that he was a thief. Tit for tat.

Yes, it had been the perfect plan and Isabel had been ready to execute it with perfect sangfroid.

So much for the sophisticated woman of the world pretending at seduction. She had tried to maintain a worldly veneer of sensual intent, as though she was well-experienced in the games men and women play. Of course, she was no such thing, but she had thought it would be so simple. Yet her pulse had begun to accelerate the moment she'd fingered the button on his waistcoat. One touch from him and she had melted like a schoolgirl, had succumbed with ease to his potent, virile charm. His kiss had sent her reeling, spinning out of control. She had pulled away, surprised at the intensity of her reaction.

It was then she had seen Danny give the signal that he'd found the brooch. But Lord Mallory—Richard—hadn't allowed her to end it. He had proceeded to ravish her mouth and her senses until she had to force an end to it, before she made a complete fool of herself.

She had not kissed a man since Rupert had died. Richard's kiss had awakened a nostalgic physical longing that had shaken her to the core. She had almost forgotten what that sweet taste of connection was like, that sense of human joining that went beyond lips and hands into realms of intimacy that were more than merely physical.

She hadn't realized how much she'd missed that closeness. Richard's kisses had pierced her heart with a yearning so powerful and unexpected it frightened her.

Why did it have to be this man of all men—a rogue and a thief—to make her feel like that? He could ruin all her efforts to land a rich, and respectable, husband like Lord Kettering. One look from him could distract her from her purpose, and she could not afford for that to happen.

Thank goodness he was leaving London.

Chapter 6

❝It's a good thing you came along, Mal-lory, or Kettering here would have wasted his blunt on that chestnut gelding. Well done."

George Amberley lifted his tankard in salute. He was a jovial chap, and one of the men who'd been a friend to Richard's brother. The fourth member of the group was Lord Northing. He, Kettering, and Amberley had all been present at the duel that had killed Arthur.

"I'm deuced grateful," Kettering said. "I never would have noticed the thin walls of his feet."

"It's easy to miss with white socks," Richard said, "but it's something I've learned to look out for."

"It pays to have a cavalryman vet your purchases," Northing said.

"Indeed," Kettering agreed. He raised his tankard. "To Major Lord Mallory and his keen eye."

They all joined in the salute, clanking their tankards and splashing ale on the tavern table.

"May I beg a favor in return?" Richard asked.

"Anything," Kettering said.

"Tell me about Arthur. You all knew him well. Tell me stories about him."

And so they did. Tales of friendship and competition, of sport and gaming, of wine and women. They laughed and drank and swapped stories for an hour or more, and Richard felt closer to his brother than he had for a long time. Finally, he asked what he really wanted to know.

"Tell me about Lord Ridealgh."

The group fell silent. They all shared glances back and forth until it fell to Kettering to respond.

"He was a hothead, a jealous maniac who thought every male who so much as glanced in his wife's direction was in love with her."

"Was he? Was Arthur in love with her?"

"Egad, no," Amberley said, and the rest of them muttered agreement.

"Then what happened? Why did Ridealgh challenge him?"

"Arthur was nice to her, that's all," Northing said. "There was a ball one night, and he spent an entire set talking with her when he found she did not enjoy dancing. She apparently mentioned to Ridealgh how kind Arthur had been to her, and that jealous fool read more into it."

"The sad thing is," Kettering said, "that we all knew about Ridealgh's irrational behavior where his wife was concerned. There was even talk about previous duels. But Arthur ignored all the tales of jealousy and gave more attention to the woman than he should have done."

"And paid the price," Richard said. "What a tragic waste. Poor old Arthur. If Ridealgh weren't already dead I would happily put a bullet through his skull."

"Someone else did it for you," Northing said.

"What? He was killed?"

"In another duel," Amberley said. "Another poor sod who'd glanced upon Lady Ridealgh. Only this chap didn't fire into the air. He aimed straight for the heart."

"And the world is a better place without that madman," Northing said.

"What became of the dashing widow?" Richard asked.

"Dashing?" Amberley chuckled. "She ain't what you're thinking, old man. Not at all the type you'd expect to fire all that jealousy."

"She kept to strict mourning, as I recall," Kettering said, "and wasn't seen about. But it's been over a year now, and with all the peace celebrations, perhaps she'll make an appearance again. I think, though, that she lives rather quietly."

Later, as Richard made his way back to Tavistock Street, he could not stop thinking about the mysterious woman who'd indirectly caused his brother's death and, not to put too fine a point on it, ruined his own life in the bargain. It was due to her that Richard was now faced with a legacy and responsibilities he'd never wanted. It was due to her that he was going to have to sell his commission and give up soldiering forever. It was due to her that there was no more adventure ahead for him.

He was determined to find this woman and confront her. He wanted to know what sort of woman it was who had wreaked such havoc with so many lives, and he wanted to make sure she knew what manner of grief and heartache she had caused. He wished he could stay in Town and seek her out, but he had other priorities. He first had to return to Greyshott and deliver that damned ruby heart.

When Richard opened the door to his chambers, he was confronted by an uncharacteristically frantic Tully. The normally unflappable batman was wild-eyed, his hair standing out in all directions as though he'd raked his fingers through it over and over.

"You look a fright, Tully. I know I'm late, but there's no need to get into such a lather over it. We can wait until morning to leave."

"It's not that, my lord. It's . . ." The fellow was actually wringing his hands.

"It's what?"

"It's the . . . the jewel, my lord. The Mallory Heart."

"What about it?"

"It's gone."

"What do you mean, it's gone?"

"It's not here. I left it right next to your shaving kit, but it was not there when I returned

110

from the stables. I've searched every corner of these rooms. It's gone, my lord."

Hell and damnation.

That little temptress had not come to seduce him. She had stolen the jewel back. No, not her. It was that blasted page boy.

"How could I have been so stupid?" he muttered, and slapped the ball of his palm against the side of his head.

"I beg your pardon, my lord?"

"Tully, my good fellow, never underestimate the guile and cunning of a woman."

His batman's eyes widened with understanding. "It was her, then? Lady Weymouth?"

"The one and only. By God, she played me for a fool with a classic decoy maneuver I am ashamed to say I didn't even recognize."

It had actually been a very neat operation, and he admitted to a sort of grudging admiration of her for it. She'd played her part well, up to a point. She had been an excellent seductress, tempting him with those eyes and that mouth. For a moment, he'd lost all reason and succumbed to her blatant invitation. Now he understood, though, why he'd been so confused about her almost horrified retreat when things began to heat up between them. She was no practiced courtesan. She was an innocent playing with fire, and she'd been scorched by her own reaction.

At least now he knew where she was vulnerable. If she thought their game was over, she did not know her opponent very well. It was time to plan an ambush of his own.

"Tully, unpack my bags. We're not leaving Town after all."

The Cummings rout was so crowded it was almost impossible to move. And it was much too warm. Isabel dropped the lace shawl to her elbows and waved a fan to cool her face.

"I see a waiter making his way through the crowd," she said. "I believe I would kill for a glass of champagne."

"No need for such drastic measures," Lord Kettering said with a smile. "He should be here shortly."

"But will he have any glasses left on that tray by the time he gets here?"

"Let's not take any chances. Come with me."

He took her elbow and guided her toward the waiter. But it was soon clear that they were not going to get close enough, and they watched as the last glass was taken from his tray.

"Rotten luck," Lord Kettering said. He turned to look at her and she almost hit him in the face with the vigorous waving of her fan. "Oh, but you are too warm," he said in a solicitous voice that warmed her even more. "If you will stay here, I will go and hunt down something cool to drink."

"Thank you, sir, I would appreciate it." She gave him her most brilliant smile and was pleased to see him flush slightly. It might only have been the overheated room, though, and not her charm, that put color in his cheeks, but she held onto the hope that she was nudging him along quite nicely.

Her smile was still in place as she surveyed the room to see if anyone interesting had arrived.

It fell when she saw Lord Mallory at the entrance.

Her heart gave a tiny lurch. It seemed he had not left Town after all. She waved her fan faster as she watched him. She told herself she had nothing to fear from him.

So what if her heart skipped a couple of beats when she saw him across the room? It was because of the jewel, that was all, and the fact that he would know she had taken it. It didn't mean anything else. It wasn't about their kiss. She had tried all day to erase that incident from her mind.

Yet the physical sensations he'd aroused earlier in the day came back in full force at the sight of him. A sudden rush of heat prickled every inch of her skin, and she was enveloped once again by that traitorous longing that had almost overwhelmed her that afternoon. She watched his mouth as he spoke to someone, watched how his lips moved to form words and then to curve into a smile, and remembered how they had felt pressed against her own.

Foolish woman! She had no business being so distracted by a scoundrel who could fire a woman's blood with a single kiss, then steal her blind before she knew what had happened. He was a cad of the worst sort, a thief, and quite possibly dangerous. She was determined to put him out of her mind.

Isabel wondered how many other woman had fallen victim to his charm, as well as his thievery. Did he single out specific women for his flirtations, women who wore jewels he most coveted? She smiled to consider that she was probably the only one who'd had the temerity to strike back. Major Lord Mallory would *not* get the best of Lady Weymouth.

Besides, he interfered with her other plans, plans that included nudging along the amiable earl who'd gone to find her a glass of champagne. They did not include a handsome, charming, red-coated thief.

Finally, he saw her.

Their gazes met across the room, and locked in a mutual recognition of strength and resolve, a brief battle of will and wit. It was something of an effort, but she remained steadfast against that calculating gaze.

Just as at the Inchbald ball, his entrance caused a mild disturbance. Though he was not the only scarlet-coated officer in attendance, ripples of attention followed him as he moved through the crowd. Was he unaware of the effect he had on people, especially females, or did he use it shamelessly to his advantage? Ladies all across the room strained for a better look.

As Isabel watched, she thought he did not in fact realize how women reacted to him. Or if he did, he did not care. He seemed oblivious to their attention.

His attention was entirely focused on Isabel.

While everyone else in the room was packed shoulder to shoulder and barely able to move, he somehow easily made his way toward her.

"Lady Weymouth," he said when he stood before her at last. He reached down for her hand and brought it to his lips. "What a pleasure to see you again so soon, Isabel."

He spoke her name softly, intimately. It was unlikely, thank heaven, anyone in that noisy room could have heard.

"I thought you were leaving Town, Richard." She infused a hint of mockery in his name as she retrieved her hand.

"My plans changed. I have unfinished business here, it seems."

"Indeed? How tedious for you."

"Not at all. It is quite an intriguing bit of business, actually, and most . . . unexpected."

"Ah. Life is full of little surprises, is it not?"

"More so than I had realized," he said.

There was something almost exciting about their banal conversation with its undercurrents of things unspoken. Isabel knew he was a thief, and he knew she knew. Richard knew she had bested him at his own game, and she knew he knew. She would like to have matched wits with him for a while longer, but it was not to be.

"Ah, here is Lord Kettering," she said, and silently berated herself for feeling disappointed that he had returned so soon.

"Success!" the earl said as he handed her a full flute of champagne, which she was tempted to down in a single gulp. "It was a prodigious challenge, but I was finally able to run a waiter to ground. Mallory! Good to see you again."

What was this? She had only introduced them yesterday, and yet Lord Kettering clapped him on the back as if they were old friends.

"I wish I had another glass to offer you," Lord Kettering said to Richard, "but it was effort enough to find two of them."

"Thank you, but I am not staying," Richard said. "I have met all whom I had hoped to meet tonight." He slanted a glance in her direction. "And I am unaccustomed to such crowds."

"Well then," the earl said, "it was good seeing you. Thank you again for your help today. I truly appreciate it."

"It was nothing, I assure you." Richard turned to Isabel. "Lady Weymouth, a pleasure as always." He gave a sharp bow, and his gaze lingered briefly on her bosom. Then he turned and made his way back toward the staircase.

"I didn't realize you were acquainted with the major," she said.

"I was not, until you introduced us. But I was a friend to his late brother, and we have spent some time reminiscing. And today he helped me avoid a bad purchase at Tattersall's. The man knows his horseflesh. A capital fellow."

A capital scoundrel. How she wished she had worn the ruby heart again tonight, just to flaunt it in his arrogant face when he'd ogled her bosom again.

And to remind him that she had soundly beaten him at his own game.

It was time to return the ruby brooch to her grandmother. She did not trust that Richard would forego another attempt to steal it. Only when it was back in its secret drawer in Gram's jewel case would Isabel feel it was safe from that rogue.

She had just closed the front door and walked down the steps when a curricle pulled up.

Good Lord. It was Richard again. Would he never leave her in peace? He'd probably hoped to sneak into her bedchamber again and purloin the jewel. He was doomed to be disappointed this time.

He bounded from the seat and his groom jumped down to hold the horses.

"Good afternoon, Isabel."

The devil. She should never have given him free use of her name. He invested it with so much seduction that it made her skin tingle whenever he spoke it. "Good morning, Richard."

"I came to invite you for a drive through the park, but I see you are on your way out."

"Yes, I am. If you will excuse me." She began to walk away, but he stopped her with a hand on her arm. She glared at him and he removed the hand, but retained the roguish smile.

"Allow me to offer my services as a driver," he said, "taking you to whatever destination you require."

"That is very kind of you, but not necessary."

"Correct me if I am wrong, but I do not believe you keep a carriage?"

"That, sir, is none of you business." The impertinent blackguard. He no doubt enjoyed letting her know that he was aware of her reduced circumstances. Isabel could not forget that he'd seen her bedchamber and likely other rooms as well.

"I am only suggesting," he said, "that if you

119

were planning to hire a hackney, I would happily take you up in this curricle instead. Surely you would not prefer the odorous, stifling confines of a hackney when you could have the sun on your face and the wind in your hair."

And sit close beside you.

The rogue. It was very tempting. "I would not want to put you to the trouble, Lord Mallory. I am going all to the way to Chelsea."

"What a coincidence. That is precisely where I was headed as soon as I'd called upon you. Please, allow me to drive you."

She should not do it. She did not trust him. If he actually had business in Chelsea, she would eat her clever little Prussian bonnet.

"It would be a great favor if you would join me. It will be a deadly dull drive all by myself."

She really should not do it. She should not. But when he held out his hand, Isabel took it before she knew what she was doing.

He stared at her hand for a moment. She was not wearing gloves. She had put them in her reticule and intended to tug them on during the drive to Chelsea. But she could not do that now without risking his seeing the jewel in her reticule. He would think her vulgar and unrefined for going out with bare hands, but he was a thief, after all, and his opinion was of no account. Let him think what he would.

He handed her up, then took the seat beside her. While his groom took a minute to calm one of the horses, Richard turned to her and took her hand.

"I cannot tell you how pleased I am to see you again."

He raised her bare hand to his lips, brushed them across her knuckles, then turned her hand over and placed a warm kiss on her palm. All the while his eyes never left hers. Heat flared from her palm, danced up her arm, and simmered all the way down her body and through her veins. Isabel was glad she was seated, for she would surely have gone weak in the knees.

Damn the man. He had turned on the full force of his seductive charm—again—and used it shamelessly against her, as though he knew he had reawakened physical desire in her for the first time in a long time. But he could not know that, and she was resolved he never would.

She was relieved, though, when he had to let go of her hand and take up the reins. She would not allow him to get the better of her, no matter how much he rattled her senses.

The groom returned to the seat behind, and they were off.

"Where in Chelsea shall I take you?" he asked.

"Manor Street, if you please."

"You are visiting friends?"

"My grandmother."

"Ah. How dutiful of you. Is she a stern old crow like my grandmother?"

"No, she is a very sweet, very gentle woman."

They spoke of their families, just as if they were ordinary acquaintances with no secrets between them, but their words were merely a façade, only the surface of more unsettling things hidden beneath them.

It was not just the jewel, which sat snuggly in her reticule, that went unmentioned. There was still that hint of something physical between them. The memory of that kiss that had almost knocked her off her feet. And even now, on the narrow seat of the curricle, his thigh brushed against hers with enough frequency that she was certain it was no accident. And each time she became aware of the hard muscle of his leg, heat pooled low in her belly, and she had to make an effort to concentrate on what he was saying.

Shortly after entering Kensington, Richard's expression grew suddenly grim, and he slowed the team to a halt. Isabel wondered if there was a problem with one of the horses. "Why are we stopping?" she asked.

Instead of answering her, he turned to speak to his groom. "Tully, go find out that fellow's situation."

The groom hopped down from his seat, apparently understanding what Richard wanted, though Isabel was at a loss. She watched as he went to speak to a crippled man in a ragged uniform huddled in a doorway. When he came back he said cryptically, "Thirty-eighth Foot, wounded at San Sebastian."

To Isabel's astonishment, Richard jumped down from the seat and handed the reins to the groom. She watched as he bent down on his haunches and spoke quietly to the crippled man. After a few moments, he pressed several gold coins into the man's hand, clapped him briefly on the shoulder, and returned to the curricle.

Was this the same man who'd stolen her grandmother's brooch? This man who gave money to ragged soldiers with crippling wounds? Isabel could not resolve the two disparate perceptions, and studied him as he checked the horses and had a word with the groom.

He swung back up onto the bench, brushing close to her so that they touched from hip to knee. She stared at him quizzically, and he looked back at her with such intensity that she could almost feel blue shafts of light boring into her soul. Their gazes locked for a long moment, then he took her face in his hand and kissed her.

It was nothing like the instant fire of the day before. It was a soft kiss, sweet and with an underlying tenderness that pierced her heart. His thumb stroked her jaw, holding her captive while his lips lingered on hers.

He pulled away first, smiled at her, and said, "When you look at me like that with those magnificent eyes, how can I resist kissing you?" Then he flicked the reins to set the horses moving again.

Isabel did not respond to his comment, though it sent a lovely warmth through her veins. A warmth she immediately attempted to cool by remembering who and what he was.

They drove in silence for a while, giving Isabel far too much time to ponder that kiss. Conversation would put her more at ease.

"That man back there—he was a wounded soldier?" she asked.

"Yes, one of thousands who served their country and are now left to beg in the streets. It makes me so angry when I see them," he said, his voice rising with passion, "especially the ones who've given a leg or an arm or an eye and we give them nothing in return."

"You gave him something."

"It was very little, just enough to buy him a few decent meals and a few nights in a real bed."

"That was very kind of you."

"It was not kindness. It was duty."

She realized this was his soft spot, these forgotten soldiers, and she could not help liking him for it. Maybe there was more to this man than she'd thought. He was still a thief, but perhaps there was some sort of explanation.

Otherwise, he was a complete puzzle to her.

When they reached Manor Street in Chelsea, Richard descended first and then handed Isabel down. He stood altogether too close and she thought he might kiss her again.

As if reading her thoughts, he said, "Do not worry. I will not outrage your grandmother by kissing you here in front of her house, as much as I'd like to. I have enjoyed our drive, Isabel."

"So have I. Thank you, Richard."

"It was my extreme pleasure. Enjoy your visit."

Isabel watched him mount the seat again, take the reins, and drive away. Richard was such an enigma, she simply did not know what to make of him. A thief and a flirt and a manipulator of people, he could also show compassion for a wounded soldier and feel compelled to offer help. And make her head spin with a kiss.

Enigma or no, it did not matter. She turned toward the door, resolved to put Lord Mallory out of her mind once and for all.

It was not until she turned to reach for the door knocker that she realized her reticule was far too light. She opened the drawstring and uttered a frustrated cry.

The brooch was gone. The wretched man had stolen it again.

Chapter 7

Richard left Tully to return the hired curricle to the stables and walked back to Tavistock Street. He touched his waistcoat pocket and smiled.

It had been ridiculously easy, especially for a spur-of-the-moment maneuver. He had not intended to steal the brooch back again today. His plan had been simply to unnerve her with his attentions, like an unwanted suitor. He knew she was attracted to him. It was not conceit to admit such a thing. It was simply a fact, and he meant to play into that reluctant attraction until she let her guard down. Then he would make his move.

But it had not been necessary. Richard had known she carried the Mallory Heart as soon as her reticule knocked against him when he lifted her into the curricle. There was no mistaking its weight and shape. Just to be certain, however, he took advantage of every bounce along the road to press against the reticule that lay beside her thigh. Even after he had no more doubts that she carried the ruby heart, he allowed his thigh to brush up against hers just for the sheer pleasure of doing so. And for the way it unsettled her.

Fortunately, Richard had commanded a great many fellows who'd come from the streets, the rookeries, even the prisons, and he had learned a thing or two from them over the years. He'd been taught the art of picking pockets by a trooper named Sands in the months after Talavera when there had been little to do. He put that infamous training into practice while he kissed Isabel.

What wicked fun this adventure had turned out to be. He had certainly not expected his quest would require him to kiss a beautiful woman. If he did not know her for a thief, he would have been very tempted to woo Lady Weymouth in earnest. Not only did she have those captivating eyes and inviting mouth, but she was also clever and resourceful. Thievery was not, of course, the best tactic for repairing one's fortunes, but he had to give her credit of a sort for her tough stand against financial ruin. Richard could not think of another woman of his acquaintance who would have gone head to head with a man she probably believed to be as big a thief as she was.

Yes, she was certainly an enemy to be admired, but an enemy nonetheless.

When Richard reached the building where he'd leased his chambers, he was surprised to find Lord Kettering coming out the front door.

"Ah, Mallory," he said. "Well met. I had hoped to catch you at home but thought I'd missed you."

"Almost. Come on upstairs. I have a nice bottle of claret I'd be happy to share."

"I'd like that," Kettering said. "I have brought something for you." He nodded toward the case he was carrying.

It was a rectangular leather case with chased silver mounts on the corners. Richard had a sinking feeling that he know what sort of case it

129

was. He motioned for Kettering to follow him up the stairs. When they reached his chambers, he said, "I'm afraid my man is out at the moment, so we will have to do for ourselves. Have a seat and I'll see to the wine."

Kettering deposited the case on a table and took a seat beside the fireplace. Richard found two clean glasses and the decanter of claret, and carried them all into the sitting room. He poured a glass for Kettering, then took the chair opposite, leaving the decanter on a small candlestand beside him.

"And so," he said, gesturing toward the case, "what is it you have brought me?"

"I hope you will not think it gruesome, but I've brought Arthur's dueling pistols. They've been in my keeping all this time, and I thought you should have them."

Richard eyed the case. "They are the ones . . ." He felt suddenly chilled, which was foolish. He'd seen more than his share of men killed with guns. But none of them had been his brother.

"Yes, Arthur's pistols were used in the duel."

"One of them killed him."

"Yes, and I can understand if you would

rather not have them in your possession. But they are a fine pair of Mantons and Arthur was rather proud of them."

"Then I shall be proud to keep them," Richard said. "Thank you for bringing them to me." He did not think he would ever be able to open the case, though. Not until he tamped down the fierce anger he felt over the senseless manner of his brother's death.

"I hoped you would take them," Kettering said. "I realize they are a dreadful reminder of his death, but I felt they rightfully belonged to his family. It was the least I could do, after your help at Tatt's the other day."

"Have you decided whether or not to take the bay mare? She's not as flashy as that chestnut you wanted, but she's a better bargain."

"I think I will. I confess I would never have considered her until you pointed out her advantages as a hunter. Perhaps I should hire you as my agent for all future cattle purchases." He flashed a grin. "You would save me a great deal of money, I daresay."

"I am at your service, Kettering. Call upon me at any time. I shall be returning to Greyshott tomorrow, but I have retained these rooms for the summer. If I am able, I hope to return in time for some of the grand fêtes I have been hearing about."

"You must not miss the Jubilee next month. I understand it is going to be something quite spectacular. I am hoping to escort Lady Weymouth." His expression held a hint of challenge, as though he were staking a formal claim on the lady.

"You have a serious interest in the lovely widow?" Richard did not know what devil prompted him to pose that question. Kettering was *not* a rival, after all. Richard had no interest in pursuing the little thief.

"I do," Kettering said. He straightened his shoulders and tried to look stern, but there was the merest glint of doubt in his eyes. "And you? Do you have an interest, too? Are we to be in competition for the lady?"

Richard chuckled. "No, my friend, I shall leave that field to you."

Kettering blew out a breath, and his whole body seemed to relax. "Thank God. I would stand no chance against you, Mallory. You ease my mind."

"No chance? What are you talking about? You're an earl, for God's sake, heir to a marquess. And plump in the pocket, no doubt. I'm only a lowly viscount with a crumbling estate as my sole expectation."

Kettering gave a wave of dismissal. "None of that matters, really. Especially considering Lady Weymouth's connections. But ladies do like a man to be dashing and gallant. You have that damned scarlet coat and a way with women I could never achieve. I wish I had half your charm. As it is, I worry that she thinks me a dull bird."

"Do not underestimate yourself, Kettering. Women like to flirt with me, as I like to flirt with them, but they want to marry men like you. I assume marriage is your ultimate goal for the widow Weymouth?"

He shrugged. "I think so. She is surely one of the most vivacious, intriguing women I've ever met. But my family might not approve."

Richard's eyebrows lifted. They certainly would not approve if they knew she was a thief. But he did not imagine Kettering was aware of that. "You mentioned her connections. I have only recently met her and know nothing of her background. Is her blood tainted in some way? Are there shopkeepers in her family? Merchants? Criminals, perhaps?" That would certainly explain her propensity for stealing jewels.

"No, no. Nothing like that. Nothing beyond the pale. They're just considered a somewhat unsteady bunch. Her mother's been married three times, and not a suitable fellow in the lot. Lady Weymouth's father was a minister in Pitt's early administration, but was apparently a bit too fond of the drink and lost his post. Her mother's now married to a ramshackle Italian count and living on the continent, thank God. She was always a bit of a wild one and I doubt Father would approve. And her younger son, Isa—that is, Lady Weymouth's brother—is barely out of university and already known to be a wastrel and a gamester of the first order."

"All families have their black sheep."

"Yes, but Lady Weymouth's family seems to have a herd of 'em. There's an uncle who writes gothic novels and a cousin who had a very scandalous divorce." He actually shuddered. "Anyway, they're not exactly the sort of connections my father would find suitable. But I admit I am tempted to throw caution to the winds. In my heart, I do not really care if they like her or not."

"You're in love with her?" Richard asked, unexpectedly rattled by the possibility.

"I don't know if it's love yet. But I am very fond of her. And even though I could never be as dashing and debonair as you, she doesn't seem to mind. I think—I hope—she welcomes my interest."

Of course she does. A rich husband would get her out of the jewel theft business. Maybe. For all Richard knew, she was seduced by the thrill of it all, and would not be inclined to give it up. Or perhaps she had no morals at all and simply saw nothing wrong with stealing. He didn't really believe that, however. His gut told him she did it for the money.

"I am sure she does," he said. "And I wish you success with her. I daresay your family will accept her in the end."

Empty words. He did not wish Kettering success. The idiot had it all backwards anyway. Isabel was not unsuitable for him, if one discounted her thievery. Kettering was wildly unsuitable for Isabel. Richard could not imagine the spirited young widow with this dry stick of a man. Kettering was a decent enough fellow—rich and titled and good-looking. But he had no fire.

Richard knew from their first kiss that Isabel was a woman of passion. Her response, before she bolted, had been enough to blister a man inside out. He sensed that she approached everything with some level of passion. How could a stiff-necked fellow like Kettering, steeped in aristocratic pride and propriety, hope to be content with such a woman? Isabel would lead him a merry dance, one in which he could never hope to keep up. Theirs would be an unwise match that would probably make them both miserable in the end.

Richard chuckled aloud at his own audacity for presuming to judge Kettering's suitability for Isabel. Did he imagine himself more suitable?

Perhaps he *was* more suitable. He was, after all, a thief of sorts. He'd stolen the Mallory Heart from her, even though she had no right to its possession. Two thieves might make a perfect match. There was an undeniable attraction between them as well. And he would match his passion against hers any day.

He was spinning idiotic fantasies. He and Isabel were not meant to be together. Even if he could turn her away from a life of crime, he did not think he could ever trust her. He would always remember how she'd come to his rooms under the pretense of letting him know she was available to him, all the while her little accomplice was doing her dirty work. This was not a woman to be trusted.

It did not matter. Richard was returning to Greyshott in the morning. If his grandfather had taken a turn for the worse, or if there was some crisis on the estate requiring his attention, he might not return to London for a long time. He might never see Isabel again.

He did see her one more time before leaving Town. Colonel and Lady Althea Bradbury invited him to accompany them to a reception for Wellington. Since many of his fellow officers would be in attendance, he felt obligated to go as well.

Like all of the social events he'd attended since arriving in London, the reception was almost unbearably crowded. Everyone wanted to see the duke, so wherever he went there was bound to be a mob, inside and outside the event. Ordinary people from all over the city lined the streets hoping for a glimpse of the great man.

Wellington seemed much more comfortable with his new rank than Richard was with his own unexpected elevation. In truth, Richard preferred the title of Major over that of Viscount. He understood Major. It fit him, just as well as his uniform. Viscount was too new and alien. He had not been groomed for it and hated how it came to him. Hopefully he would grow more comfortable with it so that when he eventually became the Earl of Dunstable, he would wear the rank as proudly as Wellington.

And hopefully draw the attention of as many beautiful women. Wellington was surrounded by them, each one agog to meet the conquering hero. He was clearly enjoying himself tonight, as his distinctive whoop of laughter could be heard from the corner of the room where he held court.

One of the beauties turned her head. It was Isabel. Her eyes narrowed briefly when she saw Richard, and they remained fixed on him as she removed herself from the group and walked toward him.

Their gazes remained locked as she walked through the crowd, creating a little buzz of anticipation in his chest. She looked stunning, as always. Clearly she did not allow her reduced circumstances to stifle her sense of fashion. She was one of the more stylishly dressed women in the room in a very expensive-looking dress of pink satin and white lace. There was a wreath of silver and green laurel leaves in her hair, which was gathered in the back in a mass of curls. One long honey-colored curl hung down to tease the nape of her neck. She wore a diamond necklace and earrings, and a diamond bracelet over her gloves.

He wondered if the diamonds were stolen.

As she approached, the crowd of people seemed to disappear and it was as though they were alone in the room. The air between them crackled with tension.

Her mouth quirked up on one side in a mocking smile. "My lord. We seemed fated to meet at every turn."

"So it seems," he said. She did not offer her hand and Richard did not reach for it. "And so you have met the great man?" He looked toward Wellington who was still surrounded by ladies.

"Yes. He is quite charming, is he not?"

Richard smiled. "So long as he is not berating you for disobeying an order or mismanaging an operation. His sharp tongue can cut deeper than any blade."

"You disliked serving under him, then?"

"On the contrary. He was the best field commander I ever served. But tell me, Isabel, did you enjoy your visit with your grandmother today?"

Her eyebrows lifted slightly. "Not as much as I'd hoped. There was something *missing* in the visit. I cannot quite put my finger on what it was, but it did rather lessen my enjoyment of the day."

Richard stifled a grin and tried to look serious. "I am sorry to hear it. Perhaps it was simply a passing blue mood. I am sure you will get over it soon."

"I hope to *recover* brighter spirits in due time. I shall simply have to tackle the thing head on."

"You ought to make an early night of it and have your cook brew up a nice tisane. That should do the trick."

"I thank you for the advice, but I am not so fragile as that. And I cannot abide an early evening when there are so many parties to keep one entertained. Do you go to the Russell card party later?"

"No, I'm afraid you will have to do without me. Though I am no more fond of early evenings than you, I must be prepared for an early departure tomorrow morning."

"Oh? You are leaving Town? Again?"

He smiled. "Yes, I am riding home to Hampshire. Unless you plan to delay me with another morning call?"

"I think not, sir. I would not want to risk my reputation by calling on a bachelor. People might get the wrong impression."

"Yes, some people might."

Their conversation was cut short by the arrival of Lady Challinor and Lord Francis Gilliard. Richard remained for a few minutes of idle chatter, then excused himself. He had no wish to watch yet another young fool—for such he judged Lord Francis to be—press his attentions on Isabel. Why did she surround herself with such ninnies? Was it because she could trust they would be too stupid to know what she was really up to?

Richard wanted to find Bradbury and Lady Althea and make his excuses. He really did plan an early morning and wanted to get a good night's sleep before the long ride into Hampshire. He located Althea's plumes and headed in that direction.

But stopped when he noticed an attractive woman holding court near a pillar on the other side of the room. She was wearing half-mourning, a gray dress with black ribbons, and a dozen gallants were fluttering about her like moths to a flame.

Was this the infamous Lady Ridealgh? The

cause of so much grief and upheaval in his family, the woman who incited her unlamented late husband to kill Arthur?

Richard had been on the watch for a dashing widow at every event he attended. Due to the wars, there was an unfortunate abundance of widows, but this one, surrounded by admirers, seemed exactly the type who could have sent her husband into a jealous rage.

He insinuated himself into her circle. She took immediate notice.

"Ah. A newcomer. I do not believe we have met, sir."

"I beg your pardon, madam. A snippet of overheard conversation lured me to your side. I fear I have no one to present me properly. It seems I must introduce myself. Major Lord Richard Mallory, at your service."

He swept her a bow, but not before closely watching her reaction to his name. There was not a flicker of recognition in her eyes.

"My lord." She held out her hand and eyed him with open interest. "I am Mrs. Daventry."

He almost grimaced with disappointment, but schooled his features and took her hand. "I am pleased to meet you, ma'am."

"Yes. Well, we were discussing the upcoming

Jubilee. Mr. Hucknell was telling us about the pagoda being built in St. James Park."

A young, eager-faced gentleman, who must have been Hucknell, began to expound on the elegance and beauty of the structure. Mrs. Daventry's gaze strayed to Richard, sending him an unspoken invitation to become more intimately acquainted.

The last thing he needed, though, was another cunning widow to worry about. Since she was not Lady Ridealgh, he had no interest in her and did not acknowledge the invitation. He remained in her group for a short time, then skulked away, trying his best to disappear in the crowd.

Isabel turned away when she saw him approach Harriet Daventry. She was stung by a tiny prick of jealousy. Why? She had no claim on the man, nor did she wish to have. He had stolen her grandmother's ruby brooch, for heaven's sake. What kind of woman could have any feelings for a man like that?

One part of her brain repeated the litany of his unsuitability, his dishonesty, his thievery. He was a man of questionable character, a scoundrel and a fraud. Yet another part of her brain shamelessly craved to be held in his arms again.

Her susceptibility infuriated her. It gave him too much power.

She ignored that traitorous part of her brain and fixed her concern on Harriet. She was probably his next victim. She wore a very fine sapphire and diamond necklace tonight. Was that what had caught Richard's eye and compelled him to cross the room and join her court of admirers?

Isabel wondered if she ought to have a word with Harriet, just as a friendly warning.

She turned around, and saw Richard edging away from Harriet's coterie. She tried to keep up her end of the conversation with Phoebe and Lord Francis and several others who'd joined them, but her gaze kept scanning the room. It was not idle curiosity that caused her to follow Richard's progress through the crowd. She wanted to know when he left the reception so she could make her own discreet exit.

She had lied about going to several other parties. Although she did indeed hate early evenings and preferred to hop from party to party each night, tonight was different. He was leaving Town tomorrow and there were preparations to be made if she was to get Gram's jewel back.

"Oh, Danny, are you sure I have to wear this thing? It reeks!"

"If yer mean fer this plan ter work, yer gotter wear them things, m'lady, smelly or no."

Isabel held her nose while Danny circled her, inspecting her costume. "Ye'll do," he said.

"I think so, too. Thank you for rounding up all this, Danny." She gestured to the clothes she wore. "And don't tell me where you got it. I don't believe I wish to know."

"I got friends what 'elped me."

"Yes, well, don't tell me about those friends, either. I don't imagine I'd approve. Now I think we'd better go. If that stableboy was right, he'll be leaving soon. Lord, I hope his groom isn't with him."

" 'E only asked fer 'is own 'orse ter be ready so it ain't likely the groom'll be wif 'im. But even if 'e is, I can 'andle 'im."

"And you are certain which route he will take?"

"Certain as can be. The boy told 'im 'bout a

shortcut, and the major thanked 'im and said e'd take it. Not ter worry, m'lady. Ever'thing's in 'and."

"All right, then. You're the expert." Isabel looked in the mirror one last time, shook her head at the sight she saw, and giggled. She turned to the door and waved for Danny to follow. "Let's git the 'ell outa 'ere, then, an' git this rum bite movin'."

Danny howled with laughter.

Chapter 8

"**F**ind out what you can about her." Richard shrugged into the coat Tully held for him. "Where she lives, where she goes, who she sees, anything."

"Yes, my lord. But you are certain I should not accompany you to Greyshott?"

"No, I'd rather you did a bit of reconnaissance on the elusive Lady Ridealgh. When I return, I would like nothing more than to meet her face-to-face. But I must know where she is."

"Yes, sir, Major. My lord, that is."

Richard smiled. His batman was no more accustomed to this viscount business than he was.

"If my grandfather's condition allows it, I will return within a few days."

"Yes, my lord. I will have the information you need by the time you return."

"Good man. Now, let's be off."

They walked together to the stables where their horses were boarded, each of them carrying a saddlebag. Richard's horse, Galahad, had been led out and a groom held him in wait. He preferred to saddle his own horse, and did so. Tully helped him strap on the saddlebags he had so carefully packed, then assisted him to mount.

"If the situation at home does not allow me to return," Richard said, "I will send for you."

"Yes, my lord."

After a few crooned words into Galahad's ear, he was off. He looked forward to the long, leisurely ride to Hampshire. The solitude would give him time to think, and there were a lot of things on his mind.

His first thoughts were for his grandfather. Richard hoped he would find him in better health. Perhaps the return of the Mallory Heart would improve his spirits, at least. Richard felt that he really ought to remain at Greyshott, now that he'd fulfilled his grandmother's assignment. He ought to spend as much time as possible with his grandfather. There might be precious little time left to them. It was selfish to consider returning to London right away, just because he was not ready to dismiss the mystery of Lady Weymouth. Once the jewel was returned, he intended to confront her about it. No more dancing around the issue. He wanted to know how she came to have it.

He could, of course, leave that confrontation until some other time. There was no urgency involved. He could stay at Greyshott and work with the steward to start putting into action some of the needed improvements and repairs, then return to London next spring.

But by then she might be Lady Kettering.

The very idea tied his stomach into knots. Richard did not want her for himself, not in the way Kettering did. But he could not bear to think of her marrying the man just to solve her financial difficulties. And he could not bear to think of her in Kettering's arms. Would she respond to the ever-so-proper earl the way she had to Richard?

There was no denying their mutual attraction. He would not soon forget that kiss in his chambers. He didn't want to forget it. He rather thought he'd like to repeat it.

Damn it all, he'd developed an unwise and irrational lust for the woman. He really should stay away.

But he did not believe he could.

What a ridiculous predicament. He'd never been so confused by a woman in all his life.

"Spare summink fer an' ol' soldier, guv'ner?"

Richard's musings came to an abrupt halt at the sound of the raspy voice. He slowed and looked around, finally seeing a hunched mass of rags huddled in a dark doorway. Some of the rags were bits of uniform. The dark figure leaned on a rough-hewn crutch and had a dirty cloth wrapped across his forehead and over one eye, then tucked up under a filthy, battered shako.

His heart lurched at the sight. He never would get used to seeing soldiers reduced to begging. Soldiers who'd fought as bravely as any officer, often more so. Soldiers who suffered crippling wounds that kept them from finding meaningful employment. Soldiers abandoned to the streets by an ungrateful government.

This soldier held out a tin cup with an unsteady hand covered in moth-eaten fingerless gloves. "Alms for a poor ol' soldier?" he said.

A street urchin, covered in black soot and

filthy rags, uncurled himself from the same doorway. "'Old yer 'orse fer an hapenny," he said.

Richard reached in his waistcoat pocket, retrieved a coin, and tossed it to the boy, then dismounted and handed him the reins. Richard walked up to the doorway and the soldier retreated further into the darkness, though he kept his tin cup outstretched. He was not as old as Richard had expected. What little he could see of the fellow's face through the shadows and beneath the dirt led Richard to believe he was a very young man.

To see a youth who'd gone to war as a boy now reduced to this pile of rags made Richard so angry he wanted to shout his outrage to the skies.

"What regiment, soldier?" he asked.

"Twenny-eighth Foot, guv'ner." The boy's voice was rough as a rusty blade, and barely above a whisper, but still held a hint of youthfulness. "Yer be a soldier, too?"

"Major Mallory, Third Dragoon Guards."

The boy brought his tin cup up to his head in half-hearted salute. "Sir," he said.

Richard gestured to his crutch. "Where did this happen?"

"Albuera."

"Ah. Nasty business, that one, especially for you lads in the Second Division. You lost more than any of us, as I recall."

"Yer was there, sir?"

"Indeed. Don't you remember?"

The boy hung his head and gave a sort of groan.

"We stole your general," Richard said, "when Long made such a mess of things. Poor old Lumley had to take over the cavalry just hours before the battle. But he acquitted himself beautifully. An excellent commander."

The soldier, still hovering in the dark of the doorway so Richard could not get a good look at him, shook his head and said, "Don't 'member much o' that day, 'cept all them Frenchies shootin' at us. Got 'it in the 'ead, see? Lost me eye. Bullet in me leg as well."

"Ah. Bad luck, old chap. It was a rough day, though. One of the worst. You are lucky to have survived. You were part of Abercrombie's brigade, right?"

The soldier hunched further into himself, as though he did in fact remember but had tried to forget. The sour odor of drink, mixed with other foul smells rising from his ragged clothes, enveloped the wretched fellow. Like so many others, he had no doubt used gin to try to erase the memories of the butchery at Albuera.

"You lads under Abercrombie and Houghton did a splendid job. Never saw such bravery in my life. The French had twice the numbers, yet your brigade kept fighting. What's your name, soldier?"

"Tom Finch, sir."

Richard pulled out his purse and spilled several gold coins into his hand. "Take this, Tom. Buy yourself a decent meal and a clean bed."

The soldier held out his tin cup and Richard dropped the coins into it. The young man stared into the cup, his one eye, the only bright spot in the shadows, was wide with astonishment. The poor fellow had probably not seen so much money in years, if ever.

"Ta, Major," he said, and clasped the cup close to his chest. " 'Tis right kind o' you, sir."

"Promise me you won't spend it all on drink, Tom. Put it to better use. Clean yourself up and try to find honest work."

"Yessir, Major."

"Remember, you were a soldier who fought bravely to save your country from Bonaparte. Never forget what an important thing you did.

Whenever life gets you down, remember what you did and fight back. You deserve better."

Richard put his hand on the young man's shoulder and squeezed. "Take care of yourself, Tom Finch."

He returned to his horse and took the reins from the urchin who held them. He tossed the boy a sixpence, mounted Galahad, and continued on his way out of Town.

The plight of soldiers like Tom Finch gnawed at his gut for several miles. There had to be a way to help them, and not just passing out coins to one here and one there. The supply of coins would need to be endless. No, the problem was bigger than that, and it belonged to the whole nation.

Perhaps there was one good thing that would come from his eventual inheritance of the earldom. He could be a voice in Lords for the veterans of the wars, especially those disabled by their wounds. By God, he would see that the government did something for them if it was the last thing he did.

Richard thought of that pile of rags in the shadows and sincerely hoped the young man would not waste those golden boys on drink, though sometimes that was the easiest escape from such a miserable existence. Perhaps Tom Finch would not take the easy route.

"Tom Finch, eh? So, we're brothers, are we?"

Isabel laughed. "It was the first name that popped into my head, Danny. I hope you don't mind that I appropriated it for my soldier."

"Naw. Yer done good, m'lady. I'm right proud o' yer. 'E never suspected nuffink, did 'e?"

"No, thank heavens. Though he gave me quite a scare when he stared asking questions about Albuera. Just my luck to pick a battle he'd been in. I only chose it because I found an article about it in one of Rupert's old magazines in the library. I almost died when he asked about my brigade."

"The 'ead wound were a nice touch."

Isabel grinned. "I thought so. He could hardly fault my memory in that case, could he? Well, I am glad it is over. Now, let me see the brooch."

"Not 'ere, m'lady. 'Tain't safe. But don't worry. I got it."

Isabel had been so caught up in her role she had forgotten they were in one of the worst parts of London, just beyond Seven Dials. She moved close to Danny and leaned on her crutch.

"That's right. Yer still a crippled ol' soldier 'til we get outa these parts."

They stayed close together, though the going was slow due to Isabel's crutch. She dare not abandon it yet. Fortunately, the two of them were so filthy and ragged that no one approached them. No one would dream that two such miserable wretches would have anything on them worth stealing. Certainly not a brooch sporting a huge heart-shaped ruby.

They made their slow way up to Broad Street. A hackney stood in front of St. Giles Church. Isabel approached it and said, "Portman Square, if you please."

" 'Ere now," the jarvey said, an outraged scowl on his ruddy face. "I ain't takin' the loikes o' yer two nowhere. Filthy buggers. Git yerself gone."

Isabel reached into the tin cup she held clasped against her breast and pulled out a shiny gold guinea. She held it up and said, "This says you'll take us to Portman Square, Berkley Mews."

"Come inter a fortune, 'ave yer?" The jarvey cackled merrily. "Awright, then, yer lordships. Git yerself inside, but don't be leavin' any dirt be'ind. I jist cleaned them seats."

Isabel and Danny climbed inside the carriage and shut the door. They were thrown back against the seat as the hackney lurched forward.

"Now, show me the brooch," she said. "I want to make sure he hasn't tricked us in some way."

Danny reached inside layers of ragged bits of jacket and shirt and pulled out the pouch. He gave it to Isabel who poured the brooch into her hand. The ruby glinted in the morning sunlight slanting through the window. She gave a little sigh of relief. It was Gram's brooch, all right. Thank heaven.

Relief was immediately pushed aside by triumph. Isabel began to laugh. They had done it again. They had beaten Richard at his own game. When she thought of him arriving in Hampshire only to find his stolen booty had gone missing again, she threw her head back and laughed and laughed. Danny joined her and their laughter filled the carriage.

When she was able to regain a bit of composure, Isabel said, "You had no trouble finding it? I tried to keep him talking long enough for you to do a thorough search."

"Naw, 'twas easy as fallin' outa bed. 'Ad it in me pocket in no more'n a minute."

"How?"

"Well, I 'membered when I took it the first time. 'Is things was all laid out real neat, like, ready fer packin'. The jewel was right beside 'is shavin' kit, an' I figgered that's where 'e meant to pack it. So I found 'is kit in the saddlebag, and sure 'nuf, there 'twas, tucked in with 'is razor and brush."

"Danny, my boy, you have the makings of a fine criminal."

"I know. Used ter be one."

"Well, I am sorry to have dragged you back into a life of crime, but after all, it's not really stealing. I'm just taking back what belongs to me."

What belonged to Gram, actually. But close enough. It certainly did not belong to Richard.

Isabel was enjoying herself as she had not in a very long time. She could not remember feeling so alive. Was it the game they played? Or was it the player?

Throughout the rest of the journey, Isabel's thoughts were full of Richard. And not only the imagined look on his face when he discovered the brooch was missing, though she would give anything to see that. She kept remembering the compassion in those blue eyes as he spoke to Tom Finch.

The words of encouragement he'd spoken, the genuine kindness and respect in his voice almost overwhelmed her. She tried to imagine what his words, and his incredible gift of two guineas, would have meant to a real Tom Finch. A poor soul left crippled, blind, or maimed, who'd been discarded by his government and society, left to fend for himself in the streets. To hear himself praised for bravery and for serving his country must do almost as much good as the gold coins.

Richard had spent many years in the army, so it should not be surprising that he felt kind-hearted toward soldiers who'd fallen into poverty and helplessness. But it did surprise her. London was full of officers returned from the war, and Isabel would be willing to bet very few of them, if any, took the time to give comfort to the Tom Finches of the world.

Isabel had been so sure Richard *did* care that he had been an easy mark for her little scam. If she wasn't so pleased to have the brooch back, she might feel guilty about taking advantage of the better side of his nature.

But she did not.

She could not regret having the brooch in hand again, no matter what means were necessary to reach that end. Besides, it was pointless to dwell on the finer aspects of Major Lord Mallory's character. He was still a thief.

Those finer aspects, though, certainly made him a most fascinating thief indeed.

She wondered what he would do next to get the brooch back? For she had no doubt he would try.

Richard arrived at Greyshott late that afternoon. He was tired and stiff from the long ride, and anxious to shake off the dust of the road. He handed over Galahad to a groom and was met at the entrance by Ralston, Greyshott's butler for as long as he could remember.

"Welcome home, my lord. Let me take your bags."

"Thank you, Ralston. How is my grandfather?"

"About the same, my lord. Your return will cheer him, I am sure."

"Good. I am glad he is no worse. Do you suppose you could conjure up a hot bath? I'd love to soak my bones for a while before presenting myself to Grandmother."

He looked forward to handing over to her the

Mallory Heart. Would she show surprise? Gratitude? She was a reserved old woman who always held her feelings in check, but he rather hoped for some expression of pleasure that he'd accomplished what she'd asked of him. He hoped it would bring her the peace she sought.

"Of course," Ralston said. I'll have a bath prepared at once."

Richard made his way upstairs and through the south wing where his suite of rooms was still kept ready for him, even after all these years. When he'd first arrived from France, it had been the most comforting thing on earth to be able to return to such familiar surroundings.

He walked through the small sitting room straight through to the bed chamber and tossed his bags on the bed. He made do without Tully in pulling off his boots and removing his dusty coat and waistcoat. He continued to undress while he heard the bath being prepared in his dressing room.

Sometime later, he entered the room clad in a silk dressing gown he'd bought in Spain. The steaming tub beckoned. A footman offered to assist him, but Richard preferred to soak in solitude and dismissed him.

He must have dozed, for he suddenly became aware that the water was cold and his skin was puckered like a prune. He stood and dried off, donned the dressing gown, and returned to the bed chamber.

The saddlebags still lay on the bed. He needed to dress for dinner, but nothing in the bags would be fit to wear, so he rummaged through the clothes press and highboy, retrieving everything he would need for the evening. He would have a shave and then call for a footman to stand in as valet while he dressed.

He pulled his shaving kit from the bag and opened it.

And froze.

The pouch holding the Mallory Heart was not there. He had watched Tully place the pouch inside the kit early that morning. There had been no mistaking it. He upended the kit and dumped the full contents on the bed. No matter how many times he checked and rechecked every item, there was nothing more than shaving gear inside the kit.

He began to rifle through the saddlebags, flinging each perfectly folded garment willy-nilly across the room as he searched every corner of each bag. But the pouch containing the jewel was nowhere to be found. What on earth had happened—

The devil!

No, it could not be. It was impossible. Wasn't it? Had she done it again? But she could not have done. There was no way Isabel could have taken the brooch. He hadn't seen her since the Wellington reception last evening. She'd been nowhere near him today.

Or had she?

He groaned at his own stupidity. Had there been hints of green and brown in the single eye that looked at him from the shadows of a tenement doorway? And the street urchin who'd held his horse. Was he not about the same size as a certain liveried page?

Richard gave a crack of laughter. The little vixen! She *had* done it again, by Jove, and what a masterful ploy it had been. A work of art, in fact. As smooth and slick as a river stone. And he'd fallen for it hook, line, and sinker.

He could not believe she had gone to such lengths, to don that elaborate disguise and park herself in a dingy doorway in one of the seedier parts of Town. It was a foolhardy, even dangerous thing to do, but confound it all, his hat was off to the lady. He had not been even remotely suspicious. Tom Finch, indeed.

He ought to have known she would not let him leave Town with the brooch. For whatever reason, it seemed she was as determined to hold on to it as he was. It was an extremely valuable piece of jewelry, to be sure. The price of the ruby alone could probably fill up those empty rooms in Portman Square. Or perhaps it had nothing to do with the jewel itself, but was simply a matter of not letting him get the better of her. It could be nothing more than mulish pride that drove her to such bold tactics.

What an interesting game this had become. And what a remarkable woman was Lady Weymouth. Damn it all, she was one in a million. It was reckless at best to admire a woman who was no more than a very clever thief. But Richard could not recall another woman who'd intrigued him as much. She would not get away with it, of course. He would not allow it. But by God, she did manage to astonish him at every turn with a surprise attack instead of a frontal assault. She would have made a formidable general.

He would have to return to London, of

course, and lay siege to her once again. And he would arm himself with every weapon appropriate to the task, for he knew precisely where to find the vulnerabilities in her formation and could easily slip inside the lines. Just as she had discovered his Achilles' heel, he knew hers as well.

He had an entertaining little skirmish in mind for the next time they met.

Chapter 9

"You do not have the Mallory Heart?" The countess glared at him. A slight twist of her lips registered her disapproval.

"Not yet," Richard said. "But I am close."

"You know where it is?"

"Yes, I believe so."

"Then why have you returned? You are wasting time here when you ought to be working to gain possession of the jewel."

"I was worried about Grandfather. I do not wish to stay away too long in case . . ."

"His condition has not worsened. It has not improved, either, so there is still danger. I will have word sent to you if it becomes necessary. Is that the only reason you have returned?"

"I wanted to pick up a few things. My second dress uniform, for one. There are so many formal events to attend that I have a need of it."

"I did not send you to London to enjoy yourself. I want you to find that brooch and bring it home."

"When my commanding officer requests my presence, I find it unwise to refuse him."

"Do not be impertinent with me, Richard. I will not stand for it."

"I mean no disrespect, ma'am. But you must understand that there are many affairs celebrating the peace, and since the nation owes that peace to Wellington's army, he and his officers are in demand. It is not only about pleasure, though several of the events have been entertaining enough. It is about duty."

"You have a duty to your family as well. Your presence in London will honor both requirements. I suggest you return at once."

"I will stay here a day or so first. You will, I hope, indulge me, ma'am. I wish to spend time with my grandfather and to meet with Venables about a few estate matters."

She gave a little huff of displeasure and turned away.

They stood in the formal drawing room awaiting the call in to dinner. The countess leaned heavily on her cane. She was so often seated—or enthroned, as Richard preferred to think of it, in all her stately elegance—that he sometimes forgot she was a frail old woman. Her shoulders had grown stooped and thin, and the cane was the result of swollen joints that had pained her for as long as he could remember.

He wondered for a moment if her health was as precarious as her husband's. Richard had been so concerned about his grandfather's health he had not taken the time to consider hers.

"Grandmother, are you well?"

She turned. "I beg your pardon?"

"You did not used to rely so much on the cane. Has the pain in your joints grown worse?"

Her eyes widened slightly for the briefest instant as though she was pleased, and surprised, to be asked. It did not reflect well on his character, Richard thought, that such a simple inquiry was so unexpected of him. There had never been any tenderness between them, even when he was a child, but she was still his grand-mother and he ought to be more solicitous.

"My pains are old friends," she said. "It has become somewhat more difficult to bear with them as the years go by, but such is life."

Ralston entered at that moment to announce dinner.

"Take my arm, Grandmother. Lean on me for a time."

Dinner was a trial, with only the two of them and little conversation between them, as they were seated so far apart. Afterwards, Richard wished to visit the earl, and his grandmother accompanied him.

The old man was propped up on a mountain of pillows and had fallen asleep with a book in his hand. He looked as pale and ill as before, but peaceful in sleep.

"We should not wake him," the countess said in a whisper. "You can visit him tomorrow."

As they were about to leave the room, a thin voice from the bed stopped them. "Henrietta? Is that you?"

She turned and went to his side. "Yes, my dear. I did not wish to wake you, but Richard is here."

"Is he?" The earl tried to sit up straighter, and his wife adjusted the pillows behind him. "Come here, my boy. Let me see you."

Richard went to his side and took the outstretched hand. "Hullo, Grandda. How are you feeling?"

The earl gave his hand a weak squeeze. "Better for seeing you. How was London? Sit down and tell me about the celebrations."

"You should rest," the countess said. "You can talk with Richard tomorrow."

"Nonsense. There, that chair. Pull it over, my boy, and tell me what you've been doing in Town."

"You will tire yourself," his wife said. "I won't have you ruining your health."

"My health is already ruined. Now, leave us be, woman. I want to talk to Richard."

The countess gave a disparaging little cluck, and left the room.

"She fusses too much," the earl said. "Drives me mad sometimes."

Richard smiled. "She only wants what's best for you. I really do not wish to tire you, Grandda. We can talk tomorrow if you'd rather sleep now."

"Bah. I sleep all day. I want to hear the news. Is everyone hanging all over Wellington?"

"They are. Especially the ladies."

His grandfather gave a hoarse cackle that deteriorated into a wracking cough. He waved away Richard's help as he coughed into a handkerchief, then sank back against the pillows and composed himself. But Richard did not miss the flecks of blood in the handkerchief, and his heart contracted in anticipated grief.

"Just lie there quietly, Grandda, and let me do all the talking. Now, let me see. My first night in Town, there was a grand ball held at Burlington House in Wellington's honor."

Richard told him everything that had happened, leaving out the bits about the jewel and Lady Weymouth. He thought his grandfather might actually be amused by the game of pass-the-heart he and Isabel played. In another time, he would have howled with laughter at the Tom Finch ruse, but Richard dared not tell him. He recollected the countess's warning about how the subject of the Mallory Heart distressed the earl, and Richard had seen for himself how very ill he was. He did not mention the brooch.

After a short while, the earl's eyes grew

heavy, and though Richard kept talking, he knew his grandfather had fallen asleep.

He spent several hours the next morning meeting with Greyshott's steward. George Venables was the son of the man who'd been steward during all the years Richard had lived there. He'd taken up the reins sometime during Richard's long absence, after the elder Venables had died. George was only a year or two older than Richard. They had played together as boys. Richard was glad to know he had remained at Greyshott, despite the dwindling resources to support the estate. George had done his best to keep it from falling into ruin, introducing every sort of economy,

George Venables was a young man full of ideas. He idolized Coke of Norfolk and his views on farming, and waxed poetic on the virtues of various crops and methods of cultivation while Richard, who understood very little of it all, listened politely. Apparently, even a sensible four-crop rotation had not been possible during the last decade when revenues had dropped and the earldom had no money to invest in new machinery or livestock.

Richard asked Venables to identify what improvements to the land were most urgent and most practical in order to bring Greyshott back to rights. They discussed drainage and reclamation projects, crop combinations and rotations schemes, hedging and ditching, tenant cottages and farm buildings, threshing machines and chaff cutters. Richard was lost in the details, but trusted Venables's judgment. Together they prioritized several projects and purchases, and Richard gave his approval, and his money, for the work to get started. He figured it was more prudent to get the land back into shape before tackling renovations to the house.

Lord, how was he ever to manage as a landowner when he had so little knowledge of agriculture or husbandry? Damn Arthur for getting himself killed. He would not have been so overwhelmed. He would have known what to do.

It occurred to him that Arthur ought to have made an effort of his own to salvage the estate. But perhaps he had done. Richard had no way of knowing and would not blame his poor dead brother for the dwindling coffers.

His head still spinning from the meeting with Venables, Richard decided to have a look at the account books for the estate. He wanted to see if he could figure out why the fortunes of the earldom had come to such low ebb.

It took very little time to learn the truth, and it was sobering. He supposed it was always difficult to discover that someone you admired and respected, someone you had looked up to all your life, was in fact quite fallible.

Richard's grandfather had squandered a great deal of the family fortune on risky business ventures and investment schemes that any sensible man would have recognized as foolish at best. There was no mysterious siphoning of the Dunstable legacy. No unexplained losses. No suspicious accounting. It was simply a matter of extremely poor judgment, time after time, until there was very little left. The foolhardy schemes had been going on since before Richard was born. It had not been a sudden loss, but a slow erosion over time.

And that erosion was almost complete.

It was a good thing Richard had amassed a substantial fortune of his own. He had never thought much about what he would do with it, beyond investing it soundly and watching it grow. At one time he imagined he would buy his own estate. Now the only thing he wanted to do was invest in Greyshott. It had once been a grand estate, listed in all the guidebooks, pictured in the *Beauties of England and Wales*. He would make it so once again.

This was the life he now faced. He would have to trade in the cavalry for husbandry. It was enough to make a man weep.

While he sat at the desk in his grandfather's study, he sorted through papers and letters and receipts, trying to get an overview of the work he would have ahead of him when he returned from London again. The earl was not overly organized. In fact, much of the documentation was in disarray. Richard made a mental note to call in the earl's man of affairs to help him sort things out.

While searching the study, Richard came across a small box tucked far back into a cubbyhole behind the desk. It was a pretty little box, made of mahogany and inlaid with lighter woods in a complex geometric pattern. The top was not hinged but opened by sliding it to the side. Curious, Richard slid it open.

Inside was a bundle of letters, yellowed with age and tied with a blue ribbon. Richard untied the ribbon and unfolded the first letter.

It was one of the most passionate love letters

he'd ever read. "I ache for you" and "my heart soars" and "the joy of your touch" were among the words that leapt from the page in a fine spidery hand. He picked up the next letter to find more of the same effusive sentiment. They were each addressed to "My Dearest Phillip" and were signed simply "M."

Phillip was his grandfather. But who was "M"?

Only one letter was dated, and that was some fifty years ago. Quickly calculating in his head, Richard determined it was during the first year or so of his grandfather's marriage to the countess. But her name was Henrietta. And given the ardent language of the letters, it did not seem likely that she could be "M."

So, the earl had had a lover. A mistress. That was not so unusual. If his wife had always been as cool and reserved as she'd been all of Richard's life, he could not blame his grandfather for seeking a connection elsewhere. It was only the fact that he'd kept the woman's letters all these years that gave the love affair more importance than a simple bit of dalliance.

Richard would love to know who "M" was, but he was unlikely ever to find out. It was ancient history and hardly mattered now. Richard tied the letters with the ribbon and replaced them in the box. He hid the box even deeper in the cubbyhole and placed several old estate diaries in front of it. He doubted his grandmother ever ventured into the study, but he hid the letters well nonetheless. Heaven forbid she should ever come across them.

Richard spent the rest of the afternoon with the earl, discussing the plans he'd made with Venables. The old man appeared weaker today, with his nurse fussing about and making conversation difficult. But he seemed so grateful, so moved that Richard was taking estate matters in hand that tears welled up in his eyes.

"You're a better man than I ever was," he said. "I made a mess of things. I wish I had done better by you, my boy."

"You did very well by me, Grandda. You taught me everything I needed to know in life."

"Except how to stay out of debt. I hope someone else taught you that lesson."

"I had a very wise commanding officer when I was a young lieutenant. I learned about sound investments from him. Since we did not expect to return to civilian life for many years, we needed conservative investments that we could simply fund and forget about. I've been adding prize money to those funds for years. It paid off.

I have more than enough to bring Greyshott around."

"My boy, I am so proud of you." A tear rolled down the pale, withered cheek.

Richard took his hand. "Thank you, Grandda. That is all I ever wanted."

The earl wiped his eyes and straightened against the pillows. "Well, then. Enough about crops and livestock. Let young Venables take matters in hand. You should be back in London for the celebrations. Wellington may be the hero of the day, but he could not have done it without you and your fellow officers. You should be fêted as well."

"I plan to return tomorrow," Richard said. "But I'll come home soon."

"I'll be waiting."

Richard sincerely hoped so.

"This is the last time, Ned. The very last time. Do you understand?"

Her brother looked properly chagrined, but Isabel wondered if he would ever mend his ways.

"Absolutely, Iz. I won't ask again."

"I mean it, Ned. I haven't another ha'penny to spare. I'm bled dry." She had raised the money for this "loan" by selling her last pair of good earrings—lovely white sapphire drops—and having them copied in paste. But there were only a few pieces with real stones left. When those were gone, she did not know what she would do.

That was not quite true. She knew exactly what to do. She had to bring Lord Kettering up to scratch.

It was not only Ned's debts that plagued her. There had been the recent expense of replacing some of the windows at Gram's house to help cut down on the drafts that aggravated Cousin Min's rheumatism. It was always something. But the well would soon be dry if she did not settle things soon with Lord Kettering.

"I'll pay you back, I promise." The look in his eyes was so earnest she almost believed him.

"How? Are you planning to find employment at last?"

He shuddered. "Nothing so drastic. But I've placed a wager on a fine little mare at Newmarket. She's a sure thing. I'm sure to make more than enough to pay you back."

"Ned! Another wager?"

"A sure thing, Iz. Not to worry. And I promise it will be my last wager. I'm packing it in."

179

She lifted her eyebrows. "Truly?"

"Absolutely. I'm through with gaming and the turf. I'm all rolled up. I've learned my lesson."

She smiled and laid a hand upon his. "Oh, Ned, I am so glad to hear it. I knew you would come around eventually. I cannot keep bailing you out of every scrape. You may not choose to believe me, but I really am down to my last sou."

"Fustian! Kettering is still sniffing about. You'll be set up in style as his countess before the summer is out, I have no doubt."

His lordship had yet to make such intentions known to her, but she hoped her brother was right. At least she thought that was what she still wanted. She could rub along nicely with the young earl. His blond hair and blue eyes were very appealing, in a neat-as-a-pin un-flashy sort of way. And he certainly had the fortune she needed. The problem was that a very different pair of blue eyes intruded on her thoughts more than was prudent.

After Ned left, Isabel sat at her dressing table and examined her jewel case. It was as full as ever, but now the majority of the pieces were copies. She wished she hadn't always loved jewelry so much. Then perhaps Rupert would not have spent so much money buying it for her. She was not entirely pleased with the newly copied earrings. Foil-backed paste could more easily imitate diamonds than that elusive fire of white sapphires. She ought to have saved her money and not bothered with the copies.

She still had Gram's ruby heart. If she didn't love it so much, or love Gram so much, Isabel might have been tempted to have it copied as well. That ruby must be worth a small fortune. But she could never do that. Especially now that it was the ball in the game of catch she played with Richard.

In fact, the only reason she had yet to return the brooch to Gram was because she awaited his next move. She was certain he would return soon with a plan to steal it again, and she was prepared.

It was perhaps reckless to let their game continue when she could simply return the brooch to her grandmother and put an end to it. There was the occasional nagging little voice in her head that warned her against risking Gram's beloved brooch in such a foolish manner, reminding her that there was always the possibility that she might not be able to retrieve it the next time Richard stole it.

Isabel tuned out the warning voice, however, because she had no intention of allowing Richard to win the game. She had a few tricks up her sleeve this time.

Young Danny Finch continued to be her trusted accomplice. It really was quite amazing what the boy knew and the specialized talents he possessed. Isabel did not like to think how he came by such questionable knowledge, but it was certainly coming in rather handy. Under his tutelage she had perfected certain skills that would give her the advantage over Richard, no matter what tactic he next used to steal the brooch.

It still puzzled her that he was so obsessed with this particular jewel when there were so many others he could steal. Maybe he really did have a fondness for antique jewelry, but she doubted it.

The first time he'd taken it had probably been a simple theft. She suspected the second time was nothing more than a competitive male reaction to her stealing it back. The third time, which she anticipated very soon, would be pure gamesmanship.

And what a game it was. Isabel had not been so thoroughly diverted for years. It did tend to distract her from Lord Kettering's slow progress, though, and she really ought to make an effort to nudge his lordship into a more definitive direction.

But not tonight.

Danny, acting as her spy, had discovered that Richard had returned to London yesterday. He had probably been invited to the great banquet at the Guildhall tonight at which the Corporation of London was to honor the Duke of Wellington. It was said that all officers mentioned favorably in the dispatches had been invited, and she imagined Richard must be among their number. A select party of women had also been invited to observe the banquet from the galleries, which sounded like a dead bore to Isabel and she was not in the least disappointed not to have been included.

But she *had* received an invitation to the Duchess of Kingston's ball, which was to follow the banquet. It was expected that most of those at the Guildhall would at least make an appearance at the Kingston ball, and Isabel hoped Richard would be among them.

She dressed with care that evening in a special gown over which she and Tessie had labored for days. They had discovered an old dress from Isabel's first season made of the finest white crepe that was still in excellent condition. They cut it apart and made a lovely Russian robe that flared open in the front to reveal an underdress of French white satin. The robe was edged in rich blond lace that had been purchased years before and never used, and a row of the same lace trimmed the bottom of the underdress. The pièce de résistance, though, was the row of embroidered pearl-studded laurel wreaths, in honor of the great duke, that spilled down the edges of the robe.

Isabel was quite proud of those wreathes. She had been among the first to adopt the emblem as a fashionable ornament, and this was surely her best effort. The embroidery had taken days, but the result was worth it. She was confident her dress would be one of the most stylish at the ball.

The final touch, though, was the ruby brooch. The big red heart stood out like a beacon against the pure white of her dress. She added a faux ruby bracelet and earrings and was very pleased with how it all looked. Most women would wear diamonds with white. The rubies would make a bold fashion statement, and there was nothing more bold than the big ruby heart on her left shoulder.

Isabel arrived at the Kingston ball with Lydia and Oliver Pearsall. The ballroom was enormous but already crowded. Moments after greeting their host and hostess, Lydia leaned over to whisper in her ear.

"He's seen you already," she said.

Isabel looked around and saw scores of red coats, but none worn by a particular dark-haired man with piercing blue eyes. "Where?"

"Just there, over on the left. Here he comes."

Isabel followed her friend's gaze and found Lord Kettering making his way through the crowd. She masked her disappointment with a smile.

"He is certainly paying you a great deal of attention," Lydia said. "Surely he will make you an offer soon."

So everyone seemed to think. Isabel hoped they were right. Despite the rather exciting game she played with Richard, she still hoped Lord Kettering would come up to scratch. She really did.

She put on her most radiant smile as he approached. "Good evening, my lord."

He took the hand she offered and kissed the air above her fingers. He had never yet kissed anything more substantial, and she was becoming impatient for him to demonstrate a bit of ardor. She was not a green girl, after all. If she did not believe it would scare him off entirely, she would grab him and kiss him for all she was worth the next time they were alone.

"Lady Weymouth, you are looking very beautiful tonight," he said. "You put every other woman in the shade. Excepting Mrs. Pearsall, of course."

"Thank you, my lord, but you are correct," Lydia said as he bowed over her hand. "Isabel outshines us all this evening."

"You are both too kind," Isabel said. "There are a hundred more beautiful women here tonight, but I shall bask in your flattery nonetheless."

"May I hope you are not engaged for the opening set?" he asked.

"I have saved it especially for you, my lord."

"I am honored."

He remained at her side as various friends and acquaintances joined them to chat and gossip and comment on the fashions. When the orchestra finally began the Grand March to open the ball, Lord Kettering led her onto the dance floor.

A country dance followed, and she was led out by Sir Walter Herrick, who'd been one of Rupert's cronies. Afterwards, she was chatting with Phoebe and Lydia and several others when a prickle of awareness danced down her spine. The air in the room had somehow changed, sending charged tingles down her arms and up the back of her neck. She turned toward the entrance, knowing what she would find.

Richard had arrived.

Chapter 10

❧

Richard saw her at once. He was in line to greet their hosts, the duke and duchess, when he saw Isabel in a group of people gathered on the left side of the ballroom. It surprised him that he could recognize her so easily even with her back turned. He had not realized he had so thoroughly memorized the slope of her shoulders, the elegant line of her neck, the burnished gold hair, the way she moved.

It was more than only recognition of familiarity. The fact was that she simply stood out from the crowd, even a crowd as dazzling as this one. Though dressed in white, she was a vivid presence. Everyone else seemed somehow muted and pale in comparison.

As though she felt his gaze upon her, she turned and looked straight into his eyes.

Damned if she wasn't wearing the Mallory Heart. Egad, she was a brazen wench. She must have guessed he would be there and worn it just to torment him. It was not nestled beneath her lovely bosom this time, but pinned on her bodice near her shoulder, its prominence no doubt meant to provoke him.

The receiving line moved slowly. Many of those just arriving had come, as he had, from the Guildhall celebration. The conversations around him were cheerful and giddy, everyone anxious for an entertaining evening after the interminable banquet.

Richard had anticipated an all-male gathering with drinking and laughter and the usual raucous camaraderie of soldiers. But the banquet was an excessively formal occasion, and not only because of the presence of the Royal Dukes and all the cabinet ministers. Several hundred select ladies had been invited to observe from the galleries. Every officer and gentleman was on his best behavior.

The food was excellent, but an endless round

of long-winded toasts and responses stretched the meal well into the evening. Richard had thought it would never end, and bolted the instant it was declared to be over. He had received an invitation to the Kingston ball, and Tully assured him the talk about Town was that it was to be an important and fashionable affair. Knowing Isabel would never miss such an event, he had been anxious to arrive.

Now that he had, he faced an agony of delay moving through the receiving line, which must have been reassembled at this late hour to greet the scores of people who had just come from the Guildhall.

When his view of Isabel was momentarily blocked, he scanned the crowd for other familiar faces. He saw Mrs. Daventry, once again surrounded by a court of male admirers, and was reminded that he no longer needed to seek out a dashing widow still in her weeds. Tully had discovered that Lady Ridealgh was not resident in Town, but had retired to the dower house on her late husband's estate in Berkshire. Richard still wanted to pay a call on the infamous lady, but that could wait for another day. His interest was fixed on a different widow this evening. One wearing a great heart-shaped ruby on her shoulder.

Richard finally made his way through the receiving line and into the ballroom. A reel was in progress and he scanned the couples on the crowded dance floor. He easily located Isabel, partnered by that popinjay, Lord Francis Gilliard. Watching her smile up at the preening fop stirred the same relentless and disquieting memories that kept him awake most nights. Memories of a soft mouth and the scent of roses and eyes flecked with so many colors a man could drown in their depths while sorting them out.

Richard kept half an eye in her direction while he chatted with some of his fellow officers and their wives.

When the set ended, Lord Francis led Isabel off the floor toward a group of ladies, one of whom Richard recognized as Lady Challinor. Isabel was smiling brightly and fanning vigorously. The energetic reel had apparently left her a bit winded.

Richard procured two glasses of champagne from a passing footman and approached Isabel.

"Good evening, Lady Weymouth. After such

a lively reel, I am sure you must be in need of refreshment."

He offered her one of the glasses. She hesitated for an instant, arched an elegant eyebrow as she looked at him, then smiled and took the glass.

She looked very beautiful tonight. Her cheeks were flushed from the dance, and her eyes, more green tonight than brown, sparkled merrily. Her white dress was stunning and as stylish as anything he'd seen in France. The neckline was tantalizingly low, revealing more of her full bosom than he'd yet seen. She had the most lovely skin. It was not as pale as was fashionable but had a sort of golden glow that echoed her hair. It was skin that cried out to be touched. Richard wanted to bury his face in that golden bosom.

He made an effort to curb the hot flood of pure lust that coursed through his veins.

"Thank you, Lord Mallory," she said, and lifted the glass in a salute. "It is precisely what I wanted." She took a dainty swallow.

"Are you engaged for the next set?" he asked.

She gave him that quirky little half-smile, and he wondered if she was recollecting the last time they'd danced, when he had flirted so outrageously with her.

"I am not, as it happens," she said.

"Will you walk with me, then? You must be fatigued after such a vigorous reel. But perhaps a turn around the room would not overtax your energy."

"Yes, let us walk."

He held out his arm and she placed her hand upon it. They left their glasses on a small table and strolled slowly along the edge of the room.

"You look especially lovely tonight, Isabel."

"Oh? You like what I am wearing?" She darted a glance to the brooch on her shoulder.

"Very much."

She gave him one of her full-blown smiles, the kind that bathed her face in a radiance that took his breath away and surely drew every eye in the room. "I am glad."

"I do not know much about these things, but I would guess that dress is bang-up to the minute. You would put the ladies of Paris in the shade. Do they cite you in the fashion magazines here in London?"

Her eyes grew warm with his praise. "I am occasionally mentioned in the *Ladies' Fashionable Cabinet*, and some of the others have now and then described my dress without mentioning me by name."

"You are a leader of fashion, then. I am not surprised. The last time I saw you"—her eyes widened slightly as though she thought he would mention that filthy, ragged uniform—"you wore a wreath of laurel leaves in your hair. Tonight, I've seen a dozen women wearing similar ornaments."

He had discovered another vulnerability. She could not disguise the pride that flickered in her eyes. "I like to try new ideas," she said, "new color combinations, new accessories."

"That shows courage. Most women I know would be terrified of failure, and so they wait for others, like you, to set the trends."

"You think me courageous?"

"Very much so. One might almost call you . . . daring."

The orchestra began again and voices throughout the room were raised in order to be heard above it. The din made conversation difficult and gave Richard exactly the opening he wanted. As they neared the doors to the terrace, he leaned down and said, "Let us go outdoors so that we may be private."

He did not wait for her assent, but simply led her onto the terrace, where several other couples strolled in the cool air. Richard took in the surroundings with a glance. There was a substantial garden below, lit along several paths with paper lanterns. It was more suited to his purpose, and so he led her to one of two stairways that curved down to the garden.

Isabel gave him a questioning look.

"The gardens are very inviting, don't you think?" he said. "Let us stroll through them."

"You are very bold tonight, sir."

He looked down at the brooch on her bodice and allowed his gaze to pass over her bosom. "As are you, madam. Delightfully so. Let us see how bold we can be."

He tugged her into a dark alcove of clipped greenery where he had spied a stone bench. He swung her onto the bench and took her in his arms.

"This is too bold, I believe," she said, though she did not pull herself out of his embrace. Her hands rested lightly on his chest.

He could feel her breath on his face as he held her close. She wore the rose-scented fragrance that he'd come to recognize as her own, and it made him hungry to taste it on her skin. He wanted to devour her in small bites.

"Not too bold for us, Isabel. There is something between us, something undeniable. We both knew it that day you came to my rooms."

"That was pure recklessness. A moment of madness."

"Yes," he said, and traced a finger over her lips as though to silence her. "Pure madness. And quite dizzingly wonderful." His finger continued to stroke her lips and he felt her body tense and her breath quicken, just as he'd hoped. "I have been waiting too long to recapture that mad moment."

He brought his finger down past her mouth until he cupped her chin in his hand. He reached up with his thumb and tugged on her lower lip, coaxing her lips to part. Then he opened his own mouth over hers and took her in a deep kiss.

And the night exploded around them as passion ignited instantly, sending shafts of heat through his body and bursts of light into his head. He wrapped his arms around her and pulled her close. Her arms worked their way around his neck and shoulders and she answered each touch of his tongue with one of her own. He felt her hunger, knew she wanted this, and held onto his control with a masterful effort of will as the blood roared in his head. He wanted to drive her wild with desire, to feed her hunger, to make her forget the caution and anxiety that he'd sensed the last time he'd kissed her like this.

Richard was relentless in his assault, but Isabel responded so thoroughly he almost forgot his purpose. He had meant the kiss to be a ravishment, to demonstrate both his hunger for her and his power over her. But it was soon evident that the ravishment was mutual when she took control and pulled him down to her, hands entwined in his hair, her tongue fencing with his in a glorious dance. They each tasted and explored and savored every new sensation in a battle for control.

He tore his mouth from hers and trailed his lips along her jaw to the flushed, warm skin of her throat. She threw her head back as his mouth traveled down her elegant neck and onto the swell of her golden bosom. She gave a little cry of pleasure, and remembering where they were, he brought his lips back to hers and captured her moan in his mouth. His hands followed the path his mouth had taken, stroking the soft skin of her throat and neck, and finally cupping her breast.

197

She moaned into his mouth again, and he knew she was lost to him. He could have taken her then and there and she would not have resisted. But he would not. Not tonight. Not here.

He teased the neckline of her bodice down slightly to give him more tender skin to stroke. She shivered beneath his touch and pressed herself closer to him. He broke away from her lips again and allowed himself the pleasure of tasting the silky rose-scented skin of her bosom, dipping his tongue into her cleavage. Each panting breath swelled the soft flesh beneath his lips, and he tasted and kissed and stroked until her moans of pleasure grew louder.

He took her mouth again—roughly, urgently—and rocked his hips against hers. His hands roamed everywhere, swift and hard, over her breasts and ribs and hips and back. Moving and moving, never stopping . . .

Until he had the brooch unclasped and in his hand. He quickly slipped it inside his coat and resumed stroking her. Now that the deed was done, he abandoned himself to the sheer pleasure of kissing and touching and tasting. He allowed pure carnal sensation to overtake him and sweep him into a conflagration of desire, passion, and need.

Need? He could not think of that now. He could not think of anything right now. But mixed up with all the other sensations and emotions was a tiny spark of need. It gave him an instant of surprise, but other sensations, physical and raw, took over and overwhelmed him. Isabel rubbed her body against his, unconsciously echoing the rhythms of the music from inside the ball but creating a more provocative dance.

She eased her thigh up to rest partially across his as she tried to get closer, tried to wrap more of herself around him. His hands answered, stroking her thighs and buttocks over the silky fabric, drawing her against him and yet still wanting more. He found the hem of her dress and pushed it up, reached underneath to stroke her bare thigh.

Her gasp of surprise brought Richard to his senses. He pulled away at last, forcing an end before they took it too far. They stared at each other, and he imagined the astonishment on his own face surely matched what he saw in hers.

"Damnation," he whispered, his lips hovering above hers. He looked deep into her eyes, dark now and glassy with desire. "Damnation."

"Indeed," she said in a breathless voice, and her lips quirked up into a smile.

He clasped her to him tightly in hopes she would not notice right away that the brooch was no longer pinned to her bodice. His hands moved slowly up and down her back.

"Isabel, Isabel," he whispered in her ear, "what have you done to me?"

He felt her soft laughter. "No more than what you have done to me, my lord."

"I would keep you here forever, but I daresay that would be unwise."

"Yes."

"We had better return to the ball."

"Yes."

He came very close to asking for more, to asking if they could meet later to finish what they'd started, but he kept his tongue between his teeth. If he hadn't already taken the jewel, perhaps he would have asked. If he hadn't been so precipitous, he could have taken her home instead, made passionate love to her, and pilfered the brooch while she slept. It was too late for that now. Damn him for a fool!

"If we return together," he said with unfeigned frustration, "everyone will guess what we have been doing. You go inside first. I will follow later."

"All right."

She pushed away as if to go, but Richard grabbed her again and kissed her, hoping to discompose her enough that she would depart in a sensual daze, giving no thought to the brooch. Her soft moan when he broke the kiss told him he had succeeded. He released her. "Go now. Quickly, my dear."

She rose from the bench and gave a little sigh of resigned disappointment. She looked down at him, flashed a dazzling smile, then hurried along the path leading to the terrace stairs.

Richard sank back on the bench and blew out a long, unsteady breath. Holy Mother of God, that had been incredible. He felt intoxicated, giddy, unsteady. He could not remember the last time he'd felt such a fierce desire for a woman. Lord, she had tasted and smelled and felt so damned good he was having trouble recovering his wits. And he was still hard as a rock.

He took several deep breaths and tried to relax. He certainly could not walk around with a tent pitched in his breeches, even if only to find his carriage and make a hasty exit.

Now that he had the brooch back again, he really must decide what to do about Isabel Weymouth. She had definitely become more to him than an opponent in their game of hearts. He wanted her. There was no point in denying it. He wanted her in his arms again and in his bed. And he wanted to know who and what she was.

The moment he reached his rooms, he would put the blasted brooch under lock and key and put an end to their game. For now, he'd better stop dawdling and make himself scarce before she discovered the thing was gone and hunted him down.

He ran a hand through his mussed hair and straightened his neckcloth. Then he stood and adjusted his coat. He inhaled the hint of roses that clung to it while running his hands over the inside pocket where he'd secreted the brooch.

Oh, no.

He checked again. And again.

It wasn't there. He knelt and looked all around the bench, feeling about in the plantings behind. It was not there.

Hell and damnation. The cunning little vixen had done it again. *No more than what you have done to me, my lord.* She had not been so discomposed after all.

He sat down on the bench, dropped his head into his hands, and laughed.

Isabel remained on the terrace for a few moments before returning to the ballroom. She stood in the shadow of an enormous urn perched atop a tall plinth and spilling masses of summer blooms in every direction, and hoped no one would see her. She needed to compose more than a slightly disheveled dress. Her head was spinning and her body tingled all over.

What *had* he done to her?

She could still feel his mouth on hers. Her skin still shimmered from his touch. If she closed her eyes, the whole scene played out again in exquisite detail in her mind. She could feel him, taste him, smell him. He did not wear fragrance as most men did, but he had an almost intoxicating scent nevertheless. There was nothing manufactured or false about it. Just a natural musky, masculine smell, mixed with a bit of leather and horse and a hint of shaving soap.

Each remembered detail, though, had been part of a deliberate, planned seduction. He had pulled away before it went too far, but Isabel was not fooled. She knew it was not propriety or gentlemanly honor that held him back. It was a deliberate attempt to entice her, to stoke awareness and desire, to make her want him. It was a masterful performance, and it had worked. He used her treacherous body against her just as she had used his compassion for disabled soldiers against him. There was no difference. Both were ruses to get the jewel. Both were pretense.

Isabel had a niggling little hope that it had not all been playacting. She had thought he was as aroused as she was. Actually, she knew he was. She had felt evidence of it when she'd flung a leg over his thigh. But that did not make the entire episode any less of a sham seduction. He had deliberately set out to drive her to the edge of madness so she would not notice when he took the brooch.

But she had been expecting it from the start, so one tiny corner of her rational brain was held in reserve in order to deal with it. She had not known when or if she would ever have the occasion to pick his pocket, but had asked Danny to teach her the rudimentary skills just in case. The training had worked. Richard had been so busy trying to distract her he had been sloppy in disposing of the jewel. It had been the work of an instant to retrieve it from his pocket and slip it into the reticule that hung from her wrist.

That sloppiness taunted her, giving her hope that some of what had occurred had not been feigned on his part, that he was as distracted, as enflamed as she was. When he'd held her at the end, it had felt so right, so comfortable, she had wanted to stay there forever with her head on his shoulder. Surely he had felt something similar?

But she had no business hoping he had felt the rightness of it. There was nothing at all right about it. He was a thief, for God's sake. A thief! She had to keep reminding herself how unsuitable he was. She could not think of him as anything but an unscrupulous scoundrel with no fortune and a taste for larceny. He could never be anything else to her.

Against all better judgment, she was not merely intrigued by him. She was excited by him. She wished and wished they had never met or that she could somehow get the wretched man out of her mind. How she wished Lord Kettering would grab her and kiss her senseless so she might more easily forget Richard's kisses.

But how does one forget the unforgettable?

If she did not have the jewel in hand, Isabel thought she might have been ready to concede defeat and let him keep the damned thing. If not for Gram, she would have walked away from this dangerous game. She no longer wanted the ruby heart. She no longer trusted its power.

Or perhaps she trusted it too well. She removed the brooch from her reticule and read its message again. "True love knows but one." But Richard was *not* the one. He couldn't be.

With an effort, she pulled herself together and shook off the remnants of their kiss. She pinned the brooch back on her shoulder and adjusted the bodice. Isabel hoped to heaven her lips were not swollen and her hair was still in place. She reached up to find the bandeau of pearls where it should be, woven among a frothy arrangement of curls. She had to trust that she looked presentable.

After a few deep breaths, she straightened

her shoulders, lifted her chin, and walked through the doors into the ballroom.

"There you are," Lydia said when Isabel approached her. "I thought you'd decided to leave."

"No, I am not ready to leave just yet."

Lydia eyed her curiously and Isabel wondered if there was still some evidence that she'd been thoroughly kissed in the garden. "Good," Lydia said. "It is time for the supper dance and Lord Kettering has been anxious to find you. You did promise him this set, did you not?"

"Yes, I did. I had not realized it was that late already."

"Your second set with the earl. That is certainly promising. You must sit with Oliver and me for supper. I will be sure to compliment your every virtue in his lordship's presence."

"Don't overdo it, I beg you. I am not feeling particularly virtuous at the moment."

Lydia's eyebrows disappeared beneath the elaborate turban that twisted around her head. She lowered her voice to a conspiratorial whisper. "What do you mean? Where *have* you been, Isabel? Or should I ask with *whom* have you been? Tell all, my girl."

Isabel waved away her questions. "There is

nothing to tell. I haven't been with anyone in particular."

"Is that so?" Lydia gave a little smile and looked away.

Isabel followed her friend's gaze to the doors leading to the terrace. Richard stood in the doorway, in all his scarlet-coated magnificence. Her pulse quickened at the sight of him. He was staring directly at her.

"No one in particular?" Lydia teased. "No handsome officer, for example?"

"No one," Isabel said, her gaze locked with Richard's. "No one at all." She reached up and fingered the ruby heart on her shoulder. He smiled and saluted her, then walked away and disappeared into the crowd.

Lydia stared at her. "Isabel?"

"Hush, Lydia. Here comes Lord Kettering to claim his dance."

His lordship approached a moment later and bowed to the ladies. Why could her pulse not race at the sight of him? He was handsome. He was rich. He was everything she wanted. That alone should make her heart flutter. If only the stupid man would kiss her.

"It is our set, I believe, Lady Weymouth."

"Yes, thank you," she said, and took his arm.

She studied him as they walked, and thought of Gram and Cousin Min and the house in Chelsea that was always in need of repair. She thought of her brother Ned and his need for a steadying influence. She thought of the back pay owed her servants. Isabel had responsibilities and Lord Kettering was the one who could help her meet them. Not some scarlet-coated rascal whose notion of helping her would most likely be to steal some other woman's jewelry.

Before Richard had entered her life like the sneak thief he was, devastating her wits and firing her senses in ways she'd almost forgotten, Isabel had been thrilled at Lord Kettering's attentions. His place on her list of the richest unmarried men under forty was, of course, a primary consideration. But she was not completely without feeling, and could not have encouraged him if she despised him or found him repulsive.

In fact, she liked him. He was kind and considerate and had the most elegant manners. And he really was quite attractive. She would be lucky to have him.

If only he would kiss her.

He looked over to find her smiling at him. His eyes lit up and he returned her smile. "Are you enjoying the ball, my lady?"

"Oh yes. It has been most . . . entertaining."

As they took their places in the line for the country dance, Isabel decided the man was too proper by half and she was going to have to take matters into her own hands. She began to consider ways to break through the earl's steadfast propriety and let him know that she would welcome a physical demonstration of his regard for her, that she wanted him to kiss her.

And if he did, maybe then she would find it easier to forget about those other kisses.

Chapter 11

❦❦❦

"**B**eggin' yer pardon, m'lady, but I think yer daft."

"Actually, Danny, I am feeling particularly clearheaded. I think my plan is a good one."

"Why doncher jus' take the bleedin' thing— sorry—back t'yer gramma? That'd put a end to it."

Isabel had considered that option, but decided against it. "I cannot be sure it would end there, Danny. He wants this brooch very badly for some reason. What if he went after it at Gram's house? No, I cannot put her in danger."

He shuffled his feet and looked at the floor. "Could be that it ain't the ruby 'e's after."

"What do you mean? He's stolen it, or tried to, three times."

He shrugged his thin shoulders. "Dunno. Just thought 'e might be int'rested in summink else."

She knew what he was thinking. Yes, Richard might be interested in her, but not in any way that mattered. She did not believe a man could kiss her like that and remain completely dispassionate about it. There was some spark of interest, to be sure, but it was purely carnal. And he exploited her weakness to feed those sexual desires. He knew she was susceptible to his seduction. She had made that clear the first time she'd gone to his rooms, unable to disguise her hunger for physical intimacy. He knew her to be a widow and probably even knew she had taken no lovers since Rupert's death. He would have guessed at her physical needs without her blatant exhibition of them.

But tempting a lonely widow was not his primary motive. He wanted the brooch. She did not know why, but he did. And whatever personal interest he demonstrated—and heaven knew he had demonstrated it very well indeed—was only a means to get the jewel.

Which meant that he would strike again. And this time, she was going to let him succeed.

"He still wants the brooch, Danny, and will try again to steal it. And I still believe my plan will work. It's the best solution I have for putting an end to this game. It will work. I'm sure of it."

The boy shrugged. "Whatever yer say, m'lady. So, who'll it be this time?"

"Yates, I think. He does the best work and this one has to be very, very good."

This was becoming the most frustrating campaign Richard had ever waged. Isabel was doing her best to make it difficult, and succeeding.

She never wore the Mallory Heart again in public. He had rather expected her to flaunt it, to tempt him with it, but she had not done so. He had attended several functions each evening, just to see if she was there and wearing his family jewel. Social animal that she was, he never had difficulty finding her. She was to be seen at every fashionable event, usually with the same court of admirers. But no ruby heart was pinned to her dress.

Kettering was almost always to be found

among Isabel's gallants, and he was the clear favorite. Richard wondered if he had overcome his objections to her family. Would he make her an offer soon?

The idea created knots in Richard's stomach. He had experienced her passion, her hunger. He knew what she needed. It was nearly impossible to imagine Kettering could provide it. Of course, one could never really know how a man conducted himself in private. Perhaps he had hidden depths, though Richard doubted it. Kettering seemed the type who would only partake of occasional decorous couplings with a wife, for the sole purpose of producing an heir, and slake his own physical needs elsewhere.

What a sad situation that would be for a woman like Isabel. In the end, she would probably take lovers of her own, and their marriage would be an empty shell.

But there he went again, presuming to know how things would be when he really didn't know anything at all. The truth was that he wanted to believe there could be no passion between Isabel and Kettering because he did not care to imagine it. He did not like to think of her in another's arms making the same little moans of pleasure Richard had found so erotic.

Isabel gave him no opportunity to hear those moans again. She did not avoid him. She even flirted with him, teasing him with that quirky smile. But she always managed to be engaged whenever he asked her to dance at a ball, and kept herself surrounded by her circle of friends and admirers the rest of the time. There was never a time when they were alone together. Rather than flaunting the jewel, she seemed to be flaunting Kettering. She made it clear with every look and smile that the earl was the one she wanted.

And so Richard had come to his last hope. If he wanted to get the brooch back, he would have to take a more direct approach.

Which was why he was now balanced precariously on the old vine growing up the wall outside Isabel's bedchamber window. He had resorted to old-fashioned burglary.

With very little effort he was able to jimmy the sash window. He quietly raised it, only to face the closed shutters. They were fortunately not barred and he was able to, somewhat awkwardly, maneuver them open. He then swung himself inside, stepping onto the broad sill. The final barrier was the heavy drapery. He pulled back a small opening that gave him a view of the room. He did not want to risk bursting in on a servant.

The room was empty. He drew back the draperies and crept down from the sill. Moonlight spilled into the room.

It was exactly as he remembered it, stark and simple. The only hints of femininity were the dressing table and a lace pillow on the bed. He wondered what the room had once looked like, before it was stripped bare. Knowing Isabel's flair for fashion, it had likely been very beautiful. How it must pain her to live like this. He could almost understand why she'd been driven to theft.

Moving as quietly as possible, he went to the dressing table and sat down. The pen-work box stood on the table, as before, and was not locked. Did the woman have no concept of security? The case was stuffed nearly to bursting with jewelry. Diamonds, emeralds, and sapphires glittered in the moonlight. He wondered again how many, if any, actually belonged to her. And if they were in fact stolen, why had she not sold them in order to refurnish her house? Why was she hoarding them?

Richard sorted through the contents of the jewel case, taking care to replace each piece in exactly the position he found it.

But there was no heart-shaped ruby.

She must have hidden it. Dear God, was he going to have to search the entire room? Distasteful as it was, there seemed no other choice.

Working as quietly as possible, he examined each drawer in the small chest, searching among undergarments and shawls and stockings and other intimate items. He held up a fine silk stocking and breathed in the scent of roses. When he realized what he was doing, he became so disgusted at the invasion of her privacy that he could not continue. He had not found the brooch, but this was taking things too far. There had to be a better way.

The game had to end. He had allowed it to go on far too long, and look how low it had taken him. Rummaging through a woman's undergarments, for God's sake. It was despicable. He'd never done anything so dishonorable in his life.

Richard crawled back out the window, closing the draperies and the shutters—a difficult maneuver—behind him, and climbing down the vine to the roof of the garden shed. No outraged servant or neighbor accosted him as he made his way to the mews, and he was fairly certain he had not been seen. Had the jewel been where he'd expected it, the operation would have been easily successful. He was tempted to caution Isabel to bar her shutters, but he did not care to admit this little escapade to anyone.

He was, however, ready to admit everything else. It was time to confront Isabel with the truth about the jewel, to explain why he wanted it, and to come to some arrangement with her for its return.

The game was over.

"It's a perfect copy, Mr. Yates. Well done, as usual."

"Thank you, Lady Weymouth. I am glad it pleases you."

She must be one of his best customers, so of course he wanted to please her. He no doubt hoped for many more such commissions. Sadly, there weren't that many pieces left to copy, so he was facing disappointment in that quarter.

"I trust you will keep this transaction confidential, as usual?"

He looked outraged that she would ask such a question. "Naturally. Discretion is included in the fee, as you well know, my lady. A transaction with Yates & Company is always a private matter."

"Yes, I know. Forgive me for being overly cautious."

He gave her a supercilious smile. "I quite understand. This is a particularly valuable piece. And quite old. I do not often get to work with Elizabethan jewelry. It was a true pleasure."

She pulled a veil over her bonnet before leaving the shop. It was not an area frequented by her acquaintances, but she preferred to take no chances. With the frequency of her visits to Yates & Company, specialists in paste copies and originals, it would be disastrous if she were recognized.

Danny held open the door of the hackney. She never traveled to this part of Town alone.

"So? Did 'e do the job proper?"

"Yes, it's an excellent copy. Lord Mallory will never know the difference."

She dressed with particular care that evening as she prepared for yet another celebration ball.

Her dress was a simple frock of embroidered crepe given extra dash with an Angouleme drapery attached to one shoulder, brought across the back, under the arm, and fastened at the bosom with the ruby brooch. The false ruby brooch.

Isabel doubted Richard would try another move like the last time, stealing the brooch while he kissed her. But she was determined to tempt him to do so. The minuscule bodice of her dress and its daring neckline would hopefully help matters along.

He was not at the ball when she arrived, but then Richard always seemed to arrive late. She tried not to watch for him too obviously, particularly since Lord Kettering was paying her special attention. He had actually kissed her gloved fingers and not the air above them. He seemed very pleased with himself for taking such a bold step. Isabel still considered dragging him off into a dark corner and pulling him into a kiss, but she did not know whether he would think it a wonderfully provocative thing to do and kiss her back with mad passion, or if he would be so shocked he would deem her a wanton beneath his contempt.

Why were the respectable, suitable men so

damned tedious? And why were the truly unsuitable men so exciting? It did not seem at all
fair.

She knew at once, as always, when Richard
arrived. He continued to cause a little stir everywhere he went. His striking good looks and his
air of command drew the attention of females
like a magnet.

Isabel had grown accustomed to the flare of
heat generated by the sight of him. She was no
more immune to it than any other woman, less
so since she had a more intimate knowledge of
those broad shoulders. During the last week,
she had done her best to ignore that heat while
she kept him at bay. Tonight, she would not ignore it. She would let it guide her.

He saw her, and the breath was sucked out of
her body. Naked desire crossed the room from
where he stood and collided with her own. His
eyes flickered with recognition of what had
passed between them. He had done his best to
make her want him. He had succeeded. One
look and she knew her planned attempt to en-
courage another seduction had nothing at all to
do with the ruby brooch.

"My set, I believe, Lady Weymouth?"

She turned to Lord Easton, hoping her face

was not as flushed as it felt. "Indeed it is, sir. I have been looking forward to it."

"Have you?" His lordship, stout and middle-aged and happily married, gave her a flirtatious smile.

"How could I not," she said, "when you always fill my ears with such flattery?"

He chuckled and offered his arm. She caught Richard's eye briefly as they approached the dance floor. He glanced down at her bosom, saw the brooch, and grinned.

She felt his eyes on her all through the set with Lord Easton. This strange, perverse connection between them, their vivid awareness of each other, charged the air and could not be ignored. She missed so many steps in the dance that Lord Easton teased her about her clumsiness being caused by her secret passion for him. He got it half right, anyway.

When the set, which had seemed interminable, finally ended, Richard was at her side at once.

"You have been avoiding me all week, Isabel."

"No, I have not. You have merely caught me at inopportune moments." She briefly touched his sleeve with her fan. "However, I am not engaged for the next set. Is there a garden?"

He lifted his brows. "It is raining."

"Oh? How inconvenient." She flashed him her best smile. "We shall simply have to be re-sourceful."

"I think we can manage something." His voice was rough-edged and very seductive. "Take my arm. We are going for a walk."

He led her through a series of anterooms where people who were not dancing were gathered in groups. She had no idea where they were going, and he probably didn't either. They finally came to a small curtained alcove, and he pulled her inside and drew the curtains. Without a word he took her into his arms and brought his lips to hers.

Their kiss was wild and torrid and unbridled. Ripples of sensation spiraled through her body, welled up, and filled her. She was lost to him.

He pulled away too soon, leaving her breath-less and bereft.

"I have been waiting all week to do that again," he said, and rested his forehead against hers. He brushed a wayward finger ever so lightly over the tops of her breasts, causing her to draw a sharp breath.

"Really? I hoped that—"

"I saw this place earlier and knew it would be

perfect for— Oh! Oh, I say." Sir Walter Herrick stood in the alcove with the curtain pulled back in his hand.

Isabel pushed away from Richard, but it was too late. Sir Walter's eyes were wide with astonishment as he looked back and forth between them. His gaze settled on Isabel and a frown of disappointment clouded his brow.

"Beg your pardon," he said stiffly, and closed the curtain.

Isabel covered her face with her hands. Please God, don't let him spread this tale. He was an acquaintance of Lord Kettering. If the earl knew she'd been hiding in a dark alcove kissing Lord Mallory . . .

Richard stepped away from her and pulled back the drapery. "I would not worry about Herrick. He will say nothing of this."

She looked up. "How can you be so sure?"

He glanced left and right, then took her by the elbow to lead her out of the alcove. "Did you see who he was with?"

"No."

"Miss Arbuthnot."

"Eloisa Arbuthnot?"

"The very one. And their intentions were the same as ours, I daresay.

Isabel's eyes widened with surprise. "But she is betrothed to Lord Billings."

"Precisely. Herrick will not say anything about us because he will not want us to say anything about them."

"Oh. Well, then." She hoped he was right. It was hypocritical in the extreme, but she really did not want Lord Kettering to know she had been kissing someone else.

Kissing Richard, though, was a matter of business, of a sort. It had not been a simple moment of pleasure. In a way, she had sacrificed her virtue in the cause of keeping him away, once and for all, from the genuine brooch. She had done it for Gram. But she had failed, for he had not yet taken the copy. In the flickering candlelight of the ballroom, and especially in the darkness of a curtained alcove, it would be nearly impossible to recognize the stones as paste.

No, that was not the reason he hadn't taken the brooch. There simply had not been enough time.

They had taken no more than two steps away from the alcove when she came to an abrupt halt. No one was nearby, so she pressed up against him with her hands on his chest, being sure he felt the brooch at her bosom. "Since Sir Walter is unlikely to return, is it really necessary for us to leave?"

He smiled and took her hands away. "You *are* a brazen hussy, are you not?"

She shrugged and felt her cheeks flush.

"Isabel, you are thoroughly adorable. Audacious and uninhibited one moment, blushing innocence the next. However, as much as I'd like to continue where we left off, I think it is best not to tempt fate again."

"I'd rather tempt you."

He squeezed the hands he still held. "My dear, you do nothing *but* tempt me. But I will not risk your reputation. Let us return to the ballroom. The night is still young, after all."

Did that mean he would welcome another interlude if it could be arranged? Isabel carried that hope in her heart as he led her back into the ballroom, and prayed her hopes were not as false as the ruby at her breast.

She did a stellar job of tempting him the rest of the evening. She could not have flaunted the brooch any more blatantly. Of course, it could have been the golden bosom she flaunted, barely covered by the plunging neckline of her bodice. He doubted it, though, and so he enjoyed an unremitting eyeful of bosom and brooch that was enough to tip any sane man over the edge.

She was so determined to thrust the brooch in his face, it almost seemed like she *wanted* him to take it, as if she was anxious for the game to continue.

And so it would. The moment Richard had seen her wearing the brooch, he had changed his mind about confronting her with the truth. She had simply been teasing him all week, smiling and flirting and keeping him at arm's length, never wearing the brooch. And then tonight she pounced like a tiger. Did she really believe he would take it from her like he did before? Had she wanted to engage in a little erotic game of passing it back and forth while they made love?

He would not be drawn into that play. He had no qualms about kissing her, to be sure. In fact, he would have been perfectly happy to spend the evening doing so. And more. But he would not steal the brooch right off her bosom again. He would not give her another chance to demonstrate her skills as a pickpocket, or her skills as an actress. He would not forgot how she'd duped him into believing she'd been so overwhelmed by his kisses that he thought her too distracted to notice when he'd lifted the jewel.

Richard was not one to be twice duped. He needed a different battle plan this time, and he had one ready to put into action.

When they returned to the ballroom, he hovered around her long enough to ensure that she had several sets promised throughout the evening. He would have enjoyed dancing with her, but he had other things on his mind. While she was dancing with Lord Francis Gilliard, who seemed as determined in his attentions as Kettering, Richard made a hasty retreat.

Sometime later, dressed all in black, he once again climbed up the old vine outside Isabel's bedchamber. He made his way through the window, as easily as before, and took his position on the broad windowsill. He made himself as comfortable as possible behind the drapery, and waited.

He would not search through her belongings again. Instead, he was going to watch to see where she put the brooch after removing it from her dress. Then, after he was sure she was asleep, he would leave his hiding place and take it.

Of course, he would be obliged to watch her undress. But she was a brazen hussy, after all.

Chapter 12

❝**H**e's here, m'lady!"

Danny had given her a bit of a start when he'd opened the front door just as she'd been about to put the key into the latch. Isabel kept late hours and never required the servants to wait up for her, so his wild-eyed appearance at the door had startled her.

She walked past him into the entry hall, where only the single candle that was always kept there for her burned. None of the wall sconces were lit.

She looked at Danny in puzzlement. "Who's here?"

"Lord Mallory, m'lady."

What? Here?

"Lord Mallory? At this hour?" She glanced up the stairs and saw nothing but darkness, as she had expected since no light shone from any of the front windows. "Where have you put him?"

"I din't put 'im nowhere. 'E put 'isself."

Isabel pulled a face. "I don't understand. What are you talking about?"

The boy leaned in close and lowered his voice. "'E snuck in the 'ouse. Climbed right in yer bedchamber winder."

"What?" He was here? In her house? In her bedchamber?

"I was out in the garden, mindin' me own business, just 'avin' a bit of a cheroot—"

"Danny! Smoking again? I've told you that you are too young to be indulging in such non-sense. And wherever did you get a cheroot?"

He gave an impatient wave of his hand. "That ain't important now, beggin' yer pardon, m'lady. Not when there be a gen'lmun 'iding out upstairs. I seen 'im climb in yer winder, slick an' silent as a cat. Like 'e knew just 'ow to get in real easy." His eyebrows lifted and he tapped the side of his nose. "Like it weren't 'is first time."

"Good heavens. You think he's done it before?"

"I'd lay odds on it. 'E knew just where to put 'is feet on that vine, just 'ow to jimmy the winder open. If t'weren't 'is first time climbin' in yer winder, then 'e's 'ad a fair bit o' practice climbin' in some other winders. A reg'lar draw latch, that 'un."

So, she had been right about him all along. He was a professional thief. She could not quell a pang of disappointment, which was foolish since she had always assumed he was a seasoned jewel thief. What was there to cause disappointment? Had she really hoped there would be some other explanation?

"He is still upstairs, then?"

"Yes, m'lady. I been keepin' watch. 'E ain't left."

"Thank you, Danny." She took the candle from the hall table and started up the stairs.

"But wotcher wan' me ter do? Come wif yer?"

She turned to face the agitated boy. "No, I will handle it. You go on to bed."

His eyes were wide with anxiety, as though he were sending her to face a monster alone. Then his expression changed as an idea seemed

232

to dawn upon him, and Isabel could guess what that idea was. His cheeks flushed pink and he cast his gaze to the floor.

"Yes, m'lady. G'night, then."

"Danny, wait. Does Tessie know about Lord Mallory?"

"No, m'lady. I ain't told no one." He shook his head and grinned. "Miz Bunch'd 'ave the 'ysterics."

"Right you are. Well done. Now, if Tessie is awake, will you send her to me, please?"

"Yer want Tessie ter come ter yer room?" His voice squeaked with incredulity.

"Yes, please. But Danny, you are not to tell her about Lord Mallory. Do you understand? Not a word."

He rolled his eyes as if he thought her quite mad, but gave a quick nod of acknowledgment and raced away toward the back stairs. Isabel resumed her climb up two flights of the main stairs to her bedchamber.

She was fairly certain she knew what Richard was up to. He was no doubt in hiding so he could steal the brooch after seeing where she kept it.

If that were true, though, there was something very puzzling about it. He knew where she kept it. He'd stolen it from her dressing table that very first time.

She came to an abrupt halt as she recalled something Danny had said. Richard's confident manner of sneaking in through her window was not a matter of professional skill. He *had* been here before. Isabel suddenly felt quite certain of it. He must have come to steal the jewel but had not found it because it was still at Yates & Company being copied. He must have assumed she hid it well, and was determined to learn the hiding place.

Well, she would make it very easy for him. She would leave it in plain sight. She would let him think he'd won.

Of course, if he meant to watch her hide it, he also meant to watch her disrobe. Instead of outrage, that notion sent a little thrill of excitement dancing down her spine. She'd been trying to tempt him to kiss her again all evening, before he'd disappeared. Just to give him another opportunity to steal the brooch, of course. But he had refused to be tempted.

Isabel smiled as she approached her bedchamber door. A little more temptation was in order.

She entered the room and casually glanced around. There were no signs of an intruder. He was hiding, of course. But where?

She went to the dressing table and used her candle to light two more that stood on either side of the mirror stand. The room was much brighter now, and she made another nonchalant survey as she removed her shawl and gloves and dropped them on the bed.

Was he under the bed? That seemed unlikely. It would be too difficult from that angle to see what she did.

She approached the clothes press, hesitating for a moment before opening it. No, he would not hide in there. It was too small, not like the large, elaborate wardrobe she had once owned but had been forced to sell. This old, slightly battered press had a central section of sliding shelves with drawers below, and was flanked by two open cupboards for hanging clothes. But the hanging cupboards could barely accommodate a few dresses, much less a very large man.

She flung the doors wide and was reassured to find no manly shoes poking out from beneath her dresses.

That left only one other option. He was certainly behind the window draperies. Since there were no telltale toes peeking out from the hem, she guessed he was curled up on the sill. It was wide enough to allow Isabel to perch in the window now and then, but must be a tight squeeze for his lordship's broad shoulders.

Poor Richard. She would try to make it worth his while.

He'd thought she would never arrive. The silly woman must have stayed until the last note of "Sir Roger de Coverley." He had thought to stretch out in some comfort and wait until he heard footsteps. But the draperies were heavy, the door was closed, and the room was in the back of the house. He might not hear her until it was too late.

So he had curled himself up on the windowsill for a very long wait. He was glad he had done so. When the door opened and soft candlelight spilled into the room, he had not heard her approach at all.

He sat still as a statue and watched through a discreet little crack he'd arranged between the draperies. She lit more candles, for which he blessed her. He would miss nothing. Absolutely nothing.

236

She puttered around a bit before getting down to business. She removed her gloves, and Richard realized he had never before seen her bare arms. She always wore long sleeves or long gloves. He had admired her gorgeous skin before, but the candlelight in the bedchamber seemed to infuse it with a special glow. Pale, but not porcelain white. A soft hint of gold gave it a tantalizing luminosity. It was the sort of skin that would turn golden brown in the sun, not bright pink.

The sight of those slender, bare arms caused a tightening in his groin.

She stood beside her dressing table, with her back to him, and removed her jewelry. First came the earrings, which she placed beside the pen-work box—not inside, though the lid was raised. Then came the ruby heart. When she unpinned it, a swath of gossamer-like drapery fell away and hung down her back. She casually dropped the brooch on the dressing table, and set her attention to removing a lace pin that held the drapery on her shoulder.

At that moment, Richard was startled by a soft knock on the bedchamber door, and the entrance of a sleepy-eyed girl with a shawl wrapped around her nightgown.

"Ah, Tessie," Isabel said. "I am sorry to get you up so late again."

The maid looked too exhausted to respond, and simply went to work. While Isabel disposed of the drapery at her shoulder, Tessie turned down the bed, pulled a nightgown out of a drawer, and laid it out on the counterpane. Richard noted with some disappointment that the nightgown was more serviceable than seductive.

As if she knew he was there and had read his thoughts, Isabel said, "No, Tessie, not that one. I'll have the one with the French embroidery and lace trim tonight."

The maid looked surprised, but returned the plain nightgown to the chest of drawers and brought out another one that she laid on the bed with such care it might have been made of spun gold. Richard could not say for sure, but it looked very sheer and delicate.

What came next made Richard more aware than ever of how low he had sunk, how dishonorable he was to be spying on a woman getting undressed. This was worse than rummaging through her undergarments. He'd become a voyeur.

He could, of course, have looked away. He

need only keep his eye on the jewel. There was no need to watch her disrobe.

But he did not look away. He watched.

The maid undid the fastenings at the back of the dress and helped her step out of it, then did the same for the petticoat. While Tessie carefully folded the petticoat and hung the dress inside the small wardrobe, Richard was provided with the delicious sight of Isabel in no more than a corset and short chemise. His eyes were drawn to her very shapely legs clad in white silk stockings clocked in silver. Long legs. Trim ankles. Elegantly shaped calves.

Dear God. He made a Herculean effort to moderate his breathing. It would not do for Isabel and her maid to become aware of panting from behind the draperies.

Isabel gripped the bedpost while Tessie unlaced her corset. Richard held his breath when Isabel, freed of her stays, flexed her back muscles and stretched like a cat. Her breasts did not disappear, as some women's did when the upward thrust of the corset was removed. He could see beneath the linen chemise the shape of full, round breasts.

"Thank you, Tessie," she said. "You go on to bed now."

"But my lady, don't you want me to help you with your hair and nightgown and such?"

"No, I can manage. I just needed your help with the dress and the stays. Go on back to bed and get some sleep."

"Thank you, my lady." The maid dipped a tiny curtsy and left.

Isabel went to the dressing table and sat down. Her bare arms reached up to remove a pearl ornament from her hair. Those soft arms and the way she held them, pulling her breasts up and tight against the chemise, were almost his undoing. After a few long, agonizing moments of watching her lifted arms move about her head, her hair suddenly fell down her back in a cascade of honey gold, burnished bright in the candlelight.

She picked up a brush and ran it through the thick waves, then pulled her hair over her right shoulder and arched her neck toward it as she brushed. The angle at which she sat gave him a full view of that elegant column of white neck, and the movement of brushing caused her breasts to bounce slightly.

His mouth had gone dry. He tried to swallow, but feared it would turn into a loud gulp, so he did not.

She brushed her hair for what seemed an eternity, twisting and turning and arching in an erotic display worthy of the most skillful houri. Finally, she swung her hair to her back and shook her head, sending waves of gold undulating against her shoulders and upper back.

Richard wondered if she had any notion of how beautiful and sensual she looked. Her husband would have seen her like this, so perhaps she did know, for she would have felt his gaze, would have known his desire. Richard was suddenly jealous of the late Sir Rupert Weymouth. Had the man realized how fortunate he was?

She next gathered the hair again, brought it over one shoulder, and began to braid it. She tied the thick plait with a small piece of ribbon, and suddenly looked very young.

Isabel then swung around on the stool so that she was almost directly facing him. She pulled her chemise over her knee to reveal a pink silk garter and a hint of golden thigh above it. She untied the garter, then lifted her knee and began to roll down her stocking with both hands. It almost seemed as though she was caressing her leg as she removed the stocking, and it made him think how much he'd like to do the same.

His groin grew tighter as she repeated the process on the other leg. Now he had bare legs as well as bare arms to contend with. It was becoming almost impossible to breathe.

She rose from the stool and took the garters and stockings to the chest of drawers he'd rifled through on another occasion. She also retrieved her gloves and shawl from the bed, folded them, and placed them in the chest as well. As she moved about, he could see the shadowy outline of her body beneath the thin linen. She was beautifully made, with a womanly shape—full breasts and hips, small waist, long shapely legs.

He hoped he was about to see more, to see what had been hidden beneath the chemise. She went to the bed where the nightgown was laid out for her. Facing him, she lifted her arms and was about to pull the chemise over her head, when she hesitated. She turned away from him, lifted her arms again, and stopped.

Something—and he cursed whatever it was—had caused her to change her mind. She took the nightgown and went to the clothes press. She opened it and moved so that she was hidden from view by the open door. He was not sure how she had done that without practically climbing inside the hanging cupboard, but disappear she did. And when she reappeared, damn it all, she was covered from neck to toe in a muslin nightgown. The only consolation was that it was extremely thin muslin, and he caught glimpses of her body underneath. The dark circles of her nipples stood out clearly beneath the sheer fabric, which clung to her more closely than the linen of her chemise.

It was not consolation enough. He wanted to see more.

Isabel gave a long, catlike stretch—giving him an even better glimpse of the lush figure beneath the nightgown—then blew out the candles and climbed into bed. Richard could see very little in the sudden darkness, and he was glad for it. While he waited for her to fall asleep, he relived every major battle of the Peninsula in an effort to forget what he'd seen tonight, what the sight of her had done to him.

He waited a long time. He wanted to be sure she was asleep before he revealed himself. Reliving the battles and reciting in his head the names of every man killed in his regiment helped to pass the time, and to douse the fires Isabel had ignited in his blood.

When her even breathing made him confident she was asleep, Richard parted the draperies and slipped quietly from his berth on the windowsill. His body groaned with stiffness, and he had to stretch a bit before he could move properly.

The brooch was on the dressing table along with the earrings, lace pin, and hair ornament. She hadn't even bothered to put them away in her jewel case, which stood open, revealing hints of her entire collection of jewels. It was a wonder she had never been robbed before. One day he would like to scold her about such carelessness.

Richard quietly pocketed the jewel and was about to crawl back out the window when he happened to glance at the sleeping form on the bed. She was faced partially away from him. The long golden plait hung outside the covers, catching the moonlight that crept into the room from the small opening in the draperies. One hand was curled beneath her chin so that she looked like a sleeping child.

He was again intrigued by the strange combination of seductress and naive innocent. Which was she?

Richard was very tempted to touch her. Just to stroke her cheek or brush away the soft wisp of gold that escaped confinement near her ear. More than that, he wanted to climb in beside her, pull her back against his chest, and watch her sleep in his arms.

But he did none of those things. He could not risk waking her. And so he simply stood and stared, and wondered what the devil had come over him.

Finally, he turned away and crept back onto the windowsill. He hoped to God Isabel slept soundly because he did not know how he was to manage the shutters and the sash without some amount of noise.

He was very fortunate, though, and he made a fairly quiet exit. Since no irate face appeared at the window, he assumed he'd escaped without detection.

Richard had participated in a fair share of stealth operations over the years, but this one ranked up there with the worst of them. He had never been so sorely tried. But then he'd never been forced to remain hidden and silent while watching a beautiful woman undress. He was breathing so heavily when he reached the ground it felt as though he'd run several miles.

But it was over. Not just this operation, but the whole war. He had the jewel again and he was not letting it out of his sight until he returned it to Greyshott. There was nothing she could do to get it back. No more tricks. No more ruses.

He would have liked to be able to leave for home the next day and be finished with the whole silly business of the Mallory Heart once and for all. But he could not. He had promised Colonel Bradbury that he would accompany him and Lady Althea to the theater tomorrow evening. The very next day, though, he would be on the road again with the damned jewel strapped to his chest, if necessary.

He would be back, though. He had to come back. There was more than a ruby brooch between him and Isabel, and he meant to find out just how much more.

When she heard the window close, Isabel rolled over and expelled a shuddery breath. She had felt his presence beside the bed, watching her while she feigned sleep, and it had been one of the most unnerving experiences of her life. And one of the most exciting. She had thought he might be contemplating joining her in the bed, and she wondered what she would do.

The bald truth was that, God help her, she would have welcomed him. Scoundrel, thief, rogue—it did not matter anymore. She wanted him. She had not felt so alive, so sexual, since the early days of her marriage to Rupert.

Isabel had enjoyed putting on a little show for Richard. She had felt his eyes on her, and had posed and preened for his benefit. It had an effect on her as well, knowing he watched. Every bare inch of skin prickled with awareness. It had felt terribly wicked to show herself to him in only her shift, with her legs exposed and no stays to bind her. But that was as far as she could take it. When it came time to reveal all, she could not bring herself to do it.

She had felt naked enough in her shift, though, and even more so in her sheerest nightgown—the one Rupert had loved her to wear. She relished the secret knowledge of Richard's gaze upon her. Even now, after he'd gone, the thought of those blue eyes watching her made her warm and tingly all over. No man had excited such feelings in her since her husband's death.

Despite being aroused and excited beyond bearing, or perhaps because of it, Isabel was suddenly overwhelmed by a great sob that seemed to have erupted from somewhere deep in her soul. She buried her face in the pillow and gave in to a torrent of tears.

Isabel hated herself for wanting him. She pounded the pillow with her fist. Hated, hated, hated herself. Not only for wanting him, but for daring to imagine an affair with him. She could not allow unfulfilled desire, no matter how painful, to rule her life. An affair with Richard, were it to become known, would change everything. She would be seen as one of those widows who took lovers, the sort who preferred their independence to another marriage, the sort men felt safe in seducing.

But she could not afford independence. She had no money and a mountain of responsibilities, a family who depended upon her. The only course open to her was to marry again and marry well. She had been solidly on that course until Richard had walked into her life and stolen Gram's jewel. And set her senses ablaze with longing.

Curse the man for interfering with her life.

Isabel might have outfoxed Richard with the paste copy of the ruby heart, but she was not so sure she had won the game after all.

Chapter 13

Lord Kettering led Isabel to a seat in his box at Covent Garden, and took the chair beside her for himself. Though he had invited a large group, he made it quite obvious that Isabel was his special guest. The evening marked a step forward in their relationship. He had called at Portman Square and taken her up in his carriage for the drive to the theater. It had been just the two of them, and though they had driven out together in his curricle on several occasions, it was the first time they'd been alone in a closed carriage.

Ever the gentleman, he had sat across from

her rather than by her side—an arrangement that was not exactly conducive to stolen kisses. Isabel had hopes that she could coax him to sit beside her on the drive back. And if that didn't work, she would invite him inside for a brandy and hope he would not be shocked by such an invitation.

But Isabel was encouraged. Lord Kettering allowed himself to be acknowledged as her escort, and there was the merest hint of possessiveness in the way he kept her on his arm and placed her in a chair against the wall of the box so no one could sit on her other side.

When he excused himself for a moment to speak to a gentleman who'd just arrived, his place was taken up by Phoebe Challinor. She leaned close and spoke in a conspiratorial whisper.

"Things are looking very promising," she said, and glanced in his lordship's direction. "You must be pleased."

Isabel was pleased. She really was. It was what she wanted, after all. A perfectly decent earl, heir to a marquisate, with buckets of money was interested in her. She would not be distracted from her purpose by fantasies of the heir to a downtrodden earldom with nothing but his officer's pay, and a bit of thievery, to recommend him. Nor by the memory of piercing blue eyes and a roguish smile, or of hands and lips that threatened to drive her to the brink of madness.

"I am hopeful," she said, and meant it. She hoped to heaven she could exorcise Major Lord Mallory from her life.

"He pays no other woman any attentions beyond what is polite," Phoebe said. "I believe he is serious, my girl. As are you, if that dress is any indication, with all your assets on display."

Isabel was wearing a bodice that was cut in a deep V in front and an even deeper V in back, revealing a great deal of skin, fore and aft. It was no more revealing than any other fashionable evening dress, but Isabel had a bit more to display in the bosom than other women. She had rather hoped Lord Kettering would notice. "One does what one must," she said and flashed a mischievous grin.

Phoebe brought a hand to her mouth to stifle a giggle. "Indeed. The right sort of bait just might reel him in."

"I don't know, Phoebe. The man is so disgustingly proper I fear I could strip naked and he would not make a move." She thought of undressing for him the way she had done for Richard last night. For some reason, the very idea sounding more embarrassing then arousing.

Phoebe pulled a face. "I take it he has not yet made any improper advances?"

"No advances of any kind. It is exceedingly frustrating." Even more so because of another man whose advances were most improper.

"Well, perhaps your good-luck charm will do the trick tonight."

"My what?"

Phoebe gestured toward the ruby heart pinned high on Isabel's shoulder. "Your brooch. I notice you wear it often when Lord Kettering is around. It looks like an old love token, so I thought perhaps you wore it for good luck."

In fact, she wore it tonight because she knew Richard was going to be at the theater. Lord Kettering had mentioned that he had invited Lord Mallory to join them, but the major had already promised to share the Bradburys' box. He would certainly drop by to pay his respects, however, and Isabel decided to wear the genuine ruby heart for his benefit. It was most likely too soon to allow him to know he'd stolen a copy, but Isabel simply had not been able to resist the temptation of flaunting it in his face. She wanted him to know he'd lost the game. And she would give him no opportunity to steal the real jewel. She was returning it to Gram tomorrow.

"It is indeed a love token," Isabel said. "Have you ever seen so much sentiment?"

"It's a beautiful piece. Did Rupert give it to you?"

"No, I borrowed it from my grandmother." Which was mostly true. Just because she had not asked for permission did not mean she'd stolen it. Not exactly.

"Well, it is quite lovely. Here's hoping all those devices of love work in your favor. Do you know what the inscription says?"

"It means 'true love knows but one.' "

Phoebe's eyebrows lifted. "And you are hoping Lord Kettering is the one?"

Isabel gave a noncommittal shrug, but her friend was not fooled.

"I shall be interested to see if it works," Phoebe said.

His lordship returned a moment later and Phoebe relinquished her chair and returned to sit beside her husband.

"I hope you are looking forward to the performance as much as I am," the earl said. "I have not yet seen Kean's Iago."

The young actor held the audience spellbound and almost managed to keep Isabel's mind off Lord Kettering and his decorous wooing. But each time she slanted a glance in his direction, she began to plot ways to get him to kiss her without coming off as a wanton. Would his lips be as intoxicating as Richard's? His tongue as daring? His touch as magical?

When the curtain came down after the first act, the earl turned to her and smiled. "Kean is quite magnificent, is he not? I have always thought Iago a most unnatural character, a sort of monster. Kean makes him believable. Thoroughly lacking in moral principle, but still human. Don't you agree?"

Isabel had not paid full attention to the actors on the stage. Her mind had wandered off too many times, but whenever Iago spoke she was drawn back to the play. "Yes, I agree. Mr. Kean has a very singular way of approaching the character, quite unlike Mr. Sowerby's Othello, for example, which seems rather pedestrian in comparison."

They spoke for some minutes about the performance. It was a most enjoyable conversation during which Isabel's admiration of his lordship grew. She found him to be more thoughtful and perceptive than she'd believed him to be.

Finally, the earl rose and said, "Forgive me for chattering so long when you must be parched. Allow me to procure something for you to drink."

"Thank you, my lord."

The box became a beehive of activity during the interval, with several people coming and going. Isabel was chatting with George Amberley, one of the earl's friends, when she felt a familiar prickle at the back of her neck. George looked over her shoulder and smiled broadly.

"Mallory. Well met, old fellow. Good to see you again. Bought any good horseflesh lately? Ha!"

Isabel had been standing with her back to the box entrance and looked over her shoulder at Richard's arrival. He was not in his regimentals, but looked as handsome as ever in a blue velvet coat that set off his shoulders to advantage. Crisp white linen and a white silk waistcoat accentuated the sun-bronzed tone of his skin, lending him an aura of virility unmatched by any of the other fashionably pale gentlemen gathered in the box.

He caught her eye at once, smiled, and moved to stand closer. George shifted his position to include Richard in their conversation.

"Oh, I say, Mallory, are you acquainted with Lady Weymouth?"

She turned full around, giving Richard a good view of the ruby brooch on her shoulder.

He eyes widened slightly in surprise, but he recovered quickly. "Yes, Lady Weymouth and I are old friends. You are looking especially dazzling this evening, Isabel."

She winced inwardly at his public use of her Christian name. And again when his gaze swept over her bosom and lingered on the brooch. Hopefully anyone watching—especially Lord Kettering, who'd just returned and was chatting with Lord Challinor—would know Richard for a notorious flirt and not make any assumptions about the two of them.

While George Amberley yammered on and on about some horse race or other, Richard kept glancing her way. Was he wondering how she'd managed to steal the jewel back? Or had he realized he'd been duped into taking a forgery?

Isabel began to think he'd figured out the truth, which meant he probably also knew she had known he was hiding behind her draperies last night. And that meant he would realize she had disrobed knowing full well he was watching.

She felt her skin prickle and flush, and he sent her a sly smile as though he'd read her thoughts. As though she'd guessed correctly and he was indeed aware that she'd undressed for him. The look in his eyes grew warmer, and she had to look away.

Lord Kettering joined them and chatted with Richard about the recent losses in the American war. Isabel moved away to stand with Phoebe and Lydia near the railing. They were discussing Dolly Richardson's headdress. Or maybe it was Lady Richmond's overdress. Isabel paid little attention to what they said. She kept watching Richard, hoping he would leave. Then she might be able to forget that he probably knew she had practically stripped for him.

Before he did leave, he came over to where she stood, took her hand, and placed a fulsome kiss upon it. Upon the glove, actually, but Isabel's skin tingled in reaction nonetheless.

"It was a pleasure, as always, my lady." A provocative twinkle lit his eyes. "I hope I shall be seeing more of you in the days to come."

More of her? More than he'd seen last night?

She felt her cheeks flame and raised a fan to her face. "Lord Mallory," was all she could manage, the wretched man had her so discomposed.

When he left, Lydia and Phoebe closed in, eyes blazing with curiosity.

"Isabel, you're blushing like a schoolgirl," Lydia said, her voice lowered so the gentlemen nearby, especially one gentleman, would not overhear. "Is there something between you and Lord Mallory?"

"No, of course not," Isabel said. She batted her fan furiously in an attempt to cool her burning cheeks.

"That man has had his eye on you since the first time we saw him at the Inchbald ball," Phoebe said. "Is he importuning you, Isabel?"

"No, no. He is simply a shameless flirt. He enjoys unsettling me."

"He does a good job of it," Lydia said. "Are you sure that is all there is? I saw the way you looked at him."

"Whatever do you mean? How did I look?"

"Like you had a tendre for the man," Lydia said. "He is, after all, exceedingly handsome."

"Don't be ridiculous," Isabel said. "We have a common interest, that is all." She fingered the common interest pinned to her shoulder.

Phoebe noticed and nodded toward the brooch. " 'True love knows but one.' Is he perhaps the one, and not Lord Kettering?"

"No, absolutely not. You are both making a great fuss over nothing. The man is a rogue and a scoundrel. He is not a gentleman to be trusted. I wish to heaven he would leave me alone."

Lydia arched a brow. "Are you certain? I confess if he looked at me the way he looked at you, I might be tempted into a bit of dalliance, scoundrel or not." She grinned and her eyes twinkled. "Actually, knowing he's a scoundrel gives him a certain appeal."

"I said the same thing to Isabel the first night we met him," Phoebe said. "There is something about him that makes a woman weak in the knees. Never saw a man fill out a red coat so nicely. Or any coat, for that matter."

Lydia leaned in very close. "No one would blame you, my dear, if you were to succumb to that . . . charm."

Isabel shook her head. "How can you say that when you know . . . Well, you know that my interests lie elsewhere."

Lydia glanced to where Lord Kettering stood, talking with Lord Challinor and George Amberley. "Yes, I know. I daresay it comes down to a choice between a respectable match with the oh-so-proper earl or a more private arrangement with the dashing major."

"Or both," Phoebe added, with a smile.

It was exactly what Isabel had been considering, especially last night while she undressed under Richard's eye. But it was impossible. She could never do it.

"Don't be foolish," she said. "You both know very well that I would lose the one if I went after the other. Besides, I am horribly old-fashioned about such things. Perhaps it is a reaction against my own mother's scandalous behavior, but if I marry again, I will not be unfaithful. It is simply not in my nature."

"Then you must be very sure," Lydia said, "that you marry the right man."

Isabel caught Lord Kettering's eye and smiled. "I intend to."

Richard had no desire to stay for the next act. Despite Lady Althea Bradbury's protest that he could not possibly wish to miss the rest of Mr. Kean's performance, Richard did not care two sticks for what was happening on the stage. Besides, he knew how it would end. He knew

Iago's treachery and Othello's crime of passion. It was a favorite play, in fact, but he had other things on his mind. Only one thing, actually.

How the devil had she managed to get the damned jewel back again?

He was so stunned he could have been knocked over with a feather when he saw the brooch pinned to her dress. He could not believe his eyes. Either he or Tully had kept the damned thing under watch since he'd pilfered it from Isabel's dressing table the night before. There was no possible way she could have stolen it.

Was there?

As he made his way to Tavistock Street, Richard considered every possibility. But there did not seem to be any way Isabel or that confounded page-urchin could have got into his rooms without discovery.

Unless Tully had slipped out while he was supposed to be on watch. Richard did not want to believe that. Tully was loyal and trustworthy to the core. Richard would stake his life on it.

Yet something had gone wrong. Isabel most certainly had the jewel once again, and Richard was determined to figure out how she'd done it. One possibility lingered in the back of his mind, but he was not yet ready to give it serious consideration.

When he reached his rooms, that remote possibility became a probability.

The ruby heart was exactly where he'd left it.

He slipped it from the protective bag and took it over to where Tully had lit a branch of candles. He examined the brooch in the light, and let out a stream of every vulgar expletive he'd learned in the army. Tully glared at him wide-eyed.

"I've been taken for a fool, Tully. Again. Look at this." He handed the jewel to his batman. "Look closely at the diamonds surrounding the ruby. Do you see the tiny black dot in the center of each stone?"

Tully squinted as he studied the brooch closely. "Yes, I think so. What does it mean?"

"Paste."

Tully's jaw dropped. "Paste? You mean these are not real gemstones?"

"They are glass, my friend. Pure sham. Expertly done, to be sure, but paste nonetheless. I've been well and truly hoodwinked by that woman."

Tully stared at him incredulously. "You mean this whole cat-and-mouse game has been over a few bits of glass? She never had the real jewel?"

"Oh, she has the real jewel. Lady Weymouth is, in fact, wearing it at this very moment."

"She's not!"

"She is, damn her eyes. And that means the game is not quite over."

Tully heaved a sigh and looked thoroughly disgusted with this latest development. "What are you going to do, then? Switch them?"

Richard considered it for a moment. Yes, he could probably make a switch, but he had no doubt she and that wily little lieutenant of hers would find a way to switch them back again. The damned game could go on and on with no end in sight.

"No," he said, "I am not going to switch them. This nonsense has gone on for too long."

"You're surrendering?"

"Let's say I am going to propose a truce, or at least a cease-fire."

In truth, Richard had rather perversely enjoyed the game with Isabel. She was a worthy opponent. But it had to end at some point. Now that there were two jewels, perhaps it was time for each of them to lay their cards on the table and come to some sort of arrangement.

He grabbed his hat and made for the door.

"Now?" Tully asked. "You're going to confront her now? Tonight?"

"Yes, tonight. I want things settled between us."

And one of the things to be settled had nothing to do with the blasted brooch. Since Isabel had deliberately left the paste copy in plain sight, knowing he would come and take it, she must also have known he was watching her undress. It had been a glorious performance meant to tempt him and taunt him.

Well, by God it had worked. Twice now—perhaps even three times if one counted the scene in the garden when she had plucked the jewel right out of his pocket—Isabel had played the part of temptress to achieve her own ends. It was past time she learned that when one played with fire one sometimes got burned.

As he made his way to Portman Square, Richard had not quite decided how he was going to proceed. Should he await her return and confront her openly at her front door? Or should he sneak into her bedchamber once again?

Since he was fairly certain she knew he'd been there the night before, he would not be surprised to find the window bolted shut from the inside. A frontal attack would likely be the best strategy. And so he decided to wait for her in the square, as he'd done once before.

Richard asked the hackney driver to stop at Orchard Street, then walked to Portman Square. It was just after eleven—still early by *ton* standards. Isabel's usual inclination to flit from party to party until the wee hours before dawn meant that Richard likely had a long wait ahead of him. He jumped the fence into the central garden and walked toward the plantings on the western side where he would take cover while he waited.

The wait was surprisingly short. Only a few minutes after his arrival, a carriage pulled up in front of Isabel's house. He recognized the crest on the door.

Kettering.

He had realized at the theater that the earl was her escort. He had watched them from Bradbury's box, seated close together, chatting amiably. Clearly he was still intent on pursuing her. Acting as her escort was a step closer to a declaration.

Richard still hated the idea. The earl was not a proper match for Isabel, but there was nothing he could do about it.

He was, though, rather glad the man was

such an upright, proper fellow who no doubt thought late hours were unhealthy. Isabel would probably thank him for his escort, wait until his carriage was out of sight, and then dash out to the next party.

But not before Richard spoiled her plans by showing up on her doorstep.

He watched them both descend from the carriage and was stunned to see Isabel leaning against Kettering, whose arm was around her shoulder. A tiny knot of anger twisted in Richard's gut as he watched the two of them walk inside the house and close the door behind them.

He could not believe it. Kettering? That haughty pattern card of propriety was her lover? Or just about to become her lover, for Richard remembered the man's insecurity about his appeal. He would wager a monkey this was the first time he'd gone home with her.

Of all the nights for it to happen, it had to be tonight when Richard was watching.

That knot in his stomach twisted tighter.

He would have to change his plans. He refused to wait while the rich, golden-haired earl enjoyed his own private performance of the buxom seductress. Damn her. That little exhibition last night had probably been a rehearsal for tonight's full production. But where Richard had merely been an audience, Kettering was to be a full participant.

Did the man know she probably only wanted his fortune, and would most likely insist on marriage in exchange for seduction? Did she know how contemptuous he was of her family and background? Did she realize that despite being captivated by her, his bloody lordship did not think she was good enough for him?

It was entirely possible that by coming home with her, Kettering had conceded that she really was not up to his standards, not at all suitable as a countess but perfectly acceptable as a mistress. Isabel might not get all she expected out of this evening.

As he watched, candlelight filled the drawing room, creeping out along the edges of the closed curtains. She probably meant to let him have her there, in the only properly furnished room in the house. She would not want him to see the starkness of her bedchamber.

Discounting last night's business, Richard was no voyeur. He had no intention of standing down in the square, staring up at that window in search of movement. He had no desire to see even a hint of what happened behind those curtains. If he didn't see it, he might be able to convince himself it never happened.

Damn her for making it matter to him.

Despite his resolve to leave, Richard did not move right away. He could not seem to tear his eyes from the drawing room window. It was some minutes before he admitted to being a fool, and began to walk away. The sound of a door opening caused him to stop.

It was Kettering. He was leaving the house already. Had he changed his mind? Had she changed hers? Or had she perhaps not gotten the promise she wanted and sent him packing?

Whatever the reason, Kettering returned to his carriage, which had conveniently, and indiscreetly, waited for him. There was something not quite right about that, but Richard had no wish to consider it at the moment.

He was going to confront Isabel, and he was going to do it right now.

Chapter 14

Richard waited for Kettering's carriage to disappear, then marched up to the door and banged the knocker. It was some minutes before the door was opened by the same maid who'd helped Isabel undress the night before. Her eyes grew large at the sight of him.

"I am here to see Lady Weymouth."

"But my lord, she has retired for the evening."

"No, she has not. She has only just returned home." He stepped past the maid into the entry.

She tried to block his way. "I am sorry, but it is late and she is not receiving visitors."

"She received Kettering. She will receive me." He walked past her to the staircase.

"My lord! Please." The maid scurried after him. "You cannot go up. Her ladyship is not well."

Not well? That stopped him. He remembered how she'd leaned on Kettering when they left the carriage. He turned to look at the maid. "What is—"

"You!"

He swung around to see Isabel standing at the top of the stairs. She was wrapped in a huge paisley shawl, but did not appear ill. In fact, her eyes were blazing.

"How dare you! Get out of my house before I call a constable."

He began to climb the stairs. "No, Isabel. We have things to discuss."

"No, we do not. Get out. Get out!"

Her voice had risen almost to a scream and he could see that she was shaking.

What the devil?

"Isabel?" He reached the top of the stairs. "What has—"

"You blackguard!"

She flew at him, almost sending him tumbling backward down the stairs. He held onto her to keep from falling, and she pounded his chest with her fists.

"Scoundrel! Beast! Devil"

He tried to grab her hands, but she wrenched away and flailed at his head and shoulders.

"Hold your fire, woman."

"How could you?" she wailed, and he realized she was crying. "How could you?"

She continued to pummel him, but the blows became weaker even as her sobbing became more intense. "I knew you w-were a thief but I n-never expected . . ." She pushed him away.

"Isabel, what the hell are you talking about?"

She wiped her eyes and glared at him. "You hurt me."

Though they made no sense, her words tore at him. "Hurt you?"

She pulled away the shawl to reveal the shoulder of her dress ripped and torn and spotted with blood.

His own blood ran cold. "Oh my God."

"Yes, take a good look at your handiwork, you bastard. And then get the hell out of my house."

He took a step toward her but she retreated.

"Don't touch me." Her voice shook and tears spilled down her cheeks. She wrapped the shawl tightly about her shoulders. "Don't you ever touch me again."

"You think I did this?"

She gave a snort that turned into a sob. "You would do anything to get my ruby brooch."

"I would never do anything to hurt you, Isabel. Never."

"But you did. You ripped the brooch away so fast the pin slashed across my shoulder. But you didn't stay around long enough to see the damage."

Damnation. "Are you telling me someone stole the jewel?" His jaw was clenched so tight he could barely form the words. "Right off your dress?"

She reached out as though to strike him, but Richard caught her wrist and held it. The shawl fell away again, and the sight of her blood sent a primitive fury racing through him. Some devil's spawn had dared to touch her, to injure her. His clever, intrepid, enchanting Isabel. Someone had hurt her, damn it, and the rage simmering in his gut threatened to boil over.

Despite her flailing fists, he scooped her up in his arms and carried her into the drawing room. The maid, whom he'd forgotten about, followed close behind and hovered in the doorway. He kicked the door shut in her face.

"Put me down, you brute."

He deposited her very gently on the sofa and wrapped the shawl about her shoulders. After removing his hat and flinging it onto a chair, he stood staring into the fire, which Lord Kettering had lit earlier while he'd sent Tessie to make tea. Richard leaned against the mantel with his back to her, one hand balled into a fist. It seemed he was chagrined at having injured her. But he had done so, and she would never forgive him for such brutality. She would never forgive herself for so badly misjudging him. She swiped roughly at the tears on her face.

"No more games, Richard. You took it too far this time. Keep the blasted jewel."

"I don't have it."

She sniffed. "Disposed of it already, have you? How very enterprising."

"Look." He turned to face her, and she caught her breath at the expression in his eyes. A dangerous combination of wretchedness and rage. He reached into his pocket, and pulled out what appeared to be the ruby brooch. "This is all I have. It's the paste copy. I came here to try to bargain with you for the real one."

"I will not bargain with a thief. A violent criminal. Besides, I have nothing anymore with which to bargain. You have it all."

"I swear to you, Isabel, this copy is all I have. I did not steal the other one. Please believe me. Tell me what happened."

"You *know* what happened."

He took a slow, deep breath. "No, I do not. I can guess, but I'd rather you told me."

"Why? Do you want to hear if the deed sounds more exciting and romantic in the telling?"

His nostrils flared briefly. "Please. Just tell me."

"Then will you leave?"

"If I can be sure you are all right. But I want to hear what happened."

She gave a shuddery sigh. "We left the theater and were on our way to Sally Thirkhill's card party."

"You and Kettering?"

"Yes. We had not gone far when the carriage came to a violent halt and the door on my side was thrown open."

He'd set his mouth in a grim line and his brow grew thunderous, but his eyes never left hers.

"Then some masked scoundrel," she said,

"some urban highwayman, reached in and ripped the brooch off my dress."

He groaned as if in pain. "Was he on horseback?"

"No. He was on foot."

"But he managed to stop the carriage?"

"The coachman said the man had stood in the street, waving his arms for the carriage to stop. He had no choice. He would have run over the villain otherwise. The blackguard had the door open before the horses came to a halt. And ran away into the shadows as soon as he had the jewel."

Richard swore under his breath, and she suddenly realized that somewhere in the telling she had come to accept the fact that Richard had not done this. He was cunning and clever, but she had never believed him to be physically dangerous. She did not want to believe it. Besides, that look of anger in his eyes was quite terrifyingly genuine.

"And Kettering did nothing to help?" he asked.

"It all happened in an instant. There was nothing he could have done. He was very upset about it."

Richard snorted, as if Lord Kettering ought to

have done more, done something to prevent that man from harming her. But he was being unfair. Richard could not have stopped what took place any more than Lord Kettering. It had happened much too fast. His lordship had been beside himself with concern. He had been most solicitous. Isabel was very glad she had not been alone.

"There was no attempt to extort anything else from you or Kettering? The man did not ask for money or take your purses?"

"No, he never said a word."

"He just grabbed the jewel and ran?"

"Yes."

"Then it was no random crime. He must have seen you wearing the ruby and followed you from the theater."

Isabel gave a shudder to think she had been stalked for the jewel.

"Can you remember anything about how he looked? Anything to help identify him?"

"He wore a mask and it was dark. And it all happened so quickly."

"Think, Isabel. His hair, the shape of his face, his eyes, his hands. Anything."

"I thought it was you, so he must have been of similar height and build. I believe he had dark hair. Oh. Oh, wait a moment. I think . . . I think he had a scar on his hand. He did not wear a glove on the hand that grabbed me, and I think I remember seeing a scar near his wrist. Oh, Richard. I ought to have known it wasn't you. You have beautiful hands."

Richard walked to the sofa and stooped down on his haunches in front of her. He reached out and touched her cheek. "Are you badly injured, my dear?"

Isabel shook her head. "It is only a scratch. But I was s-so frightened."

In the next instant, he was beside her and holding her in his arms. She fell into the comfort of his warmth without protest.

"My poor Isabel. You are still trembling. I swear I will kill whoever did this to you."

Her head rested on his shoulder. "I thought it was you."

"No. I wanted the jewel, but I would never harm you. Never."

"I know."

He nudged her head off his shoulder and looked into her eyes. "You do?"

She nodded.

"Isabel."

He closed the short distance between their

mouths and kissed her. Softly and with such tenderness it almost broke her heart. It was a kiss of comfort and caring, without the urgency of their previous encounters.

His lips moved against hers in gentle exploration. He kissed her upper lip, the corners of her mouth, her lower lip. He moved to her jaw, her throat, and the hollow beneath her ear, his lips light as moth wings, barely grazing her skin. It was almost more than she could bear, and she gave a soft moan.

And suddenly everything changed. His mouth returned to hers, urged her lips open, and plunged his tongue inside. All the pent-up desire she had felt the night before when undressing for him surged to the surface. Her tongue fenced with his as he deepened the kiss. His hands roamed over her body, stroking her breasts and hips and belly.

And then his body was pressing hers down and down until she was lying on her back and Richard was on top of her. His mouth left hers and trailed down her neck to her bosom. His tongue dipped into her cleavage while his hand reached under her skirts and stroked her silk-clad leg.

Every sense was heightened. Every thought

was concentrated on Richard and his hands and his mouth. Her body arched and stretched in immodest reply to his caress. Her wits deserted her entirely when his hand crept up above her garter to her bare thigh.

Flushes of warmth washed over her, from the tips of her toes to the roots of her hair, pooling deep between her legs. She was engulfed in heat and longing. Such longing! Desire burned so hot she felt literally on fire, and found herself swept up into a conflagration of passion and need. She wanted him, needed him inside her. She had never wanted anything so much in her life.

"Oh my God. Please, Richard, please!"

Her cry emboldened him. He wanted nothing more than to invade her, to possess her, to transport her. When he stroked higher up her inner thigh and found the moist curls of her sex, he was lost. Pure mindless lust drove him, but he had just enough reason left to make certain it was not ravishment.

"You want this, Isabel? If not, speak quickly before it is beyond stopping."

"Don't stop. Please don't stop."

"You want this?"

"Yes!"

"You want *me*?"

"Yes, damn you. Please don't stop now!"

He crushed her mouth with one more ravenous kiss while he pushed her skirts up around her waist. He nudged apart her knees with his own, and she adjusted her position beneath him. He reached for the buttons of his breeches, but she was already there. Fumbling together, they managed to release the fall, allowing his erection to spring free.

He wriggled his breeches down past his buttocks and positioned himself at the entrance to her sex. He had no thought for finesse or extended foreplay and plunged inside her with one mighty thrust.

Isabel cried out, but arched to receive him. He reached his hands beneath her bottom and lifted her hips to give him deeper access, and she wrapped her legs around him. She bucked hard against him, meeting him movement for movement until she stiffened, convulsed, and called out his name. She melted beneath him and he pumped and pumped into her warmth until an explosive climax ripped through him. He pulled out just in time and spilled his seed on her belly.

He collapsed his full weight upon her and

caught his breath. After a moment he lifted his head. Isabel looked up into his face and smiled.

Sometime later, Richard stoked the fire, returned to the sofa, and pulled Isabel to his side.

"You are not trembling anymore," he said.

"You made me forget what happened. You took away the fear."

"I'm glad." He dipped his head and kissed her tenderly. "But next time, I want to take away more than that." He glanced down at their clothing—rumpled but more or less intact. "Next time, I want to take your breath away."

"You did that already, my lord."

"Then I want to take away your reason, and every stitch of clothing."

She gave a girlish giggle, but did not deny the possibility of a next time. They both knew this would not end tonight.

"You know, don't you," he said, "that I have wanted to make love to you since the first time I set eyes on you?"

"I was never sure if you were staring at my bosom or my brooch."

"Both, I confess." He trailed a finger along

the edge of one breast. "They are equally magnificent."

She laughed softly, then turned in his arms to face him. "Why did you steal it? What made you a thief?"

"I am not a thief."

She gave a little snort.

"Actually," he said, "I thought *you* were a thief."

She flinched. "Me?"

"Well, you did steal the brooch from me."

"Only after you stole it from me. How could you possibly believe me to be a thief?"

"I have seen the state of your house, my dear. But for this room, it is stripped bare. I suspected you had become a jewel thief to make ends meet."

She straightened and stared at him. "But I thought the same of you."

"What?"

"I know your family's fortune is in jeopardy."

Damn. Did all the world know their private business? "And so you thought I'd become a thief to refill the family coffers?"

"Well . . . yes. Why else would you do it? For the thrill?"

"I think I had better explain. I am not a thief,

Isabel. Taking the jewel from you that first time was the only truly dishonorable thing I've ever done in my life. But I felt justified."

"Why?"

"Because the jewel belongs to my family."

She scrunched up her face in an adorable look of puzzlement. "What?"

"It is known as the Mallory Heart and has been in my family since the time of Queen Elizabeth. I can show you a long gallery filled with portraits to prove it."

"But I don't understand."

"How did you come to have it, Isabel?"

"I borrowed it from my grandmother." Her cheeks flushed slightly. "I admit I didn't ask her permission. It was wrong, I know, but I was afraid she would refuse, and I just love that brooch. I took it without asking. I suppose that is closer to stealing than borrowing."

"Your grandmother? The one in Chelsea?" Richard remembered the humble little row house on a pokey little street in an unfashionable part of Town. What was a woman living in such a place doing with his family's priceless heirloom?

"Yes, and she is going to die when she learns the brooch is missing. It is very important to her. I don't know why, but it is. She keeps it hidden in a secret drawer in her jewel case. She's not even aware that I know about it, which is why I was afraid to ask to borrow it. How on earth can I tell her I've lost it?"

"How long has she had it?"

Isabel shrugged. "I don't know. A long time. All of my life and long before that, I'm sure."

Could her grandmother have been the one to steal it all those years ago? "Who is your grandmother?"

"Mrs. Theale. No one important. She was, I think, the daughter of a country squire. Now she's just another impoverished widow."

Richard did not miss the scorn in that last sentence. Isabel was not a woman who would easily accept that fate for herself. He had recognized that much from the start. It was why he'd had no difficulty imagining her a jewel thief. A woman who put on a great show of affluence while stripping the private areas of her home to the bare walls might have been desperate enough to dabble in a bit of larceny.

He was glad he'd been wrong about that.

"She and my grandfather lived in India for many years," she continued. "He worked for the East India Company, but not in any capacity

284

that made him rich. He did not leave her much when he died. Just some jewels and a few pieces of furniture."

"Do you think your grandfather gave her the ruby heart?"

"I don't know. But I confess I always suspected he did not. I used to imagine that she had a secret lover who'd given it to her. Why else would she hide it?"

A secret lover? Richard suddenly remembered those love letters he'd found at Greyshott. Passionate letters to his grandfather from someone who signed herself "M." Was there a connection?

"Does your grandmother's first name begin with M?"

She gave him a puzzled look. "No. Her name is Emmeline. Why?"

Blast. E not M. Emmeline. M. Or was it Em? "Does anyone ever call her Em?"

"Yes, lots of people. I think my grandfather called her that. Why all these questions about her?"

Richard pulled her close and held her tight. "Isabel, my dear, I think you have just solved a fifty-year-old family mystery."

"What do you mean?"

"Let me tell you a story."

And he told her about the Mallory Heart. He told her how Queen Elizabeth had presented it to Robert Mallory, the first Earl of Dunstable, when the title was bestowed on him. The queen was known to love jewels, and this one had been given to her by an admirer who had fallen out of favor. But it was an important and valuable item, and a significant mark of honor from the queen. Because it was such a sentimental piece, the earl had given it to his bride to wear at court. And thereafter, every succeeding earl presented it to his countess.

"Except for the current countess, my grandmother," Richard said. "Around the time of her marriage to my grandfather, the Mallory Heart went missing. The story was that it had been stolen. But now I don't think so."

"Why not?"

"Because I recently found a batch of fifty-year-old love letters to my grandfather signed by 'M.' I have a feeling that was a secret code for Em, or Emmeline. I believe they were from your grandmother. And I think he must have given her the brooch."

Isabel's eyes grew round with astonishment. "Do you really think so?"

It was a wild theory, but it might explain why his grandfather wanted it back so badly. Perhaps after all these years he regretted not giving it to the countess and pretending it had been stolen.

"I cannot be certain, of course," he said. "But it makes sense. It is certainly more appealing than to believe your grandmother is a thief."

"Oh, no. She is not a thief. I promise you that."

"And neither are you."

"Nor you."

"Well, we each did a pretty good job of it, did we not?" He gave a bark of laughter. "That wounded soldier act was priceless. Who is that little partner of yours, by the way? The one who played the page and the street urchin?"

She smiled. "That is Danny Finch. He is the under-footman here. He was my husband's tiger for a time. Prior to that he was a street urchin in earnest. A pickpocket."

"Ah. He is no doubt the one who taught you that particular talent."

Isabel chuckled. "That, and a few other things. He really is a good boy. I could not bear to turn him out after Rupert died."

"But you had to turn out others?"

"Yes." She squirmed a little, as though she did not want to discuss her circumstances.

"Weymouth did not provide for you?"

She shook her head. "We had lived very high, Rupert and I. It was not until he died that I learned we had been living on credit."

"Yet you did your best to hide your financial situation, keeping only this room furnished for visitors."

"Yes."

He ran his fingers down her arm. "There is no need to be ashamed, my dear. Many of us fall on hard times now and then."

She covered his fingers with her hand. "It is not very pleasant, is it?"

She still assumed his fortunes were as dismal as her own. The notion provided a sort of bond between them, and he was not yet willing to shatter it with the truth.

"Since you had a copy of the Mallory Heart made," he said, "can I assume the rest of your jewelry is paste as well?"

"Most of it. I only have a few good pieces left. Which is why ..." She did not finish her thought, but Richard was fairly certain he knew what it was.

"Which is why you look to marry a fortune.

An offer from Kettering, for example, would solve all your problems."

Her shoulders hunched inward, cringing at his words. But then she pulled away and searched his eyes. "Can you blame me? There is an ugly term that could be used to describe me, I suppose, and I have no wish to have that vulgar label hung around my neck. But is it so wrong to want to return to the life I once led? To have nice things again—real jewels instead of paste, and dresses from a real modiste, not made over from old ones?"

"No, of course not." Though it was somewhat disappointing to think she merely coveted expensive trinkets and stylish clothes. The disappointment made no sense, though, since he had found much to admire when he believed her to be a thief, which was a much uglier label than fortune hunter.

"A woman has no other recourse, Richard. We are completely dependent upon the men in our lives. And I have no man in my life at the moment."

"Except me."

She smiled and snuggled up against him. "A lot of good you do me. A jewel thief."

"I'm not!"

"I know. But you have as much reason to resort to such desperate measures as I do."

He did not, but Richard decided to keep that bit of intelligence to himself. He had a sneaking suspicion that if she knew he had a sizable fortune of his own, she would profess undying love for him in order to get her hands on it. He would never be able to trust her affections, and he did not want her on those terms. "And so I am no good to you."

She brought her mouth close to his. "On the contrary, my lord. You are very, very good indeed."

Chapter 15

Their second loving was a beautiful thing.

He built up the fire and lay her down on the Turkey rug in front of it. They took turns undressing each other and laughed at the memory of Isabel's performance the night before.

"I wanted to jump out from behind that curtain," he said, "and ravish you on the spot."

"And I was secretly hoping you would."

"Vixen."

She was fascinated by his naked body. He was larger and more muscular than Rupert, his chest and belly covered in silky dark hair, where Rupert had been smooth as marble. And there were several scars that made her wince. A long one on his thigh from a French saber, he explained, and one along his ribs from a bayonet. Another on his shoulder where a musket ball had grazed him.

It was a soldier's body—solid, well-kept, and slightly battle-worn. Isabel thought it quite a magnificent thing to behold. And to touch.

He studied her with equal curiosity, with his eyes and hands and mouth. He gave particular attention to her full breasts, which he fondled and kissed and sucked until she was driven nearly to madness. But he was not singular in his focus. Other parts of her claimed his attention: her hips, her thighs, her buttocks, the backs of her knees, even the slight roundness of her belly, which he kissed until she giggled with ticklish delight.

There were no barriers between them. Nothing held back. Nothing refused. They explored each other with lips and tongues and fingers, slowly at first, then ever more frantically as passion built. He lavished her hungry flesh with miracles she had not thought to experience again, and some she'd never known before.

He twice brought her to climax before entering her, once with his fingers and once with his wicked tongue. By the time he finally pushed himself inside her she had been aching for him to fill her and had shouted out her need.

Their passion was no longer gentle, but she did not care. She savored each deep, hard thrust that bound them in a frenzy of mutual desire.

Isabel clung to him so tightly at the moment of climax—hers and then his—that it felt as if they must surely be bound together for all time.

Afterwards, he used the paisley shawl to cover them, and gathered her close, chest to breast. Feeling the steady beat of his heart, she thought of another heart, one now lost to her except for the paste copy—the big ruby heart with its piercing arrows, its lover's knot, and its message of love.

True love knows but one.

Was Richard the one? The truth about the jewel and why he had taken it, the knowledge that she'd been wrong about his character, had turned her own heart inside out. Isabel was very much afraid she'd fallen in love with him.

But was he the one? Her one true love?

She had pinned her hopes on Lord Kettering—for his fortune, of course, but lately she had begun to grow quite fond of him. She would have welcomed a match with him, she would have been happy.

But now? How could she allow him to continue to court her now that she had lain with Richard? Isabel was not the sort of woman who could be casual about such things. She had only been intimate with one other man in her life, and she had been married to him. Though the first time with Richard had been spontaneous and frenzied, it was not the madness of a moment. She had known what she was doing. She'd been half-hoping he would make love to her for some time now. And he had given her the opportunity to stop.

But she had not stopped and she had no regrets. She snuggled up against him as he slept, breathing in the scent of him, the scent of their lovemaking. She would not have missed this evening in Richard's arms for all the ruby brooches in the world.

It changed everything, of course. Richard had nothing to offer in the way of a fortune, no financial security to improve her circumstances, even if he were inclined to do so, which for all she knew he was not. In fact, the only offer he was likely to make her was to invite her to become his mistress. The devil of it was she was just as likely to accept. There was no turning back after tonight. She wanted Richard any way she could have him. Again and again.

Which meant she could no longer in good conscience allow Lord Kettering to believe she welcomed his addresses. It was not fair to him, and besides, his strict sense of propriety would never permit him to offer marriage to another man's mistress. The very notion would outrage his pertinacious sensibilities.

And so she would have to find other things to sell, other methods to retrench. Ned would have to pay his own debts. Thomas the footman would have to be let go. Gram and Cousin Min would have to make do with less, the collapsed flue in their morning room fireplace would have to be repaired at some other time.

But Gram would understand. She knew the message of the ruby heart. *True love knows but one.* She would understand.

If she did not first murder Isabel for managing to lose the precious love token.

"I am tempted to return the paste copy to the secret drawer and say nothing."

Richard glanced at Isabel who sat beside him in the curricle, holding her bonnet in place as they bounced along the streets leading to Chelsea. "We have to tell her, Isabel."

"Yes, I know. I am just not looking forward to doing so. I don't know which will disappoint her more—learning the brooch is gone, or learning I took it in the first place without asking."

"I know it will be difficult for you, but it is very important that I learn the truth about how she came to have it."

"I know it is."

He felt her gaze upon him as he steered the team around a corner. His blood warmed and he wondered if she, too, was remembering last night, when they had done more than gaze at each other. Was she undressing him in her mind, just as he had undressed her a thousand times since collecting her this morning?

"If the jewel in my reticule were not paste," she said, "if it was the real Mallory Heart, what would you do? And don't say you would steal it again. As entertaining as it was, that game is over. Assume we had made our peace and the jewel was still in our possession. Would you make Gram return it to your family?"

Richard had struggled with the same question all morning. "I suppose it depends on what she tells us. If my grandfather gave it to her in love, then he must have meant for her to keep it. I would not have taken it away from her. But if they parted bitterly and she kept it out of spite, then I might have been tempted to cut a bargain. As it happens, I have nothing to take away from her anymore."

"I wish it *had* been you in that mask last night. At least I'd know where to find the jewel. Now it's lost forever."

"Perhaps not."

"What do you mean?"

"It will be a difficult piece to fence. It is too distinctive. I'm guessing our thief will have it taken apart, the diamonds reset or sold, and the ruby cut down into several smaller stones."

"Oh, I can't bear to consider it. That beautiful ruby!"

"But that type of work will take time. Our man will have to find an expert gem cutter who won't ask questions and will keep his mouth shut. Not your average Bond Street jeweler. More likely some scapegrace working in a back alley. I've asked Tully to nose around and see what he can learn. A piece like the Mallory Heart will not go unnoticed. Someone will know where it is. It's just a matter of slipping the right coins into the right pockets."

"Oh dear."

"Speaking of which, does your boy Danny still have connections in the streets?"

"I daresay he does. I don't ask where he goes on his time off, but he grew up around the rookeries of St. Giles. He may still have friends or family there."

"Perhaps he can be of some help to Tully. When I return you to Portman Square, I'll have a quick chat with the boy. Ah, this is the street, is it not?"

The hired groom took over the reins when they had descended from the curricle. Richard gave him instructions to exercise the team and turned to follow Isabel up the front steps. She stood before the door for a moment, unmoving. Richard took her hand and tucked it in the crook of his arm.

"It'll be all right, my dear," he said.

"No, it won't. She will be devastated."

"She must be told. And I need to know the truth." He reached up and lifted the knocker.

The door was answered by a stick-thin elderly woman with wooly gray hair sticking out in all directions from beneath an incongruously frothy lace cap. Her eyes, behind a pair of gold spectacles, lit up when she saw Isabel.

"Oh, my dear girl. What a lovely surprise. Come in, come in."

"Thank you, Cousin Min. I have brought a friend to meet you and Gram. This is Major Lord Mallory. Richard, this is my cousin, Miss Minerva Cuthbert."

The old woman's eyes widened, looking enormous behind the slight magnification of the spectacles, and her mouth formed a startled O. Richard reached for her hand and brought the bony fingers to his lips.

"Miss Cuthbert. Your servant."

"Oh." Her lips had not moved, already having been formed in the perfect shape to accommodate the single syllable. She gave a little sigh, and then repeated, "Oh."

"Shall we have tea in the parlor, Cousin Min?" Isabel retrieved a packet from her reticule and handed it to her elderly cousin. "I've brought some good Darjeeling."

The old woman snapped to attention when she saw the tea. "How delightful. You are too kind to us, my dear girl. Yes, let us gather in the parlor. This way, my lord."

Richard left his hat and gloves on a hall table. Isabel removed her bonnet and left it beside his hat. She wore a scrap of delicate lace in her hair that must have been her notion of a matronly cap. Richard bit back a smile. He could not imagine Isabel, ever so stylish, in caps.

Miss Cuthbert led them down the short corridor to the stairs. They passed a dining room on the left and a small study or morning room on the right. The rooms were bright and cheerful, the furnishings a bit threadbare, but good quality.

He followed the ladies up the stairs. Miss Cuthbert bent her head close to Isabel and said, in what she must have assumed was a whisper but was loud enough to have been heard in the last balcony at Drury Lane, "A major *and* a lord? What a coup, my dear girl. I do wish he'd worn his red coat."

Isabel looked over her shoulder and grinned.

They came to a small parlor in the front of the house. There was a coal fire in the grate even though it was a warm July day, and a fine gilt mirror hung over the mantel. The furniture—a settee, two chairs, and a tea table—was all from the last century, not fashionable but functional. All good, solid English pieces, but for one intricately carved and inlaid Mogul chest between the windows.

A woman with thick, beautiful white hair sat

in one of the chairs before the fireplace. She was dressed simply, but there was something about the way the spotted muslin scarf was draped over one shoulder that gave her a casual elegance. Her lace cap was as abbreviated as Isabel's.

It seemed Isabel had inherited her sense of style from her grandmother.

The woman looked up and smiled at their entrance. Her face was lined but the bones beneath were elegant and refined. She was still a beautiful woman, though she must be in her seventies.

The resemblance to Isabel was striking. Mrs. Theale must have looked much like her granddaughter when she was younger. When Richard's grandfather had loved her.

She reached out a hand. "Isabel, my love. What a nice surprise."

Isabel took her grandmother's hand and kissed her on the cheek. "Good morning, Gram. You are feeling well, I hope? I have brought a visitor."

"And tea!" Miss Cuthbert announced with enthusiasm, waving the packet Isabel had brought. "I'm going to pop downstairs and ask Mrs. Hammett to brew us a pot."

"Oh, wait a moment, Cousin Min." Isabel

fumbled in her oversized reticule and brought out another package, a linen napkin gathered up and tied in a knot. "Mrs. Bunch made an extra batch of ginger biscuits. I thought you and Gram might enjoy them with your tea."

Miss Cuthbert took the napkin and smiled. "What a special treat. You know I have a weakness for ginger biscuits. Thank you, dear girl." She darted a glance at Richard, gave an excited titter, and left the room.

"You are too good to us, child," her grandmother said. "You spoil us, you know. Which reminds me, the new windows in my bedchamber have been installed. No more drafts to keep me awake at night. Thank you for taking care of that for me."

"I do not want you catching a chill, Gram. But you have not allowed me to introduce our visitor."

The old woman turned her gaze upon Richard, and he found himself looking down into eyes flecked with green and brown and gold—the same intriguing mélange of color as her granddaughter's. He felt as if he was looking into the future, at Isabel fifty years from now.

She smiled at him and he stepped closer to stand beside Isabel.

"Gram, I'd like you to meet a friend, Major Lord Mallory. Richard, may I present my grandmother, Mrs. Theale."

She visibly paled at his name and the smile wavered. She appeared shaken, but managed to lift a hand. Richard took it and bowed over it. "I am pleased to meet you, ma'am."

Isabel watched her grandmother closely with concerned interest, and placed a hand lightly on her shoulder.

"Lord Mallory." Mrs. Theale retrieved her hand and looked down as she placed it in her lap. When she lifted her eyes a moment later, she had composed herself. "Your grandfather is the Earl of Dunstable, I believe."

"Yes, ma'am."

"You are Phillip Mallory's grandson."

"Yes, ma'am. I believe you were acquainted with him some years ago."

She lifted an eyebrow. "We were more than acquainted, my lord, as I think you know."

She waited for a response, looking squarely into his eyes, but Richard said nothing. It was up to her to reveal the secrets of her past. Or not. He held her gaze.

"We were lovers," she said at last. "We had a scandalous affair."

* * *

To hear it confirmed so outright was something of a shock to Isabel. She had not been entirely convinced that Richard's theory was true. It was hard to imagine one's sweet old grandmother involved in a passionate affair.

She pulled up the other chair to sit at Gram's side, close enough so she could reach over and take her hand. "There is no need to drag up old scandal, Gram. Or painful memories."

"There is nothing painful in my memories of Phillip Mallory. Except for the inevitable parting, it was a glorious time." She turned to Richard, who had taken a seat on the settee. "How is he?"

"Not well, I'm afraid."

"I am sorry to hear that."

"Do you mind telling me about your days with him, ma'am?"

"Why? It was a long time ago."

"But I believe you must have been a very important part of his life."

She hunched a shoulder. "For a time."

"Tell us about him, Gram."

She looked at Isabel and frowned. "You, too? Why all this interest in ancient history." Her eyes suddenly widened and she sucked in a sharp breath. "Oh. You think there might be blood between you? That you are perhaps cousins?"

Isabel had thought no such thing and the notion startled her. Dear God. She looked at Richard and saw his own restrained shock. He had not considered it, either.

Gram gave a soft chuckle. "Do not worry, my child. Your mother was born before Phillip and I became lovers. You and Viscount Mallory are not related, I assure you."

Isabel expelled a breath, so obvious an expression of relief that Gram laughed aloud.

"Here we are!" Cousin Min bounced into the room with Mrs. Hammett on her heels carrying a tea tray. "Darjeeling and ginger biscuits. What could be finer?"

When Mrs. Hammett had gone, Cousin Min looked about and realized the only place for her to sit was beside Richard. That seemed to fluster her and she stood awkwardly, shifting her weight from foot to foot.

"Will you pour for us, Min?"

Gram always knew how to soothe Cousin Min's excitable nature.

"Oh, but we have guests, Emmeline, and it is your house. You must have the privilege of pouring."

"I confess I am a bit fatigued," Gram said. "Would you be a dear and do the honors for me?"

"It would be my pleasure," Cousin Min said, beaming with delight to have something important to do. She poured and delivered each cup with the dignity of a duchess, and passed around the plate of biscuits.

When she had taken her seat beside Richard, she was more sure of herself and no longer flustered about sitting beside a handsome man.

She almost lost her composure when Gram spoke again.

"We were just talking about Lord Mallory's grandfather," she said, "the Earl of Dunstable. He and I had a rather passionate affair many years ago."

Cousin Min choked on her ginger biscuit and began coughing so hard Richard held her teacup to her lips and forced her to take a sip. When she recovered, she stared wide-eyed at Gram.

"Did I shock you, Min? I am sorry, but it's true. You wanted to know about those days," she said to Richard. "I haven't spoken of that

306

time for years, but I do not mind telling you about it."

She took a long sip of tea and then stared at the coals glowing in the grate. She seemed to be composing her thoughts, and so no one spoke. Cousin Min leaned forward in obvious anticipation of the tale.

Finally, Gram looked at Richard and said, "Phillip, your grandfather, was my first love. My father had a small farm in Hampshire near Greyshott. Phillip and I fell in love when we were very young. But he was destined to be an earl and I was nobody important, the daughter of a minor squire. His family, quite naturally, sought a more distinguished match for him.

"My father was convinced by the earl to marry me off and remove me as a threat to Phillip's future. I am certain money or other favors exchanged hands, though my father never admitted it to me. He arranged a marriage for me with Mr. Theale and I moved away."

"Oh, Gram. How awful."

She gave a shrug. "Such things were done all the time. Still are, I have no doubt. Important families want to keep their bloodlines as blue as possible."

307

"Then what happened?" Cousin Min prompted.

"I married Theale and had a child. I was content enough. But I met Phillip again some years later. His father had died and he was now the earl, and he had just become betrothed to Lady Henrietta Beauchamp. It was a brilliant match for him, but not a love match. Our mutual attraction was instantly rekindled, as though no time at all had passed. When he declared that he still loved me, I was overjoyed. We began an affair. We tried to be discreet, but somehow it became known and there was a minor scandal. Theale packed me off to India with him, and Henrietta married Phillip. That was the end of it."

"You never saw him again?" Isabel asked.

"Once, just after Theale died and I returned to London. I saw him walking down the street with Henrietta." She had such a wistful, sad look in her eyes that Isabel could almost feel the pain she had felt at seeing him again, and not being able to speak to him. It would have been like losing him all over again.

"I did not wish to interfere in his life, or Henrietta's," Gram said. "It would only bring pain to all three of us. So I used my widow's jointure to buy the lease on this little house, away from

Society, and made sure there would be no possibility of an encounter by keeping to myself. But I still have my memories to treasure."

Gram looked at Isabel and must have seen the sympathy in her eyes. She squeezed her hand. "Do not be sad for me, my child. It was a very long time ago. I had a good life with Theale. He was somehow able to forgive me and I grew to admire and love him. He made me happy. And he gave me your mother. But I never forgot Phillip Mallory. He was my first love. My one true love. The one that burned brightest."

"Emmeline," Cousin Min said, her eyes misty with tears, "you have never mentioned any of this before."

"It was a private memory, Min. Until our Isabel met Phillip's grandson. They deserved the truth." She turned her gaze on Richard. "He gave me something, your grandfather."

Richard eyes flickered briefly. "Did he?"

"Yes, something I've kept all these years. It is actually my most precious possession. A great ruby heart suspended from a lover's knot."

Chapter 16

Isabel rose and stepped to the tea table. She fumbled about with her empty cup, arranging it precisely on the tray, and randomly moved other items around. It kept her hands busy and her back to Mrs. Theale. Clearly, she was reluctant to face her grandmother. She shot Richard a glance that was full of guilt and anxiety.

"A ruby heart?" Miss Cuthbert said. "How lovely. But I do not believe I have ever seen it, have I, Emmeline?"

"No, Min, I'm afraid I keep it locked away," Isabel's grandmother said. "I never wanted Theale to see it, for he would know who had given it to me. I always kept it hidden in a secret drawer in my jewel case. Even after Theale died, I never took it out much. I certainly never wore it, but I cherish it. It is quite valuable, I'm sure, and I probably ought to have sold it to help out with household expenses and such, but I simply cannot bear to part with it."

Isabel's face, which her grandmother could not see, was a mask of wretchedness. It almost broke Richard's heart to see it. This was not going to be easy for her. But she squared her shoulders and turned to face the inevitable pain she was about to inflict on her beloved grandmother.

Before Isabel could say anything, Mrs. Theale caught Richard's eye.

"Your grandfather told me a story about the jewel," she said. "I never knew if he was simply being romantic, though in my heart I always believed what he said."

"What did he tell you?" Richard asked.

"That there was an old tradition associated with the jewel. He said that it was passed to each earl upon inheriting the title, and that each new owner of the jewel was meant to present it to his true love." She smiled wistfully. "Phillip told me I was his one true love, and therefore I should have the jewel, even knowing we could never be together. I confess I was reluctant to take it, realizing how valuable it must be. But there is an inscription on the jewel, in Latin. He said it meant 'true love knows but one' and I was the one. Since I felt the same about him, I took the jewel as a memento of that true love."

Dear God. No wonder there were no portraits of his grandmother wearing the jewel. His grandfather had never given it to her. The tradition of the earl bestowing the jewel upon his countess had not been a simple ritual of rank to him. He had taken the inscription literally. And perhaps he'd been correct.

Then why did he now want it back? After all these years, did he suddenly have regrets about giving it to Mrs. Theale instead of to his countess?

Isabel could no longer contain the tears she had so obviously been holding back. Richard wanted to go to her, to put his arms around her and share this burden, but he kept his seat. Miss Cuthbert had begun to sniffle as well.

Mrs. Theale rose from her chair and said, "Would you like to see it?"

Richard and Isabel stood at the same time, no doubt with the identical intention of stopping her. Isabel shot him a look that told him this was her ordeal, her sin to confess. He remained standing but did not move. Isabel reached for her grandmother's arm.

"Sit down, please, Gram," she said. "There is something I must tell you."

The old woman looked puzzled, but sat down. "What is it, child?"

Isabel knelt before her and took one of her hands, grasping it tightly. She did not speak right away, and he knew she must be struggling to find the right words. Finally, she rested her forehead on her grandmother's knees. Even the line of her back spoke of misery.

Mrs. Theale stroked her hair. "Isabel?"

"Oh, Gram." Isabel raised her head. "I am so ashamed. I am so sorry."

"Whatever for, child?"

"I knew about the brooch," Isabel said. "I saw you put it in the secret drawer once when I was a little girl. I used to sneak into the jewel case and gaze upon it." The words spilled quickly now that she'd begun. "Then lately I decided I wanted to wear it, and I borrowed it. I didn't want to tell you because I didn't want to confess that I knew about the secret drawer. Somehow I knew the jewel was important to you. But I took it anyway. I am so sorry, Gram."

"Isabel." She touched her granddaughter's

cheek with tender affection. "You had only to ask. I do not mind if you want to wear it. It's a beautiful piece. You may borrow it any time."

"But I can't, you see, because the unthinkable has happened. Last night it was stolen from me. The brooch is gone, Gram. Gone." Tears streamed down her cheeks. She dropped her head back onto her grandmother's knees. "I am so, so sorry."

Mrs. Theale's brow furrowed and she closed her eyes briefly. When she opened them again and looked up at Richard, there was a world of anguish in her gaze. But she quickly mastered it and schooled her features.

"It was stolen?" She asked the question of Richard.

"Yes, ma'am. A thief ripped it right off Lady Weymouth's dress."

Miss Cuthbert gasped.

"Dear God." Mrs. Theale looked down at the head on her lap and laid her hand upon the golden hair. "Were you harmed, my child?"

"No. Not really." Isabel's voice was muffled against her grandmother's knees. "All that matters is the jewel is gone. I'm so sorry, Gram."

Isabel seemed to be crying in earnest now. Mrs. Theale continued to stroke her hair and softly croon, "There, there," while the rest of them sat in miserable silence.

"I am optimistic we may be able to recover it," Richard said in an attempt to relieve the moment with even the tiniest ray of hope. "I have a man looking into it for me. I cannot promise anything, of course, but we'll do our best to get it back."

Mrs. Theale looked up and offered a wan smile. "That is very kind of you, my lord. Of course it belongs to your family more than it does to me. That is why you are involved, I daresay."

"I saw Lady Weymouth wearing the jewel and recognized it from old family portraits."

"Indeed? I hadn't realized it was that important. Then I am very sorry it has been lost and will hope your man has luck in tracking it down."

Isabel lifted her head. "Can you ever forgive me, Gram? I know I should never have taken it, but now . . . Oh, how you must despise me."

"Don't fret, my child. I could never despise you. Such things happen. It was not your fault."

"Oh, Gram. How can you say that? If I hadn't taken the jewel, it would never have been stolen."

"I do not blame you, Isabel. It was not your fault it was stolen."

"Oh, Gram. You are much too kind."

"Kind? After all you have done for me? Nonsense. I do not know how Min and I would have survived all these years without your help. Heavens, child, if not for you and Rupert I would have been forced to give up the lease on this house and move into rooms somewhere far less genteel than Chelsea. The loss of one jewel means nothing in comparison."

"Since I never saw the ruby heart," Miss Cuthbert said, "I cannot fully appreciate the significance of losing it. Other than sentimental value, of course. But at least Emmeline still has her diamond parure."

"Oh, which reminds me," Isabel said.

She rose to her feet with fluid grace and retrieved her reticule from the floor beside her chair. She pulled out a large shagreen case of irregular shape. Richard marveled at all that had come out of that bag this morning.

"I have brought the parure back, Gram. I thank you for allowing me to wear the diamonds. But after what happened with the ruby brooch, I don't think I should borrow them

316

again. I might be a target for jewel thieves, for some reason."

"Good heavens!" Miss Cuthbert said. "What a frightening thought. Then you must surely take care not to wear any of your other beautiful jewels. The emerald necklace especially."

Richard glanced at Isabel and lifted his eyebrows in question, but she looked away. The old ladies did not know, then, that she had sold off her jewelry and had paste copies made. Isabel was too proud even to allow her own family to know of her financial situation. Foolish, stubborn woman. He wanted to shake her and hug her at the same moment.

They stayed only a short time longer. Isabel's grandmother hugged her close before they left, telling her again not to worry about the brooch.

"You did not offer her the copy."

Isabel sat beside Richard on the curricle seat, feeling thoroughly drained and morose. It had been a very emotional morning for her. She could not decide if she was glad he'd been there to share it with her, or if she had made a terrible mistake bringing him along. He needed to learn the truth about Gram and the brooch, but she was afraid he'd learned much more.

"No," she said, keeping her eyes straight ahead, "it seemed somehow distasteful to do so. A cheap copy could never replace the genuine token of love your grandfather gave her. Besides, she would have asked questions about how I happened to have a copy, and I did not want to get into the details of our little game. To know we had used her precious brooch as a pawn between us would only have added insult to injury."

"And you would have had to explain how you knew so much about paste copies."

She felt him glance at her, but she did not look at him. She did not want this conversation.

"They do not know, do they?"

She kept her eyes on the team and did not reply. What was there to say, anyway?

"No, of course they do not," he said. "You sell your own furniture so they can keep theirs. You sell your own jewels so your grandmother does not have to part with the few pieces she has."

"It is none of your business, Richard."

"Stubborn Isabel. You beggar yourself so they can live comfortably."

"So what if I do? Gram should not be forced

to give up the few nice things she owns when she has a family to help her."

"A family? Or just you?"

Isabel shrugged. "I just do what I can. When Rupert was alive and I believed we had substantial funds available to us, I made sure Gram had everything she needed. It was the least I could do. She and Min have no resources."

"And you do?"

"I am young, at least, and still have the possibility of . . ." She almost bit her tongue.

"Of marrying again," he said for her.

"Perhaps." Though she no longer knew how she was to go about the thing now that she and Richard were lovers. Lord, what a coil.

Richard was silent throughout the rest of their journey back to Portman Square. Was he thoroughly disgusted with her for being such a fortune hunter? She had hoped he, of all people, would understand.

Perhaps he did. Perhaps he was thinking of his own family and how he would have to marry a fortune just like Isabel. What a pair they were.

It would have been so much easier if she hadn't fallen in love with him.

When they arrived at Portman Square, she

brought him upstairs to the drawing room and asked Tessie to send Danny to them. Neither of them took a seat. Instead, they stood and regarded each other from opposite sides of the room. He was surely thinking, as she was, of what had happened between them last night in this same room. On the sofa, against the armchair, on the floor. There was nowhere to look that did not bring to mind some memory of their passion.

His mouth began to twitch up into a smile, and his gaze was a naked caress. Her skin flushed and prickled in response to what she saw in those blue eyes.

She was never sure which of them moved first, but they were suddenly in each other's arms and his mouth was on hers. Passion flared instantly. Their kiss was full of remembered intimacies, deep and lush, laced with hunger and longing.

They pulled away quickly when they heard footsteps approaching. By the time Danny walked into the room, they stood several feet apart, neither looking at the other. Something in their eyes or faces must have given them away, for Danny looked back and forth between them and grinned.

"Yer sent fer me, m'lady?"

Isabel straightened her skirts and tried not to smile. "Yes, Danny. I believe you know the ruby brooch was stolen from me last night."

Danny darted a glance toward Richard, then cocked an eyebrow.

"No, it was not his lordship. Not this time. It was an ordinary common thief. Lord Mallory would like to ask you a few questions."

Danny's spine straightened. "I din't take it."

"We know you didn't," Richard said. "We were hoping you might be able to help discover who did."

"Why? Cuz I still got me chums in the rookeries?"

"Precisely. You've seen the brooch. You know it is too distinctive to remain unnoticed. Perhaps one of your friends knows something or saw something. I'd pay well for information."

Danny eyed him suspiciously. "I can arsk 'round, I 'spect. If m'lady says I should."

"I would be grateful, Danny," she said.

The boy shrugged. "All right, then. I'll poke me nose about." He looked at Richard. "But yer might ask that feller yer set to watch the 'ouse. Bet 'e seen a thing or two."

Richard frowned. "What fellow?"

"That man o' yers, the one I bang into ever time I leave the 'ouse."

Isabel shot Richard a questioning glance, but he shook his head. The anxious look in his eyes gave her a moment of panic. "Are you saying a man has been watching the house?" she asked.

"Yeah. 'Is lordship's man."

"I sent no man to watch the house," Richard said. "It wasn't my man you saw."

"Sure 'twas. 'E said as much."

"What?" Richard eyes blazed with anger.

"Perhaps you'd better explain, Danny," Isabel said. "Start at the beginning. When did you first see him?"

" 'Bout a week ago. Not very artful, that one. I seen 'im creepin' in the bushes ever time I left the 'ouse. One day 'e were loungin' against a lamp post on the square, big as life. I walked up to 'im real friendly like an' jus' started talkin' 'bout the weather an' such. Told 'im I 'ad the afternoon orff and was 'eading to the Star and Garter fer a pint. Which weren't true, beggin' yer pardon, m'lady. But I figgered it'd be in the line o' duty, so ter speak, ter find out 'oo 'e was. So I says would 'e join me, and 'e says sure."

"And what did he tell you?" Richard's voice held a note of command that brooked no refusal. Isabel could imagine soldiers scurrying to do whatever that voice, and those steely eyes, told them to do.

"Nothin' much at first," Danny said. "But I kep' a steady flow o' gin down 'is throat, and 'e were singin' like a bird soon enuff. Said 'is name were John Pettiford and 'e come from a place called Gray-somethin' where the earl o' Dunstable lives. I knew that was yer family's name, sir, so that was all I needed ter 'ear. Figgered 'e was yer man, and left 'im passed out on the table."

"Good God," Richard said. "He's one of the footmen at Greyshott. What the devil was he doing here watching your house? You didn't see him before a week ago, Danny?"

"No, sir. The first time I seen 'im was the night o' some fancy ball at a duke's 'ouse. Yer was wearing that dress with the wreaths on it, m'lady. Right pretty, it was, so I remember it real plain. You went off in a carriage with Mister and Miz Pearsall."

"That was the night of the Kingston ball," she said. The night Richard had lured her into the garden and kissed her senseless.

"That was the night after my arrival back in town," Richard said. "He must have followed me from Greyhshott. Hell and damnation."

He reached into a pocket and pulled out a coin, which he tossed to Danny. "Thank you, lad. You've been a great help."

"Do yer still want me ter sniff 'round the stews? Find out 'oo's cuttin' gems and such?"

"That won't be necessary. Thank you, Danny."

The boy recognized a dismissal when he heard it. He gave a little bow and left the room

"Why don't you need him to question his friends?" Isabel asked. "I thought you wanted his help."

"I don't need his help. I know who took the brooch. John Pettiford has worked at Greyshott since before I left for the wars. He worked in the fields until an accident with a scythe sliced through his arm. He has a scar that runs from his elbow to his wrist."

"Oh, my God. It was him!"

"Apparently. I just wish I knew why. I never told you this, but I was sent to London on a mission to find the Mallory Heart. I was sent by the countess. My grandmother. She said my grandfather, who is gravely ill, wanted the jewel restored to the family before he died. Now that we know she never had possession of the jewel, that the earl gave it to your grandmother, I can only question her motives."

"You think she wanted it for herself? After all these years?"

"I don't know. But Pettiford is her personal footman. The countess has a lot to answer for, by God. I have to go home."

"Yes, of course." She tried to sound supportive, but the thought of Richard leaving now, after only one night of love, made her heart squeeze up tight as a fist.

He seemed to sense her despair and took her in his arms again. He held her tight, one hand on the back of her head pressing it into his shoulder.

"Isabel, Isabel. I wish I did not have to leave just now. Especially after last night. But it can't be helped. I have to go."

She nodded her head against his shoulder.

"I have to find out what game the countess is playing. And I need to spend time with my grandfather before . . . I just need to be there. I don't know when I can come back."

She lifted her head and looked into his eyes. "I understand."

"I will write to you."

"I would like that."

"And I will be back, Isabel. I will."

He dipped his head and kissed her. There was a hint of promise in that kiss, and Isabel would hold him to that promise. She kissed him back with a fierce longing that she hoped he understood was more than physical desire.

Chapter 17

〜〜∘〇〇∘〜〜

"Richard." The countess sat at the desk in her private sitting room, writing letters. She did not look surprised to see him. John Pettiford would have alerted her. "You have returned."

"As you see."

Richard strode into the room he had entered on no more than a handful of occasions in his life. It had always been his grandmother's private domain and visitors were not made to feel welcome. As boys, he and Arthur had dared each other to go inside, but there was no fun in it when they did.

It was an entirely feminine room, done in shades of pale pink and lavender and cream. The rug was French, the pile worn down and the colors faded. The fabric of the draperies and upholstery was old and split, and carried the faint smell of mildew, which battled unsuccessfully with a sickeningly sweet potpourri that Richard would forever associate with his grandmother. The result was a cloying atmosphere that was far from inviting.

The room had not changed much since he first came to live at Greyshott as a boy. It had seemed unpleasant then and still did.

Richard entered nonetheless, uninvited, and took a chair adjacent to the writing desk. A musty cloud rose from the upholstery when he sat. He crossed his legs and made himself comfortable.

"Why did you send me after the Mallory Heart?" he asked without preamble. He had no patience for mincing words.

She replaced her pen in the stand, closed the pounce pot and ink bottle, and straightened the sheets of parchment. It was several minutes before she turned to face him. She appeared pale and thin. Richard wondered again about her health.

"I do not know why I sent you," she said at

last. "I ought to have known I could not trust you to get the job done. Fortunately, I have no more need of your assistance."

"John Pettiford."

"Yes."

"Why did you not simply send him in the first place? Why did you need me?"

"To find the woman with the jewel. You could go where John could not. Once it was located, it was clear you were not going to do your duty. You fell victim to that young woman's charms, just as the earl fell victim to her grandmother. I did not believe you would have the fortitude to take the jewel from her."

"You knew she had it? You knew all along where it was?"

"I knew who had it, yes. Or at least I suspected. The earl never admitted to it and I never believed his story that it had been stolen."

"Then why now? If you knew where it was, why send me off on a quest fifty years later?"

"I told you. Lady Aylesbury saw a young woman wearing it. I knew it had to be Emmeline Theale's daughter or granddaughter. Emmeline herself never appeared in public, and rightly so, after the scandal she caused, so it had to be a younger relative. I knew you would find

329

her. I did not know that you would become besotted with the girl and let her keep the jewel."

Besotted. He hadn't expected that either. How much had Pettiford seen? "And so you sent Pettiford to rip it right off her dress. Did you know he cut her in the process? And scared her half to death."

The countess shrugged. "I trust the damage you did to John's face more than compensates for whatever harm he caused the girl."

Pettiford had been the first item on Richard's agenda when he returned to Greyshott. The fact that he'd dared to injure Isabel angered Richard more than his grandmother's manipulation. After bloodying the man's nose, he'd told him to pack his bags and leave. He would not have that villain in his employ. But if the countess had seen his face, then the man obviously had defied him and not yet left the estate.

"Nothing compensates for what he did to Lady Weymouth. I trust he will be gone by morning."

"You have no right to terminate one of my employees."

"I have every right. It is my money supporting the estate now, and I'll be damned if that money is used to pay John Pettiford's salary. If I see him on the estate ever again I swear I will shoot him."

She looked slightly abashed. "I depend upon John. I need him."

"I will assign another footman to you. You may choose any footman you want, but it will not be Pettiford."

She frowned. "I do not care to be ordered about like one of your soldiers, Richard. But all right. I will choose a new footman. I am sorry John was so rough with the young woman, but he was only doing as he was told."

"And so now you have the Mallory Heart."

She lifted her chin and glared down the length of her aristocratic nose. "As I ought to have had it these last fifty years. It is mine by right."

She was wrong, of course. Unless his grandfather had decided she was indeed the love of his life after all, then she had no right to it.

"Every countess before me has worn the Mallory Heart," she said. "I am the first one to be so slighted. But no more. Before the earl dies, he will see it pinned proudly on my breast."

Dear God, he hoped not. The sight would kill the old man, as she must know. Richard would have to warn him.

"Will that make you happy, ma'am, to know you have thwarted his wishes, to flaunt the jewel in his face?"

"It will indeed. It should have been mine all along. And now that it is mine, I will have further revenge. No one else will ever wear this jewel. I plan to take it with me to the grave. No other countess—including *your* countess—will ever see this jewel again. That is how I repay the wrong done me."

Richard was astonished at her words. Surely she had gone a little mad. Or had there always been a vengeful nature beneath the stately reserve?

"It is a fifty-year-old wrong, Grandmother. Can you not find it in your heart to forgive him? Has there been no happiness at all in your life with him?"

"You can never understand." She heaved a weary sigh. "Ours was a rather glamorous match, you see. The betrothal parties were dazzling events. The cream of Society celebrated with us. Then, just weeks before our wedding, the scandal broke. His liaison with that woman became public. It was a great humiliation to me, but my father insisted the wedding go forward. I was to be the Countess of Dunstable, after all, which was supposed to be enough to make up for the public embarrassment."

"But it wasn't enough?"

She shook her head. "Over the years, the money ran out, the farms failed, and the earl's investments did not pay out. The London house was sold and this estate ran to ruin. So I was not the grand lady I'd hoped to be. Nothing was as I'd hoped it would be."

"The jewel would not have made a difference, Grandmother."

"It was a symbol of all I did not have. Do you know I never laid eyes on it until yesterday? When I held it in my hand for the first time, I felt triumphant. At last, I could pay back the earl and all the Mallorys for the wrong they'd done me. The jewel represented all I never had, and it will forever after represent all the Mallorys will never have. For none of them, none of *you*, will ever have this jewel. It is mine now. Mine forever."

He did not have a response for such a speech. A great sadness swept over him as he considered how little happiness she had allowed herself over the last five decades. What an incredible waste of a life. Two lives, really, since the earl could have found little contentment with a woman so hell-bent on making herself miserable.

"I am tired now, Richard. Would you send my maid to me, please?"

"Of course."

Richard left the room in a troubled state of mind. He felt as though everything he ever believed about his family had crumbled into dust during the past month. His grandfather's love affair and bad business decisions, his brother's duel over a woman, and now his grandmother's vengeance. Not one of them was the person he'd believed them to be.

He suddenly felt very much alone in the world. Richard longed for Isabel in that moment, a yearning so powerful it was a physical ache. He wished he had brought her with him, for he wanted nothing more than to crawl inside her warmth and feel connected to someone. To someone he loved.

But then, Isabel was not who he'd believed her to be, either. She was not a thief. She was not a selfish woman who cared only for an extravagant lifestyle. Yes, she was a fortune hunter, but with cause. He still found it hard to believe how she'd stripped her own home practically to the bare walls, and had sold all her jewelry, so her family would not suffer. And she was too proud for anyone to know what she did.

Richard, however, was proud as well. Proud to know her, to know what sort of caring, compassionate woman she was. He even liked that she had a weakness for Society entertainments and high fashion. It made her less of a paragon and more flesh and blood. Beautiful golden flesh and hot blood.

Yes, he was proud of her. He would be proud to give her his arm, his name, his life. His love.

His grandmother was right. He was well and truly besotted. When he returned to London, he was going to make damned sure she did not accept an offer from Kettering or any other rich lord. If she wanted a fortune, by God she could have his. He was going to have to tell her the truth. And if she only wanted him for his money, then so be it; but he would do his best to make her love him.

He found the maid in her mistress's dressing room, repairing a ripped seam. Before sending her to the sitting room, which was only a few doors away, he questioned the woman about the countess's health.

"She tires easily, and she has her bad days now and then. Sometimes she has trouble get-

ting up from her chair, and often needs someone to lean on when she walks. Frankly, I do not
believe she will allow herself to become ill while
the earl is ailing. She finds the strength somewhere to care for him and as long as he needs
her, she will be there."

Richard believed there was probably some
truth to what the maid said. The countess, however, was not one of those women who don't
survive their husbands long, simply because
they no longer have the will to live without
them. But he now believed she was exactly the
sort of woman who could die peacefully knowing she had made her husband's last days miserable through her revenge.

Richard had to speak to his grandfather before it was too late. But there was one bit of business to take care of first.

As soon as the maid left, Richard looked
about the dressing room in search of his grandmother's jewel case. He found it on a shelf and
tried to open it, but it was locked. By some quirk
of serendipity, the maid had left the key ring
from her chatelaine on the dressing table.
Richard quickly found the right key and
opened the jewel case.

He lifted the top tray filled with rings and

earrings and hair ornaments, and saw the Mallory Heart sitting on a bed of silver tissue below. He reached inside his waistcoat pocket and pulled out the paste copy. It was the first time he'd seen the two pieces together. The copy was an excellent likeness. The countess would never know the difference. He carefully placed the paste jewel on the tissue, tucked the real jewel in his pocket, and locked the case.

"Richard, my boy . . . is that you?"

"Yes, Grandda. I've come home. How are you feeling?"

The old man was agitated. His hands shook and his body twitched under the bedcovers.

"Not so well, I fear." His voice was a raspy whisper and each breath rattled in his chest.

Richard had heard that sound a thousand times in field hospitals. He knew well what it meant. Dear God, he'd almost been too late.

"Grandda, I want to show you something. Do you see this? Do you know what it is?"

The earl gave a little cry that turned into a spell of coughing. The nurse rushed over and pushed Richard aside. When the coughing subsided, he sent her back to her chair. He needed a moment of private conversation before the end came.

"She told me." The earl's voice was so soft Richard bent low to hear him. "She told me . . . she had got back . . . the Mallory Heart." Each sentence was an effort, each breath a trial. "She showed it to me . . . pinned to her dress . . . and gloated. Gloated."

"I know. Don't fret, Grandda. It's all right."

"No . . . it is not. She should not . . . have it."

His breathing became more and more labored. The nurse approached again, but Richard sent her back. There was nothing she could do for his grandfather now.

"Belongs to . . . someone else."

"I know," Richard said. "I met her."

The earl's eyes grew enormous in his thin face. "Emmeline?" The name was whispered like a prayer.

"Yes. And she is still very beautiful."

The old man managed a smile. "Is she? Wish I could have . . . seen her. One . . . more . . . time." He clutched at Richard's sleeve. "How did Henrietta . . . get the . . . jewel?"

Richard bent down close to his grandfather's face and lowered his voice so the nurse could not overhear. "She does not have it, Grandda. She thinks she does, but it is a paste copy. This one, the one I have, is the real one."

"Thank . . . God. Must get it . . . back to . . . Emmeline."

"I plan to do so."

"Promise . . . me."

"I promise. And shall I tell you something remarkable? I have fallen in love with Emmeline's granddaughter."

The old man's eyes brightened slightly and he smiled. "Pretty as . . . Em?"

"The spitting image."

"Will you . . . marry her?"

"I hope so. I haven't asked her yet, but I plan to."

Suddenly, the old eyes filled with tears. His mouth turned down and his chin wavered. "Emmeline should have . . . been my . . . countess. Now . . . at least . . . her blood . . . will be joined . . . with mine. That is . . . good. You tell Em . . . how pleased . . . I am. Tell her . . . tell her . . . I will wait . . . for her to join me . . . in . . . eternity."

His head drooped to one side, exhausted from the effort of talking. His eyes closed and his breathing seemed easier. Richard squeezed his hand and kissed his cheek.

"Call for me," he told the nurse, "if he gets worse. I want to be with him."

The earl never opened his eyes again. A few hours later, with his wife and grandson at his side, he took his last breath and passed away peacefully.

"Isn't it lovely!"

Isabel strolled along the Bird Cage Walk on Lord Kettering's arm. The Chinese bridge and pagoda were almost complete for the Grand Jubilee next week. The long-delayed Jubilee. It had originally been planned as a celebration of the peace to be held when the allied leaders were in London. But it kept getting postponed and the foreign leaders had long departed.

And so now it was to be a celebration to honor the one-hundredth anniversary of Hanoverian rule, as well as the anniversary of the Battle of the Nile, which was to be re-enacted on the canals in St. James's Park. All of London was agog with excitement. Isabel and Lord Kettering were not the only ones taking a look at the preparations.

"I understand fireworks will be discharged from the bridge," he said. "It should be a spectacular sight. Are you sure I cannot convince you to join me?"

"It is kind enough of you to escort me to the celebrations throughout the afternoon. But I promised my grandmother and cousin that I would take them out to see the fireworks in the evening. They so seldom get out, and are more excited about the fireworks than anything else. It will be a treat to take them."

"You are very thoughtful to do so. I confess I had hoped to have you alone during the fireworks. It should be a very romantic setting."

Isabel knew he was leading toward a declaration, and she did not know what to do. She had not heard from Richard since he'd left London two weeks before. She had expected he would return for the Regent's fête at Carlton House in honor of the Duke of Wellington. Given his title and his military rank, he was certain to have been invited.

But he had not returned, and he had not written. She did not even know if he had located the genuine ruby brooch, and so had no news to report to Gram. She despaired of ever seeing Richard again, which was why she continued to allow Lord Kettering's attentions. What if she gave him up and Richard never returned? Or returned with a rich viscountess in tow?

What a quandary. She had been tied in knots over it for two weeks,

"I am sure Gram and Cousin Min will enjoy the fireworks," she said.

He smiled and seemed aware that she was deflecting the conversation from romantic topics. They strolled along and watched more of the preparations for the Jubilee, speaking of the various plans and rumors they had heard, and of all the nobility, English and otherwise, who were expected to attend.

"That reminds me of sad news," Lord Kettering said. "Did you hear that the old Earl of Dunstable passed away?"

Isabel almost stumbled at his words. "Lord Mallory's grandfather?"

"Yes. Only he will be Lord Dunstable now. That is why we have not seen him about, I daresay."

And why he had not written. He had likely been too busy with funeral arrangements and such to think about Isabel. But now that he was the earl, and in mourning, she would not be surprised if he did not return to London for a year or more.

This news did not improve matters. It merely added to the quandary.

What was she to do?

"I daresay you are right," she said. "How sad for his family. Thank you for telling me. I shall send a note of condolence."

"Ever the thoughtful lady. May I hope that your kindness extends to a gentleman who regards you most highly? A gentleman with hope in his heart?"

Oh, no. Not now. It was too soon, and she could not think straight. "My lord."

"You must be aware of my regard, my admiration, my affection. Tell me now, dear lady, if there is no hope for me, and I will never mention it again."

"I cannot tell you that, my lord." She did not want to close that door forever. Not yet. "There is always hope."

He lifted her gloved hand to his lips. "I am encouraged, Lady Weymouth. Dare I risk it all? Would you . . . would you be my wife?"

Oh, dear God. She had not expected an offer right this moment. And just after she'd learned of Richard's bereavement. What was she to do?

This was the moment she had been waiting for since the spring when Lord Kettering had first been introduced to her and asked her to dance. It was a dream come true, everything she wanted. A brilliant match for her.

Except that she loved someone else. Someone who might not love her at all, and who might never come back to her. Someone who was likely to marry a rich bride as soon as he left off mourning.

What was she to do?

She took a deep breath. "I am honored, my lord. More than you can know. But you have caught me unawares, I fear. May I have time to think it over before I give you an answer?"

"Of course, my lady. I realize I have perhaps moved too quickly, but my feelings could no longer be contained."

Too quickly? The man had not yet even kissed her.

"I shall take heart that you do not refuse me outright, and hope for an answer soon."

"Thank you, my lord. You are very understanding. I will give you my answer at the Jubilee."

"Four days cannot pass too quickly, then. I look forward to our day together, and to your answer."

So did she, for she did not know what that answer would be. Her head said yes, but her irrational heart cried out for Richard. If she married Lord Kettering, she would be giving up Richard forever. Was she willing to risk that loss?

True love knows but one.

Chapter 18

◦◦◦◦◦

His life would never be the same. Richard could no longer be a solider. He had known that since coming home, but now that he was the earl, the knowledge stared him in the face daily. And it was not a comfortable sight.

Managing an estate was not something he understood or enjoyed. He would much prefer charging into battle than spending an afternoon studying drainage options with George Venables. But this was his life now, unappealing as it was. His soldiering days were over.

He would have to return to London to formally resign his commission. And there were a few other pieces of business awaiting him in London. One in particular.

Isabel.

Memories of their one night together invaded his brain with increasing frequency. Richard was determined there would be other such nights, though his grandfather's death meant it might be a while before those nights could become a permanent arrangement. Assuming Isabel would have him. He liked to think so, but one could never be sure about women. But he at least wanted to make her an offer as soon as possible, before Lord Kettering stole a march on him.

It had been two weeks since his grandfather's death. During that period of seclusion he had worked with Venables as well as his own man of affairs in setting certain projects in motion, and ensuring the appropriate flow of funds in support of the estate. He would leave matters in good hands if he took a short trip to Town.

The countess was a more difficult problem. Her health had indeed declined since her husband's death. Her moment of triumph had not lasted. She did not, of course, know what Richard had said to the earl or why that seemed to have helped him to a more peaceful death. She had given him a moment of anguish and that, apparently, was enough. Once he was gone, there had been no rejoicing, no glow of happiness. The possession of the jewel did not seem to have brought her any peace.

But she was as reserved as ever, so Richard could never be sure what was in her mind.

His feelings for her had become confused. He could almost understand her sense of betrayal, carried around for fifty years. But having met Emmeline, Richard better understood how a man who had loved such a vibrant woman would have difficulty forming a close union with a woman as cold and severe as the countess.

Before leaving for London, Richard stood before his grandmother's portrait in the Long Gallery. The coldness was there even at so young an age. No wonder his grandfather could not bring himself to give her the Mallory Heart. He'd given the brooch to the right woman. He'd married the wrong woman.

Richard was bound and determined not to make a similar mistake. He was going to listen to his heart. And to the Mallory Heart as well:

True love knows but one.

While Tully prepared the carriage, Richard took leave of his grandmother.

"I do not imagine I will be gone more than a week," he said. "Will you be all right?"

"You have been away a dozen years or more and we somehow managed to survive."

"Promise me you will follow the physician's orders in all things. You must take care of yourself, ma'am."

"Yes, yes. But tell me, will you see *her* when you're in London?"

There was no sense pretending he did not know whom she meant. "I do not know. I do hope to see her granddaughter, however."

"Hmph. I suppose you mean to marry the chit."

"If she'll have me."

"How strange and cruel fate can be. I sincerely hope I do not live to see such a match."

He allowed her that parting shot, bowed, and took his leave.

"What should I do, Gram?"

"I cannot tell you that, child. You must follow your heart."

Isabel leaned her head on Gram's shoulder. "My heart is all scrambled up. I can't follow what I don't understand."

"Do you love him?"

"I'm fond of him. I like him."

"Why would you marry him if you do not love him?"

"Because I need a rich husband."

Gram nudged her head off her shoulder and sat up straight. "What do you mean, you need a rich husband? Why? Rupert left you a comfortable living."

"No, Gram, he didn't. He left me nothing. I am nearing the end of my limited resources. I need to marry a fortune."

"Child, why did you never say anything?"

"I did not want you to worry. And I knew things would turn around eventually. Everything was fine until I met Richard."

"Ah. So he is the cause of all this turmoil. I ought to have known. There was definitely something in the air between you two. Well, then. It sounds as if your heart has spoken."

"It tells me that I love Richard. But my head tells me he may not love me, and is unlikely to want to marry me. Both of us need to marry a fortune, and neither of us has one. I am afraid all Richard can offer me is an affair. And in the meantime, I have a perfectly nice, rich man who has offered me marriage."

"That is certainly a dilemma."

"Made worse because I have no idea what, if anything, to expect from Richard. Does he love me? Does he want me to be his mistress? Does he want to marry me, even though neither of us has money? How can I decide without knowing?"

"You must decide for yourself, not for Richard. If you decide to marry Lord Kettering, it must be because *you* want it. Or not. Since you do not know Richard's mind, your decision must stand regardless of his intentions. You must be able to live with your decision, regardless of what Richard does. Even if you were never to see him again."

"You are right, as always, Gram."

"You are fortunate, my child, in that the decision is yours and yours alone. You have no parents, or grandparents, directing your actions. You have no one to please but yourself."

Isabel kissed Gram's cheek. "I knew I could count on you for sound advice. I do not know what I will do, but I have a better idea how to make the decision. Thank you, Gram."

Richard did not travel straight to London. There was one other unfinished bit of business to address, and now was as good a time as any.

The swing west into Berkshire was not too far out of the way.

The Ridealgh estate was a large one, with extensive grounds in the style of Capability Brown—no longer fashionable, but still beautiful. The main house was Palladian in style with a central section of pediment over columns, flanked by two wings with echoing facades. The dower house was a smaller version of the central portion of the main house, brick instead of stone.

Richard presented his card to the butler and was led to wait in a small receiving room. The walls were filled with a fine collection of Italian paintings, and Richard took the time to study them while he waited.

"Lord Dunstable."

She had a beautiful voice, melodic and slightly deep, like a mezzo-soprano. He turned toward the voice, and was rather stunned to see a short, stocky woman with florid cheeks and several chins who appeared to be in her late thirties. But for a pair of very expressive brown eyes, her features were quite plain.

"I am Lady Ridealgh. You wished to see me?"

He took her outstretched hand and bowed over it. "My lady. Thank you for receiving me."

"Please accept my condolences on your grandfather's death."

"Thank you."

"And for Arthur's death as well. That is why you have come, is it not?"

"Yes. I wanted to understand why he died."

"Of course. Would you care for tea, my lord? Or something stronger?"

"No thank you, Lady Ridealgh. I will not take up too much of your time."

She took a seat and gestured for him to take one across from her. "I am glad you came," she said in that disconcertingly lovely voice. "I am so sorry about Arthur's death. I have carried that guilt around for over a year now, and I am glad for the chance to set the record straight."

"Tell me what happened."

"There was no affair, my lord. There was never an affair."

Now that he'd seen her, he believed it. Though attraction was not always purely physical. There was that voice.

"Your brother was kind to me, that is all. We enjoyed talking together about art and music and such. He was a lovely man. I ought to have known better. Ridealgh was jealous of any man who so much as looked at me."

"And so he got the wrong impression."

"He always got the wrong impression. Poor old Ridealgh believed every man was wild with desire for me." She laughed, and it was as musical a laugh as he'd ever heard. "Can you imagine? You see what I am. But Ridealgh was a bit mad, you see. He thought I was beautiful. I suppose that is why I loved him. It is difficult to resist a man's worship, however undeserved."

"Could you not have talked him out of the duel?"

"When I said he was mad, I meant that quite literally. No one could talk him out of anything once his mind was fixed. It was not his first duel over me. Or his last. His mind was in a constant turmoil, poor thing. He is thankfully at peace now."

"Thank you, Lady Ridealgh. I am pleased to know there was no impropriety on my brother's part."

"None whatsoever. I am not the sort of female who inspires impropriety, though Ridealgh thought otherwise. I confess, I rather miss him. Though the duels had become a bit of a nuisance."

A nuisance? His brother's death was a nuisance?

She'd had him fooled until that comment.

Lord Ridealgh was not the only one whose mind was unsound.

Richard rose and thanked her, then made his escape as quickly as possible. He'd learned what he wanted to know, anyway. Arthur had done nothing to incite Ridealgh's challenge. His life had been taken by a madman.

And people said lives were wasted on the battlefield.

The next morning, Richard made an official visit to the regimental agent at the Horse Guards, giving formal notice of his intent to sell his commission. He was no longer a soldier. He'd sold out.

He was feeling so melancholy as he left the Guards, as if he'd lost yet another loved one, that he almost failed to notice all the activity in St. James's Park. It was only a sudden burst of rocket fire that snapped him to attention. He instinctively reached for the sword he no longer wore.

"It's the fireworks, soldier." A uniformed officer on his way into the Horse Guards chuckled as he walked by. "No need for your sword. No battles in the park today, just a stray rocket for tomorrow's celebrations."

Richard then noticed all the activity, the crowds of people milling about, the tents being set up on the park grounds, and the rather amazing Chinese bridge over the canal. This must be for the Jubilee he'd been hearing so much about ever since he had arrived back on English soil.

As he walked down the parade toward the park, figuring he might as well take a look at the preparations, a familiar voice hailed him.

"Mallory!" Lord Kettering approached and fell into step beside him. "Or Dunstable, I should say. Sorry to hear about your grandfather, old chap. Sad business."

"Thank you, Kettering. What brings you to the Horse Guards?"

"Oh, I was just taking another look at the Jubilee preparations. Quite a sight, eh? And what about you? What brings you back to Town?"

"I've just sold my commission."

"Oh, yes, you would have to do that, would you not, now that you're Dunstable? Can't play soldier anymore. Well, the wars are over. It's for the best, I daresay."

Play soldier? The fool. He'd like to see just how much fun his lordship would have with a company of French soldiers unleashing volley after volley of gunfire in his face, choking on thick clouds of smoke and the acrid stench of blood and death, watching his men fall and lay crushed beneath the weight of their dead horses. Play, indeed.

"Are you planning to attend the celebrations tomorrow?" Kettering asked.

"I don't know. I'm still in black coats so I don't know if it would be appropriate. But you? You will be going, I have no doubt."

"I would not miss it. It is going to be a very special day for me."

Richard's gaze took in all the preparations. "Yes, it looks as if it will be quite special indeed."

"I'm sure it will, but that is not what I meant." He leaned in close. "I am hoping to make a special announcement tomorrow."

Richard's heart sank like a stone. Oh, no.

"I will let you in on a secret," Kettering said. "I have asked Lady Weymouth to marry me, and I expect her answer tomorrow."

Richard felt suddenly sick to his stomach. "And you apparently expect a positive answer."

Kettering grinned. "A fellow can hope. Besides, just between you and me, I believe I'm as good a catch as she's likely to reel in. She would be a marchioness one day."

"A tempting prospect, I'm sure." Not to mention the fortune that went along with it.

Damn, damn, damn. She was still going to go through with her plan to marry a rich man. If only he'd told her about his own tidy little fortune, he might be the one beaming like a fool.

"Do you love her, Kettering?"

His lordship gave him an indulgent smile. "Love? I'm not the sentimental sort, Dunstable. I am fond of her, as I believe she is of me. A deeper affection will grow over time."

Richard could not even begin to imagine a loveless, pedestrian marriage for Isabel. She was too passionate, too full of life to settle for that. A man who was merely fond of her would be a misery. She needed a man who loved her to distraction.

A man like himself.

But it was too late. She was going to marry this stiff-necked pattern card of propriety. Richard was sorely tempted to tell the man he'd already had her, to offer a few pointers on just which spots made her moan the loudest. How would he feel about taking another man's leavings?

Richard was fairly certain he would find a way out of marrying her in that case. He was almost bursting to tell Kettering the truth, but he would not do that to Isabel. Perhaps if she married his lordship, she and Richard could emulate their grandparents and have a scandalous affair. If that was the only way he could have her, by Jove he'd take it. But he wanted more.

The next day, all of London and beyond filled the streets leading to the Parks. The traffic was so thick that anyone who happened to be going in the opposite direction from the crowd was unable to pass. Shops were closed. Theaters were dark. All attention was on the celebrations. Park gates opened at two o'clock, and masses of people poured in from every level of society. There were fairs and pavilions and temples, and even a balloon ascension.

Richard stayed away from it all. He did not want to risk running into Kettering and Isabel. He did not want to hear an announcement that would break his heart. So he stayed inside his rooms on Tavistock Street all alone—he had given Tully the afternoon off to participate in the revelries—and tried to keep his mind occupied with a volume of poetry.

A mistake. Poetry to a broken heart is like salt on a wound.

He took out the ruby brooch and studied it. Its blatant sentiment had the same effect as the poetry. He wrapped it carefully and put it away. He needed to take it to Mrs. Theale, but like everyone else in London, she was probably at the Jubilee celebrations. He would drive to Chelsea in the early evening when she would more than likely be at home.

It was fortunate that he had brought his carriage to Town this time, for he could not have found one for hire anywhere in the metropolis. The streets were still crowded and he had to take a circuitous route north of the Parks and back around south to Chelsea. It took him twice as long a he'd expected.

When he reached Mrs. Theale's house, there was another carriage parked in front. He pulled in behind it, tossed the reins to the indefatigable Tully, and walked to the door. It was opened by Isabel.

Isabel.

Chapter 19

⧗

She stared at him as though he were a phantom. She could hardly believe her eyes. She wanted to fling herself into his arms, but strangely, he did not look as though he would welcome such a display.

"Good evening, Isabel." His voice was flat. He did not smile. He did not look happy to see her.

"Richard. I did not know you had returned."

"I returned yesterday. I have come to see your grandmother."

And not Isabel? She did not know what to make of his stiff manner. Perhaps all those notions she had spun were correct after all, the ones about him having to marry a rich wife now that he was the earl. Maybe he was trying to spare her feelings by keeping his distance.

"Come in," she said. "We will soon be leaving to see the fireworks, but Gram will be pleased to see you."

"I have brought her the brooch."

"Oh, thank God. She will be thrilled to have it back. Come on upstairs."

She led the way and neither of them spoke. Isabel did not understand this awkwardness between them. It frightened her.

"Look who is here," she announced brightly. "It is Major Lord Mallory. Oh. No, it is Lord Dunstable now, is it not. We heard about your grandfather. I am so sorry about his death."

"We were all sorry to hear of it," Gram said.

Richard shared a look with Gram, one so filled with sadness that Isabel began to think perhaps that was the cause of his stiff reserve. He was grieving for the old earl.

"And so you are Major Lord Dunstable now," Cousin Min said.

"No, only Lord Dunstable. I have sold my commission."

"Did you?" Isabel studied him. There had been such regret in his words, that here was another possible reason for his cool manner. He'd lost his grandfather *and* his commission. Two things he loved.

"No more red coats?" Cousin Min said. "What a pity."

That brought the first hint of a smile to his face. "I shall have to find something to do with all that red wool. Cushion covers, perhaps?"

Cousin Min tittered.

"Gram, he has something for you."

"Yes, ma'am, I do. I have recovered the brooch." He reached into a pocket and pulled out a tissue-wrapped bundle. "Here it is. Back where it belongs."

Gram took it and smiled. Her eyes were decidedly watery, Isabel noticed. She had pretended it didn't matter that the brooch had been lost to her, but it had mattered a great deal.

"I do not know how to thank you, my lord."

"Keep it safe. That will be thanks enough. And I have a message for you as well."

"A message?"

"Yes. From my grandfather."

"From Phillip? A message for me?" Her voice had begun to tremble ever so slightly.

"His last words were of you, ma'am."

"Oh." It was almost a cry.

"He said to tell you that he will wait for you." Richard's voice cracked, and so did Isabel's heart. "He said he will wait for you to join him in eternity."

Gram's face collapsed and she gave a great sob. Isabel went to her and took her in her arms. They both cried. Cousin Min cried as well. Isabel was fairly certain that Richard's eyes were not dry, either.

When they had collected themselves, Richard said, "I have something else as well." He held out a packet of letters tied in a blue ribbon. "He kept these for fifty years. I thought you might want them back."

Gram took the letters and clasped them to her breast. "You do not know what this means to me," she said in a shaky voice. "I did not know he kept them. I am so glad he did. Oh my. This is all quite overwhelming."

"He never forgot you, Mrs. Theale. He said he ought to have married you."

"Dear Phillip. How I wish I could have seen him one more time."

"He said almost the same words about you."

"A love that lasted through time," Cousin Min said. "How utterly romantic."

Gram chuckled. "Lord Dunstable . . . Richard . . .

I do not have words to express my thanks. But I do have something." She held out the jewel. "It is yours now."

"Oh, no, ma'am. It is yours. I promised my grandfather I would deliver it to you."

"And so you have. And now I have a duty as well. Phillip told me that each new earl takes possession of the Mallory Heart. He is to hold onto it until he finds his one true love, and he is to bestow it upon her. Here, my lord. It has served me well. It is yours now."

Richard held out his hand, though it seemed he was reluctant to do so. Gram placed the jewel in his hand and closed his fingers around it.

"Keep it, my lord, until you find your one true love."

He tucked the jewel back into his pocket, and Isabel experienced a moment of sheer anguish. She had hoped, had dreamed, that she could be his one true love, as he was hers. But he had put the brooch away.

Richard bent and kissed Gram on the cheek. "I shall keep it safe until then," he said.

"I hate to mention it," Cousin Min said, "but are we not going to be late for the fireworks display? I should so hate to miss it."

* * *

It was not until they were packed among thousand of spectators that Isabel and Richard had a moment alone.

"Did you accept him?" he asked. "Are you going to marry Kettering?"

She looked at him with eyes glittering with the reflection of the rockets bursting about them. "You knew? That is why you have been so distant."

"He told me he asked you, and he expected an acceptance today. Did he get it?"

She smiled, and it lit her face more brilliantly than any fireworks. "He did not."

"Truly?"

"Truly. I could not marry a man I do not love."

Richard let out the breath he'd been holding. "Thank God. Thank God."

Under the bright explosions in the sky, under the eyes of a thousand spectators who did not even notice, he took her in his arms and kissed her. The rest of the world disappeared and it was only Isabel and Richard—joined, connected, one.

He broke the kiss and said, "I have something for you." He took the Mallory Heart out of his pocket and pinned it to her pelisse. "True love knows but one. My love knows only you."

"Oh, Richard. I so hoped you would say that." She pulled his head down and kissed him. Several people around them began to cheer, and this time it was not for the fireworks.

"Will you be my countess, Isabel? Will you marry an earl with a rundown estate that will take years to repair?"

"I know all about economizing, my lord. I will be a great help to an impoverished earl."

"You would marry me, knowing I have no fortune to offer?"

"I have learned that there are more important things in life than a fortune. I will happily marry you, and fortune be damned."

"And what if I had a fortune? Would you still want me? Or do you prefer a bit of slumming?"

"If you had a fortune? Hmm. I don't know if you would be quite so deliciously unsuitable."

"Then I suppose the marriage is off."

"Why?"

"Because, my vixen, I do have a fortune. Not as great as Kettering's, but sizable enough."

"You're joking."

"I am quite serious. I happen to be a fortune hunter's dream."

"Oh my God. Richard!"

"If you will marry me, my love, I promise to

take care of Mrs. Theale and Miss Cuthbert and any other ramshackle relations who show up on our doorstep. And any new ones we create together. So, now that you know the truth, will you still agree to marry me?"

"With pleasure, my lord. For you have stolen my heart. And not the one made of rubies this time. I love you, Richard."

He took her in another kiss, this time under the watchful eyes of two elderly women who clapped and giggled with glee.

Epilogue

"Turn your shoulder slightly to the right. Ah, perfect. Don't move, my lady. Now, think happy thoughts."

Richard watched as the artist studied his subject, seemed pleased with the arrangement, and began to sketch. Richard had gone to a great deal of trouble to obtain a commission from Sir Thomas Lawrence, who was a favorite at Court and recently knighted. He wanted the best artist available to paint Isabel's portrait, to hang alongside those of the previous Countesses of Dunstable.

They were set up in the Long Gallery, the

same room in which the portrait would eventually hang. The light was best here, Lawrence had said, and had posed Isabel in a chair elevated on a makeshift platform in front of one of the widows. The heavy velvet draperies that hung straight down had been pulled to the side to give a deep swag behind Isabel's chair. As Richard watched over his shoulder, he saw that Lawrence was using the full swag as a backdrop, with only a small section of window showing on the left. Isabel's white dress would look beautiful against the deep red drapery. And he hoped Lawrence would be able to capture the special golden hue of her skin. Richard wanted a true representation of the woman he loved—her beauty, her spirit, her passion. A picture he could happily stare at for the rest of his life. It was only a preliminary sketch, but Lawrence had already caught her line of jaw perfectly. Richard was encouraged.

Lawrence stiffened and stopped drawing. Without turning around, he said, "Do you mind, my lord?"

"Oh. I beg your pardon." Richard moved to the side so that he was not staring over the artist's shoulder. He supposed that could be a bit disconcerting, but he really was interested in the face taking shape on the page. He looked up at his wife, who chuckled.

"No laughing, please," Lawrence said. "Keep your face serene for just another moment."

He sketched for a few more minutes, then rose, and adjusted Isabel's skirts and the position of her hands. He stood back and studied her again. "I suppose you are determined on wearing that brooch."

"Oh, yes," Isabel said.

She reached up to finger the Mallory Heart, pinned beneath her bosom. Lawrence moved her hand back onto her lap.

"It is a bit large," he said, "but if you are set on wearing it, then we shall simply have to deal with it."

"It is a family piece," Richard said. "All the countesses have been painted wearing it."

Lawrence turned and looked at the series of portraits lining the opposite wall. He went to stand before the picture of the first Lady Dunstable and said, "So I see. It is a very old piece, then."

"Yes," Richard said. "It was given to the first earl by Queen Elizabeth."

"Indeed?" Lawrence moved down the line of portraits. "It's a very sentimental piece. I'd have guessed it was a love token."

"It was," Richard said. "The queen had been given it by one of her admirers. When she presented it to the first earl at the time she bestowed the title on him, she told him to give it to the woman he loved."

That part of the story had been confirmed when Richard had found a document signed by Queen Elizabeth among the first earl's papers. Isabel's grandmother had been right. The jewel's message was meant to be taken literally, and the jewel presented by each earl to his own true love. "And so all the earls have done ever since." Including his grandfather.

"A lovely story," Lawrence said as he moved from one portrait to the next. "And so every countess has been painted wearing the jewel as a token of love."

Except one.

Lawrence stopped in front of the painting of Richard's grandmother. He turned to Richard with a questioning look in his eyes. "The last countess is not wearing it."

"No. The brooch was . . . lost for a time, but is now recovered." Richard glanced at Isabel and smiled.

"Poor lady," Lawrence said. "It is a shame that she is the only one without the jewel."

Richard had come to understand that she must have felt that shame profoundly every time she came into the Long Gallery. Her resentment had grown and festered for over fifty years. In the end, she had not cared that her gloating over possession of the jewel might have hastened her husband's death. She wanted him to die with the knowledge that she had bested him at long last.

She never knew that she had not in fact done so. Less than a month after the earl's death, the countess had passed away as well. As requested, she was buried wearing the Mallory Heart. The paste copy.

Isabel had not worn the real jewel again until their wedding, almost six months later, when Richard could finally put off his black coats.

"If this was painted by anyone but Reynolds," Lawrence said as he studied the portrait of Richard's grandmother, "I would offer to paint in the brooch for you, so that she could have her love token just as all the other ladies do. But I'm afraid I would not dream of tampering with Reynolds' work."

"Nor would I dream of asking you to do so," Richard said. The absence of the jewel in his grandmother's portrait was an important symbol to him and Isabel. It was a reminder of the love shared between their grandparents, a love that had lasted through time and beyond, a love that had somehow, miraculously, been passed along to Richard and Isabel.

Lawrence walked back to his easel and sat down to resume the drawing. "Now that I know the story of the jewel—"

"The Mallory Heart."

"Yes, the Mallory Heart. Now that I know its story, I can invest it with more meaning. We must be sure to have a glint of light reflecting off the ruby. We must make it clear that it is a symbol of love, of passion, of desire." He chuckled softly. "How extraordinary, my lord, that all the previous earls must have married for love."

Richard gazed upon his wife and smiled. "As did this one."

"Yes!" Lawrence exclaimed with sudden enthusiasm. "That's exactly the look I want, my lady. That blissful glow in your eyes. It's absolutely perfect."

And so it was.

374

Keep your resolution to get more passion with these irresistible love stories coming in January from Avon Romance!

Sin and Sensibility by Suzanne Enoch
An Avon Romantic Treasure

Lady Eleanor Griffin's overprotective brothers fully intend to choose her bridegroom, and Eleanor knows she might as well enjoy herself now, before a man dull enough to satisfy them appears. But when she meets her brothers' best friend, her idea of enjoyment takes a whole new turn, and her brothers' wishes are the last thing on her mind . . .

The Protector by Gennita Low
An Avon Contemporary Romance

After a covert mission goes awry, Navy SEAL Jazz Zeringue has no doubts he'll be rescued, but he's certainly surprised when his savior turns out to be the mysterious and beautiful agent Vivi Verreau. Vivi doesn't trust him and is trying very hard not to like him, but they'll have to work together if they're to escape from dangerous enemy territory alive.

Seducing a Princess by Lois Greiman
An Avon Romance

Having set out to avenge a great wrong, William Enton, third baron of Landow, finds himself with nowhere to turn in the most lawless part of Darktowne. Then a vision appears from the dirty alleyways, a woman who seems to know him at once. But she is the princess of thieves, and nothing is as it seems, including the woman he is quickly coming to love.

What an Earl Wants by Shirley Karr
An Avon Romance

Desperate for employment, Josephine Quincy dresses as a secretary would—as a man—and lets her new employer, the rakish Earl of Sinclair, make his own assumptions. But he is no fool, and just when she thinks her game is up, she realizes she has a bargaining chip she never dreamed of—the powerful Earl's attentions . . . and perhaps he in turn is gaining possession of her heart.